PACIFIC RISING

JOHN W. DENNEHY

SEVERED PRESS
HOBART TASMANIA

PACIFIC RISING

This book is dedicated to the late James Petrongelli, MGySgt, USMC

Courage is endurance for one moment more…

ONE

Maki followed her parents down the bustling streets of Tokyo. Rain poured in a deluge as people shuffled along the sidewalk. Car horns honked and shoes slapped at puddles. Traffic sat still, car after car, jam-packed like she'd never seen. Shopkeepers were closing early.

Everyone moved in haste, worried about the storm. Afraid.

Rain batted off the rubber hood of her pink slicker. And Maki's knapsack thumped against her back with each step. Her hood muffled the street sounds. Winds blew hard, impeding her progress. Maki held her mother's hand tightly and used the larger adult for support to help plod ahead.

"Move out of the way!" her father shouted, trying to clear a path through the throng. He dragged his family along behind him.

"This way, Maki." Mother pulled her hand.

"Why are we rushing?" Maki said, struggling to keep up.

"Shush now, and move…" Mother pressed ahead. "No time for talking."

People dashed in sundry directions, with no rhyme or reason to the movement on the sidewalk. Nobody adhered to conventional paths of travel. Everyone shoved other pedestrians, trying to make their way through the city, a mass hysteria of people in flight with panic-stricken eyes. Father paused and wiped the thick lens on his glasses.

"Why doesn't everyone keep to the side?" Maki complained.

"There isn't any order." Father shook his head, dismayed.

"Why not?" Maki kept at him. She was surprised he'd heard her over the commotion, and even more amazed that he'd responded.

"Just keep moving," Mother interjected.

Maki looked around, confused. She wondered why this storm had spawned such concern. At a tender age of twelve, she had experienced numerous tropical storms and a few hurricanes. This storm hadn't garnered much consideration at first.

Her mother wasn't currently working, and her father had taken a much-needed vacation day. They planned to spend the afternoon on a shopping venture, expecting a bit of rain and wind. All of them had dressed for the weather and prepared for a tropical storm.

They'd headed out late morning, and Maki bounced through puddles carefree, splashing them with her rain boots. Her family took a late lunch at her father's favorite delicatessen in downtown Tokyo. A news station aired on a flat-screen television, mounted to the restaurant wall, and reported on the storm.

When the broadcast zipped headlines across the monitor, her father stood up and headed toward the television. Maki read the words: "Emergency Weather Alert."

The news station reported on the tropical storm being upgraded to a severe hurricane on short notice. Her father worked as an engineer and came back to the table scratching his bald head, obviously unable to comprehend such a mistaken forecast. Already the ocean kicked up massive waves, and camera crews shot film of rough surf battering the shoreline. The images were ominous, as though the Pacific had come to life and would pound the ancient coast.

Now, her family scrambled through the city, hoping to catch public transportation back to their small apartment in northern Tokyo. Most of the cabs were occupied. Even if they found one available, they'd sit in traffic, like waiting in a parking lot.

People moved along the sidewalk with fearful eyes darting about. The merchants closing shops had dire looks of concern cast on their faces. Maki wondered how wind and rain could stir such alarm.

Even her parents were afraid, and they usually took everything in stride. Her family handled burdens stoically. Hysteria engulfed everyone. And her father pushed his way down the sidewalk, clearing a path for Maki and her mother. Typically non-confrontational, he snapped at people to move it along and get out of the way.

His efforts were futile. A tide had turned and sent a wave of people headed in their direction.

Maki wondered what might happen if they didn't get to shelter soon.

Then, her father came to an abrupt halt. He looked up past the tall buildings, toward the sky. Maki glanced at the grey overcast, and torrents of rain cascaded on her face, blurring her vision.

A moment later, a ferocious roar resonated amid the far towers, rattling windows.

Something dark and massive shifted beyond the skyscrapers. Through the downpour, she glimpsed the monster near the harbor and understood why people rushed in the opposite direction.

And then a flood washed down the street, hurling people through swelling currents.

****

Earlier, General Yoshi had reported to the command center for the Japanese Self-Defense Forces, eager to learn about recent developments. He'd stood behind a console watching video feed and data recordings, as a lump grew in his throat, and dread engulfed him.

A tremor reverberated along the ocean floor, and rough currents churned over the surface. Ten-foot waves rose and undulated across the Pacific Ocean. Hurricane winds battered the Japanese coastline.

Something broke the surface of the water, and a rock-like shape plied through the turbid waters. The general scratched his chubby face.

Yoshi sighed and pointed at the screen. "Zamera returns!"

"What do you mean?" This from Major Nagasaki.

"A fierce Kaiju," Yoshi muttered as images returned to mind from his youth, rampaging over the countryside.

"Nonsense," Nagasaki replied. "Merely an old folk tale."

Shaking his head, Yoshi pictured the Kaiju nestled at the base of an underwater mountain range, asleep, dormant for decades. Then, the hurricane stirred this pre-historic creature to life.

The shifting of tectonic plates must have brought it out of a decades-long slumber.

Watching the screen, Yoshi figured the Kaiju had fallen into a crevice after it was attacked with a small nuclear weapon in 1965. Perhaps the sea floor had closed around it and put Zamera into a deep sleep. The earth had shifted again, and a major storm brewed in the rough seas, waking the creature.

The rocky form in the water spiked further above the surface, and massive legs kicked in the turbulent current. Major Nagasaki gasped in horror. The head resembled a triceratops, with horns protruding from protective armor.

Stout rear legs and a long tail, its back was lined with jutting plates, stalactites poking in sundry directions. It cut through the water effortlessly. The front legs paddled, shorter, demonstrating the creature was accustomed to walking on hind legs. Claws extended from its limbs, sharp and deadly. The creature's entire body was covered in dense, protective scales, resembling armor-plating.

The head led to a long muzzle with fangs. A meat eater, the Kaiju blinked its eyes, alert, and no longer groggy from sleep. Yoshi shook his head, alarmed. Hunger obviously churned in the beast's stomach and drove its every move.

Yoshi feared its appetite could only be satiated through revenge. Battles from the distant past came to mind. The Kaiju had ravaged the countryside while tracked armored vehicles shot it with cannons and rockets, and fighters whizzed through the air, launching missiles. All efforts were to no avail, futile. Only the last resort of a nuclear weapon had driven the monster away.

Now, the Kaiju had returned and swam through rolling waves, headed toward the coastline where it had wreaked havoc many years ago.

Nearing shore, the creature's jagged back rose from the water, cutting through twelve-foot waves. It swam into the harbor of the city the monster decimated in 1965.

The attack during Yoshi's childhood had slipped into the distant past, a foggy chimera, which he sometimes doubted ever existed. For a moment, he stood staring at the screen, watching the monster, and everything came rushing back and seemed like yesterday.

The Kaiju moved toward shore, as though it had merely taken an afternoon nap, leaving it punchy and hungry. Still in mind for a fight, it pressed ahead swimming hard against the current.

Spikes protruding from its back created a wake trailing the monster. The Kaiju encountered boats pitching in the stormy water. It flailed in the violent water, approaching the boats, and batted a large vessel with its claws, ripping striations in the hull. An eerie metallic sound resonated over the equipment in the command room. The ship held together as crew members screamed in fear and agony.

Zamera dove under the water. Then, it swam into a small boat, tossed in the turbulent sea. A pleasure yacht that hadn't returned to port before the storm, the boat appeared defenseless. The Kaiju bit into the hull and snapped the yacht in half like a toy. Wood splintered in its mouth, along with pieces of fiberglass. Tasting flesh and blood sent the beast into a frenzy. People spilled from the broken hull into the harbor. The Kaiju maneuvered its large head above the water, like a serpent gobbling up the fare.

Then, it swam toward a fishing trawler and knocked the ship out of his path with a swing of its massive head, and a blow with long horns.

A crew of sailors tumbled into the sea, screaming for help, as the vessel went into a roll and capsized in rough waters. Ten- and twelve-foot waves crashed over the sides of the ship, and a fissure ran down the hull, splitting the boat in two.

The Kaiju snaked its head through the water and scooped up sailors who'd fallen overboard. The monster chomped madly, snapping bones and tearing flesh, and then it scarfed them down. Large chunks of human flesh and jagged bone went down the hatch, unchewed, bound for slow digestion. But the Kaiju seemed too hungry to care.

Now, Zamera resumed its journey toward the large city. Tail whipping back and forth, the monster churned through the water, crashing into the broken vessel, bashing the fragmented boat to pieces. Sailors clung to the shattered hull in a desperate attempt to stay alive. The massive tail thrashed again, and sent a chunk of wreckage plummeting toward the ocean floor.

When its stocky legs found purchase on the sandy bottom, the Kaiju lunged upward from the water and propelled a thirty-foot tidal wave hurling towards Tokyo.

The Kaiju took a few steps, pounding the surf like thunder, and let out a massive roar.

TWO

James Penton accelerated his Jeep Wrangler through a heavy downpour as rain pelted off the canvas soft-top. He went to the gym a few days each week during lunch, a privilege of serving in the Marine Corps for close to thirty years. Now, he had to get back to the office and be quick about it.

Weather predictions had forecasted a mild tropical storm, but the base command recently upgraded it to a hurricane.

The little island of Okinawa sat in the Pacific Ocean on the outskirts of the storm but would take a battering. Penton wheeled the Jeep into a parking lot behind the hangar serving Marine Aircraft and Logistics Squadron 36, known as Blade Runner. The Jeep rolled up to a reserved spot. It was designated for the Aviation Ordnance Chief of Marine Aircraft Group-36, Marine Corps Air Station, Futenma.

Master Gunnery Sergeant Penton double-timed it to the building and entered a hatch near the rear. He marched down the corridor soaking wet, boots smacking the recently buffed tile floor. The scent of Pine-Sol wafted in the air. Beads of water dripped from his desert utilities, heavily starched and pressed with sharp creases.

He'd followed regulations and worn his cover on his head from the Jeep until he entered the building. Now, he held the hat in hand, also starched and ironed. Penton sauntered down the hallway, stretching out the long legs of his six-foot frame.

Turning a corner, he entered his office and headed directly for the coffee pot. Penton didn't say a word to anyone until he'd taken a swill of lifer-juice. His mug had the Blade Runner squadron emblem plastered on it. An M-16 rifle and a Cutlass sword were shadowed by the Rising Sun, flanked by a wrench and key.

Then, he walked over and took a seat on the edge of his desk. "What's the latest on the storm?" Penton said to his office assistant.

"The storm has definitely been upgraded to a hurricane," replied Lance Corporal Sally Johnson. "The eye is headed directly toward Tokyo, but we're expected to get some really high winds."

"We'd better clear the flight line. I'll head down to see Top Anderson and get some of his Marines from the ordnance shop to help."

"You want me to wait here?" Lance Corporal Johnson said.

"Stick around in case we get a call from the Brass." Penton took another swig of coffee. He shook his head at the distasteful blend.

"That bad?"

"Helps build a cast-iron stomach." Penton patted his gut. No love handles on him, anywhere. He'd stayed in shape his entire career, running, lifting weights, and he kept the beer drinking to a minimum.

Penton chugged the rest of the coffee down and put the mug on the counter. He headed out the door, leaving his cover on the desk.

He walked down a corridor, resembling the painted concrete block walls of a public school, then rounded a corner and stepped through a set of double doors. The next hallway was unfinished, lined with metal lockers, stuffed with flight suits and gear. Walls were merely exposed block, and the floor was bare concrete.

Penton pushed through another hatch and stepped into an immense hangar bay. The area was empty except for a few cargo boxes. All the aircraft were tied down on the runway, grounded due to the storm.

Several doors ran along the back wall of the hangar. Most of them were swung wide-open, with Marines dressed in oily coveralls headed in and out. Aircraft maintenance specialties filled the backrooms, airframe and welding, and a host of aviation support occupations. Penton headed to the first shop, a thick metal door clamped shut.

He rapped on the door. A moment later, it creaked open and a young private first class greeted him wearing a sidearm.

"Master Guns," the private first class said, swinging the door wide.

"Afternoon." Penton nodded. "Top around?"

"He's in the back."

Penton stepped into the ordnance shop. He walked by a couple of metal desks with industrial chairs behind them. All the desks were unoccupied, except one taken up by a disheveled staff sergeant. Behind the desks an office area was shared by a master sergeant and a first lieutenant.

He glanced into the office and found it empty. Then, he cut to the right and entered a secure area where metal fencing divided the room in half.

The ceiling was the height of the hangar outside, and so the chain-link fence ran about three stories high. Inside the protected area, a few young Marines huddled around a metal table, assembling two .50 caliber aircraft machineguns. A few others hunched over a deep sink, filled with chemicals, hard at work cleaning machinegun parts.

Penton shook his head. The young men had their arms in the sink and didn't bother with protective rubber gloves. He looked at the gloves hanging on the wall in front of them. Both pairs were stretched out, swollen in size, a reaction between the rubber and the solvents used to clean the guns. *The chemicals damaging the gloves should make them realize they need protection*, Penton thought, shaking his head in dismay.

Top Anderson wasn't in the cleaning and assembly area.

Then, he heard a familiar laugh from inside the cage. Penton walked over to the weapons locker opposite the cleaning area. Comprised of twisted metal, the cage rose about two stories high. Huge bolts connected the bottom to the concrete flooring.

The cage was packed with aircraft machineguns, enough to equip almost every bird on base. Penton walked over and found Top Anderson standing with a corporal and a sergeant, apparently working through a new inventory procedure. They handled the task lightly, carrying on with banter and laughing.

"Look who's come to pay us a visit," Master Sergeant Anderson said to them.

"Top, how are your folks doing?" Penton said.

"We're doing just fine." Top Anderson smiled. "Nice of the highest ranking enlisted Marine on base…to come pay us a personal visit."

"Not sure the base sergeant major would agree." Penton chuckled.

"He's a pencil pusher," Top Anderson replied. "I'm talking about Marines that *still* work for a living. Ain't nobody higher up in this Marine Corps than a master guns, at least that's what I always say. And you've got that exploding pineapple in the middle of your chevrons, there."

Penton grinned coolly at the comment. Anderson was likely the best candidate for his replacement.

He noticed Corporal Alvarez laughing more than necessary. She was fit and wore a Naval Aircrew badge, one of the few younger Marines in her unit who had earned the grueling flight time to qualify. Penton and a few others wore Combat Aircrew badges.

"What brings you by?" Top Anderson turned serious.

"The storm…" Penton looked around. "Let's head into your office.

"Sure." Top Anderson nodded, then turned to the Marines beside him. "Carry on." He handed Corporal Alvarez the clipboard. "And report to me later with the results."

"Sure thing," Corporal Alvarez said, smiling flirtatiously at Penton.

Penton figured she was the one running the inventory. She likely had more brains than most of her peers and took the lead, even though a sergeant was in the working-party. Probably told staff sergeants what to do when she was a lance corporal.

He followed Top Anderson to the office.

"What's the deal?" Top Anderson placed both hands on his hips.

"Turns out the storm is much worse than expected."

"All the aircraft are grounded, and tightly fastened down." Top Anderson looked over at Penton curiously. "The ordnance is all accounted for and safely tucked away. We've got all of the weapons back in the shop."

"Not here to question your ordnance crew. I've got enough to deal with checking up on every ordnance unit in MAG-36."

"What is it then?" Top Anderson's eyebrows shot up with interest.

"The storm is coming at us hard. It's been upgraded to a hurricane. We've got to get the aircraft into the hangars, and keep a couple of choppers ready to roll out in the event of an emergency operation."

Anderson smiled and shook his head. "Glad it's got nothing to do with me."

"Can I count on you to help get this done?"

"Sure thing." Top Anderson nodded. "I've got a few Marines in the turret shop and down in the trailer shop that I can spare."

"Thanks," Penton said. "I knew I could count on you."

"No problem." Top Anderson chuckled. "We go way back."

Penton looked over the small office space. The lieutenant had a shiny metal desk with a model of a Harrier perched on top. While Top Anderson's desk was painted olive drab, the filing cabinet nearby had a camouflage Marines bumper sticker plastered on the side. A poster of a recruit getting throttled by a drill instructor hung on the wall, and a model of Huey with an aerial gunner hanging out the door was on the filing cabinet.

The Brass always go for the fixed-wings, he thought. *And the enlisted prefer the rotary-wing. The jets are shiny, but you don't get to fly in them.* Penton smiled to himself and thought back to his flying days out of Marine Corps Air Station, New River in North Carolina. Wind had always whipped off the Atlantic Ocean, ruffling his flight suit as he fired away with aircraft machineguns, dinging metal buoys placed in the water by the military for target practice.

"Reminds me of the storm that hit us in North Carolina," Penton finally said.

"Had a few of them back at New River." Top Anderson grinned. "But I remember the one you mean... Hugo. Blew right through the base and tore up a CH-46."

"Yeah." Penton laughed. "Tipped over a stake-bed truck, and the metal rails flew into the Phrog. Cut the fuselage up pretty bad."

"And who left the truck on the flight deck..."

"None other than ole Diddy-Bop Sabini. An Italian stallion from Philly."

"Believe that Shit-Bird got himself a bad conduct discharge."

"You should know," Penton added. "You're the one that gave it to him."

They both had a good laugh at Sabini.

Penton gave Top Anderson a slap on the shoulder before stepping toward the door, then he paused. "I've got to run down to VMM-262, and tell them the good news," Penton said, shaking his head.

"The Flying Tigers. Always have been a good outfit. I'd use their birds for any emergency."

"That's what I was thinking." Penton smirked. "But let's not tell the Dragons they're second best."

Top Anderson nodded, smiling wide. "Secret's kept with me."

Penton started out the door. "Have your Marines mustered at 1300," Penton said over his shoulder. "And I'd appreciate if you'd help supervise some of this."

"A little rain never hurt anyone," Top Anderson said, chuckling.

"Recon sunshine." Penton had spent much of his career soaking wet. Marines get aquatic training in boot camp, jumping from a diving board with full combat gear. And drill instructors march recruits outside to sit in the rain without a poncho to indoctrinate them into functioning in the elements. Exposure to the weather gets even worse when training in the fleet.

When Penton stepped past the threshold, Top Anderson cleared his throat. Penton faced his comrade and noticed a serious look in the master sergeant's eyes. "What's wrong?" Penton pressed.

"We've forgotten about VMA-214. Not enough hangar space to hold all of our Ospreys and the Harriers here TAD for the next few months."

Penton thought about the Black Sheep Squadron of Harriers, stationed at the base for six months while training and deployed. He shook his head and walked into the hangar, wondering what to do with the excess birds.

****

Penton headed off to visit a few squadrons and advise of worsening storm conditions. He told senior enlisted personnel about his plans to have the aircraft brought into the hangars. Everyone moved into action immediately.

Then, he walked over to the ordnance shop for the Flying Tigers. Penton entered through an open door and found Chief Warrant Officer Thomas behind a desk doing paperwork. The shop was sparse and didn't store any machineguns. Mostly greasy tools and equipment lay scattered about the narrow space.

Thomas looked up and smiled. "Master Guns," he said. "What brings you our way?"

"Storm has kicked up. And so, we're telling everyone to get all the aircraft into hangars ASAP."

Thomas nodded. "Anything is better than sitting around filling out evaluations."

"Precisely why I didn't become a sergeant major; too much paperwork." Penton grinned and placed his hands on his hips. "Going to need you to do something for me…"

"What's that?" The industrial chair creaked as Thomas sat back to look him over.

"I'd like two Ospreys from the Flying Tigers kept down at the MALS-36 hangar, ready to go in case of an emergency."

Thomas shrugged. "Sounds like a good idea."

Penton nodded, then turned to leave.

"What are you going to do about those Harriers?"

Penton turned back and laughed. "That's what everyone seems to want to know." He shook his head. "Going to shove as many as we can into the MALS-36's hangar."

"That sounds like a plan, too. Let me know if you need anything else."

"Appreciate it," Penton said and headed out the door.

He went from hangar to hangar, running through the heavy rain. Returning to MALS-36, Penton dripped all over the floor. Top Anderson's people were mustered around the hatch to the ordnance shop waiting for him.

"You look like a drowned rat," Top Anderson said.

"This is worse than you'd believe," Penton said, shaking his head.

"How so?" Top Anderson crossed his arms.

"Wind is blowing hard off the flight line. We don't have much time."

The hangar doors opened and rain whipped inside. Several Marines came over from the Flying Tigers, pulling two aircraft with aviation support tractors.

"Get a forklift and move those cargo boxes out by the trailer shop," Penton said to a few ordnance Marines standing around.

"Aye, aye," they responded in unison, and quickly moved out.

A few minutes later, the hangar stood clear and a few birds were safely tucked away. Stacked in tight, but they were accessible in a moment's notice.

"How many Harriers do you think we'll fit in here?" Top Anderson said.

"Only about half of them," Penton replied, shaking his head.

"Leaves a handful outside in the storm."

"Thankfully, you gave a bad conduct discharge to ole Diddy-Bop Sabini, so he can't leave a truck out there with loose parts to pelt the multi-million-dollar aircraft."

Top Anderson grinned from ear to ear.

Penton shook his head and laughed at his own comment.

"Those were the good old days," Top Anderson said. "Back during the Cold War, we could punch someone in the head to straighten them out."

"No kidding." Penton grinned proudly.

"Now, you've got to sweet talk them into doing their freakin' jobs or wade through a mountain of paperwork to get rid of them."

"Sure do miss the old Rehabilitation Platoon."

"That was a motivator if you ever saw one. Marines would go off with an attitude and come back like they were straight out of boot camp."

"Suppose having them spend a few months… breaking big rocks into little rocks made an impression."

"Damn right it did." Top Anderson laughed and clapped him on the back.

"Yeah, I remember picking up a private after he finished there," Penton said, shaking his head, amused. "The staff sergeants were tougher than drill instructors, and they had them all on line, except instead of holding rifles, they held sledgehammers and goggles."

The two of them broke out laughing, reminiscing about the past.

Then, a look of concern cut across Top Anderson's face. Penton turned to see what had caught the master sergeant's attention.

A young Marine squirmed on the flight deck, and a cable used to tether a Harrier had broken loose. The free line whisked around in the wind like a venomous snake.

Penton broke toward the commotion.

He stretched out his strides, but the wind resisted his efforts. Rain pelted him as he ran from the hangar. Penton reached the scene before anyone else reacted. Grabbing the Marine by a shoulder, he yanked him out of harm's way, and then lunged at the dancing cable.

The line moved, almost partly alive, waving in the air. Penton took a blow to the head. Blood ran down his temple and around his cheek. Everything turned fuzzy for a moment. He gathered himself and snatched out again, grabbing hold of the hazardous cable.

As it writhed in his hands, Penton backpedaled and stretched it out. He pulled the line taut to prevent further movement. Then, he called a young Marine over and had her hold the cable in place. Penton stepped to the eye-bolt in the flight deck and removed the other end. The line went slack. He coiled up the cable, wrapping it around his palm and elbow. And then he handed it to the Marine who'd secured the other end of the line.

Penton crouched by the Marine on the deck and looked him over. A gash in the youngster's chin dripped blood into a puddle, rapidly expanding from the torrents. The private first class was dazed but not severely injured. He sat up and then tried to get to his feet.

"Stay put for a moment," Penton said.

"I'm fine." The kid sounded embarrassed.

"You took a blow to the head."

"Doing okay now," the Marine insisted.

"We're going to get you checked out. This isn't the time for heroics... we're not in combat. Better to keep our Marines healthy and able for the real thing."

The young private first class nodded, acquiescing.

A corporal knelt by the fallen Marine. Penton noticed Aircrew wings and recognized Alvarez from the inventory. She slipped the private first class's arm over her shoulder and helped him to his feet.

Penton reached for the private first class's free arm.

"I've got it from here, Master Guns," she said.

"We should get him in a tractor and take him over to Navy Hospital pronto." Penton stood down as she'd instructed. For some reason, the corporal had stepped onto the scene with authority.

"He's strong as a bull," Alvarez replied. "I'll walk him into the hangar, then drive him over in my POV. We'll make sure he's in good hands."

"You certain that you've got him? Maybe you could use some help."

"If we offer Jonesy any more help, he'd kill us all."

"He's your charge," Penton said.

"Maybe you should head over there with us," Corporal Alvarez said. "You took a good blow yourself."

Penton shook his head. "Not much for sitting around Navy hospitals."

Corporal Alvarez smiled, then she led the injured Marine, ambling toward the hangar. Penton spun around and found himself eyeballed by a bunch of Marines.

"Don't just stand there," Penton said. "Let's get a move on!"

They scattered back to their work-detail assignments. A few hopped into a tractor and started pulling a Harrier inside. Others worked more diligently, unfastening the cables tying the birds to the flight deck. They were more careful to keep a grip on both ends of each line.

Penton walked back into the hangar and found Top Anderson staring at him wide-eyed, with a sardonic grin on his face.

"What?" Penton snapped, not comprehending.

"You... that's what," Top Anderson commented as if explaining himself.

"What's so funny?" Penton pressed.

Top Anderson shrugged, still grinning.

"Really don't get this…" Penton shook his head.

"Well, you should get my drift."

"*Now*, you're starting to piss me off."

"Let's put it this way," Top Anderson explained. "For a guy on the verge of retirement, you act like someone still trying to move up the ranks."

"Just trying to help out a fallen Marine."

"Once a Marine, always a Marine," Top Anderson said. "Not sure how you'll handle retirement. A younger guy could have stepped over and addressed that situation, but you put yourself in harm's way… like always."

"No big deal," Penton said. "A minor incident."

"Looked pretty serious to me." Top Anderson laughed. "Probably should put you up for the Navy and Marine Corps Medal."

"That's what they gave JFK for rescuing the crew of the PT 109." Penton shook his head. "Not an award for something like this. You have to put yourself in a perilous situation."

"All kidding aside," Top Anderson said. "You did put yourself in a fairly hazardous situation. Why do you think I stayed right here?"

"Looks like the birds are getting put away just fine," Penton said, changing the subject. He looked around the hangar, and it was getting jam-packed with dripping wet Harriers, along with the two Osprey.

Top Anderson nodded in agreement. "Yeah, things are coming together, here. So, you should probably get checked out. That was quite a blow. Make sure you don't have a concussion."

"Rather head back to my quarters and grab a Scotch."

"Figured you say something like that."

"Can you take it from here?"

"Sure thing," Anderson said. "Go take care of yourself."

Penton walked across the hangar as rainwater dripped from his uniform, leaving a trail of stippled dots along the dry floor. He headed back to the office, grabbed his cover, and told his assistant where he was going.

Then, he busted out the rear hatch and stepped into a raging storm.

THREE

David Hardy rolled out of his bunk and landed on the metal deck, thankful he didn't spend more time than necessary aboard a submarine. He gently kicked at the bunk below, waking Petty Officer Jacob Stiles from a heavy sleep.

"Time to get a move on it," Hardy snapped.

"Give me ten more minutes, Chief," Stiles pled, groggy. Stiles sounded like he was talking to his mother while home on leave.

"Now!" Hardy ordered, kicking the bunk harder. "SEALs don't get more shut-eye than necessary."

Stiles whipped back the blankets and sprang to life.

"Fix the rack, and make it like we've never been here." Hardy shook his head. "Then, grab your gear and join me in the briefing room."

"Aye, Chief." Stiles hustled to straighten out the bunk. He tucked in the sheets with sharp angles, like a recruit in boot camp.

Hardy grinned, then grabbed his pack.

Opening the hatch, he entered a small passageway filled with gauges and pipes, similar to walking into a boiler room of an industrial building.

He headed aft toward a briefing room, thinking a two-man team might not be the best choice for this operation. But even as a highly decorated senior chief petty officer, with his entire military career spent in the Navy SEALs, he didn't get to make the final calls.

Walking down the narrow corridor, he stepped through a series of hatches and tread on metal grating. The submarine did not have accommodations found on larger ships. Hardy didn't mind roughing it. In fact, he preferred being in the field, weathering the elements. Sitting aboard ship led to boredom, but something about the claustrophobic space in a submarine really made him want to get topside and start the mission pronto.

He entered the briefing room. A Navy lieutenant and a commander leaned over a map spread out on a steel table located in the center of the room. They wore khaki dress uniforms and had the same corporate look found on many officers in Navy Intelligence. The railroad tracks on the Navy lieutenant's collar looked brand, spanking new.

"Afternoon, Chief," Lieutenant Smith said to Hardy.

"Good afternoon, gentlemen." Hardy stepped to the table.

"Will Petty Officer Stiles be joining us?" said Commander Johnson.

"He'll be along in a moment."

"Not like Navy SEALs to be tardy…"

"Think we're about 15 minutes early." Hardy pulled a face.

"Didn't mean offense." Commander Johnson forced a smile and raised his eyebrows to Lieutenant Smith, as if indicating the SEALs were testy, or worse, overly sensitive.

Hardy didn't pay the man any mind. The commander's job was to feed information to the SEALs so they could go out and get the mission done, while others stayed back in support roles, pushing paper and earning commendation medals to make them feel important.

Stiles busted through the hatch, holding his pack in one hand and a cup of coffee in the other. "Sorry, I'm late to the show," he said, even though he was early.

"Now that *we're* all here," Commander Johnson said. "We can get started."

"Sure thing," Hardy said, dismissively. He figured Stiles directed the comment at him for failing to keep up with the older SEAL, rather than an admission of tardiness.

"Lieutenant, would you do the honors of explaining the mission?" said Johnson, desperately trying to demonstrate he oversaw the operation.

The lieutenant nodded and smiled. "Gentlemen, please step up to the map." The young officer indicated toward the chart.

Hardy moved closer to the table, and Stiles stepped alongside him.

Like many special operations, a warrior left the base with a general understanding of the mission, often getting the classified information only after boarding ship. This mission was unsettling from the start, though. Hardy didn't know much about the task, but the sheer number of just two SEALs felt a bit low, considering the submarine moved through hostile waters.

"We're located right here." Smith pointed to the map.

"Wow," Stiles said, growing wide-eyed.

"Didn't think we'd sailed that far," Hardy commented.

"The captain got this sub moving at a good clip," Johnson spoke up, proudly.

"So, what are we positioning to do?" Hardy glanced over the map, noting the submarine would surface off the coast of North Korea, not far from the Russian border.

"Good question," said Lieutenant Smith.

The commander cleared his throat and stepped up to the table. "Folks, we need to make clear... this is a very delicate operation. You are to go directly from this room to your launch-craft. Understood?"

Stiles nodded. "Yes, sir."

Hardy looked at the commander. "We understand... This isn't our first rodeo."

The commander grimaced. "You have quite an impressive record," he said. "That's why you were chosen for this mission. But, I'm not sure you've ever had to do something of this magnitude."

"So, what is the op?" Hardy shrugged.

"You're both aware of the recent treaty at the UN, resolving to decommission all nuclear weapons at an accelerated pace?"

They both nodded, understanding.

"North Korea somehow got hold of an old Soviet mobile nuclear missile," Johnson said. "And we believe the thing is armed with a warhead."

"An OTR-21, Tochka," Lieutenant Smith cut in. "We refer to it with NATO call numbers as an SS-21, Scarab B."

"The missile was built back in 1989 and is a durable weapon," Johnson continued. "It's highly mobile and could be used for an initial strike."

"Weighs just 4,400 pounds," Lieutenant Smith added.

"Why not just send in a UN task force and take control of the situation?" Hardy pondered out loud. He looked around the room gravely at the Navy Intelligence officers, thinking he was ultimately responsible for the SEALs on his teams.

"Our intelligence reflects the missile is not heavily guarded," Johnson replied. "Apparently, the North Koreans seek to avoid attracting attention. The thing was transported by truck with only a handful of guards."

"*Now*, you are making sense," Hardy said.

"We have ample opportunity to strike quick and immobilize the damn thing."

"What's the game plan?"

"Lieutenant, go ahead and take it from here."

"You will launch from the Seawolf in a SEAL Delivery Vehicle and travel by stealth to the shoreline." Smith pointed to the map. "Once ashore, you will track the missile to a location two clicks away where it is stored on a trailer awaiting further truck transport."

"How are we going to catch a truck?" This from Stiles sounding dumbfounded.

"The truck hasn't arrived yet. And the missile is strapped to a trailer, parked in an old warehouse," Johnson replied.

Stiles nodded, registering the point.

Hardy looked the map over. The mission entailed traveling through the water for over three miles, then landing on shore and humping over hilly terrain for another couple miles. They'd likely encounter five to six trained soldiers if everything went right, but possibly many more. No chance of a helicopter extraction. He shook his head in disbelief.

"Something wrong, Chief?" Commander Johnson said.

"Think we're kind of light on team members," Hardy replied with another shake of his head.

"We don't want to send in too many operators," Johnson reasoned.

"The direct action should go off without a hitch," said Smith.

"Don't doubt that a bit," Hardy said.

"What are you concerned about, then?" The commander's tone suggested that he didn't want to be questioned on the record.

"Once we strike at the missile," Hardy said, "all of North Korea is going to be out searching for us."

"Precisely why we need a small team," Johnson explained.

Yeah, so they don't find too many bodies to tie the operation to the United States, Hardy thought, but he didn't say anything. He just glanced at them and held his tongue.

"So, are *we* all set," Commander Johnson said, shutting down the discussion.

Hardy didn't take the comment as an actual question.

"Sir, all set," Stiles and Hardy replied in unison.

Lieutenant Smith pointed out a few more particulars. Then, the SEALs stepped out the hatch and made their way toward the launch vehicle. Every sailor they passed eyeballed them, as though understanding the two SEALs were the reason the submarine trolled through hostile waters in the Sea of Japan.

****

Stepping into the launch zone, Hardy and Stiles were dressed in black one-piece utilities and carried scuba gear. They'd packed to the hilt for the mission with machineguns, grenades, pistols, and combat knives.

The SEALs climbed a ladder inside the submarine.

Hardy took the lead. Twisting open a hatch in the roof of the sub, he climbed into a compartment near the back of the boat.

Hardy slipped inside the tight space and Stiles followed him.

Both SEALs donned their scuba tanks and masks, put on their fins, and then got into the two-man SEAL Delivery Vehicle. Sailors filled the compartment with water, and a hatch opened at the rear of the cargo unit. Then, Hardy piloted the SDV out into the open sea while Stiles handled navigation.

The stealth delivery vehicle serves a two-man open submersible with a propeller on the back. Hardy and Stiles were tucked into a cockpit space near the front and drove the vehicle through the open water. Occupants of a two-man SDV remain exposed to the elements, unlike a SEAL Pod, which holds a six-member team and operates like an enclosed mini-submarine.

The SDV shifted sideways and Hardy fought to correct its course. A storm brewing topside was more severe than the weather forecast. Hardy shivered from the cold water.

He thought about what they'd encounter on the mission. A SEAL Pod was more suitable for the rough waters. A bigger delivery vehicle would have withstood the currents better and held a larger team. The two-man team was much too small for this assignment.

Military Intelligence wanted to avoid drawing any attention to this clandestine operation. They weren't taking any risk with an insertion by helicopter, or even chancing the use of a larger delivery vehicle.

Hardy shook his head again. The measures taken to conceal the mission drastically reduced its chances of success. Leave it to the bureaucrats to stack the deck against them. And if the SEALs on the ground somehow pulled off the operation, everyone in Washington would think the idea was planned well from the get-go.

The SDV moved along swiftly, traveling thirty meters below the surface, occasionally drifting from side to side by the turbulent currents. Utilizing the SDV's compressed air system, they conserved the air supply in their scuba tanks.

Hardy was prepared in case they ran into trouble and needed reserves later.

FOUR

Rear Admiral Keyes sat on a posh sofa in the ship's command center. He held a cup and saucer made of bone china. As Keyes sipped coffee, he glanced at the Navy logo on the cup, thinking about the comment he'd just heard.

Keyes had come a long way from the rough neighborhood where he'd grown up in Atlanta. Now, he found himself surrounded by middle-class white males. Many of them had little common sense, and some were educated beyond their intelligence.

Afloat on the USS *Ronald Regan*, the aircraft carrier was known to members of the fleet simply as the Gipper. The ship took part in a task force located mid-point between Pearl Harbor and Tokyo. Keyes commanded the massive 7th Fleet, with a span of control encompassing Japan, South Korea, and Okinawa.

Keyes was simply the most powerful person in the western Pacific.

Sitting across from Keyes, a diplomat attached to the ship stared at him in earnest, and his executive officer, Commander Maxwell James, sat wide-eyed, with an amused look of disbelief.

Keyes glanced down at the coffee, which he took without cream or sugar, and avoided prolonged eye contact with either of them, lest someone might get the impression that Keyes supported either viewpoint.

He hadn't made up his mind on the issue facing them and didn't want to weigh in until he considered it further, or received supporting intelligence.

Clearing his throat, Keyes turned to the young lieutenant commander seated beside him. Susan Williams was from Navy Intelligence and reported directly to Keyes.

"Tell me the status of our SEAL operation," Keyes said.

"Chief Petty Officer Hardy and Petty Officer Stiles have disembarked from the Seawolf, located in the Sea of Japan, near the coast of North Korea."

Keyes shook his head, dismayed at the formality that young officers always employed when addressing someone with the title admiral. "So, they got off the boat?"

"Yes, sir," she answered. "They detached their SDV without incident. Now, they are making their way toward shore. We believe the mission is progressing without any complications."

"Believe?" Keyes snapped. He put the cup and saucer down on the coffee table and shifted to face her.

Lieutenant Commander Williams looked back at him, aghast.

"*Believe*," Keyes repeated. "You are with Navy Intelligence, the finest intelligence gathering body in the world. And you *believe* that the mission is tracking according to plan. You should *know* whether it is on target."

"Excuse me, sir," Williams responded. "I stand corrected. We are certain that the SDV disembarked without incident, and the SEAL team is on target. Hardy and Stiles are en route to their touchdown location... and their timing is within mission parameters."

Keyes glanced around the room and let out a sigh. He didn't particularly enjoy lambasting a young officer, but the potential seriousness of various issues at hand caused him to pound on her. He meant to use her as an example to others who might question his authority. "Within parameters," Keyes repeated. "Sounds like they are barely making progress within the allotted schedule. Am I right?"

She nodded in agreement. "We expect the storm conditions are slowing them down."

"But they are still progressing toward shore," Keyes said. "Correct?"

"That is correct, sir." Williams wiggled and adjusted her skirt.

"What is the status of this storm?" Keyes said to his executive officer.

"The storm has been upgraded to a hurricane," Commander James answered. "Changed from a tropical storm to a category three... fairly quick."

"How bad are we talking?" Keyes shook his head.

"The eye of the storm is headed directly towards Tokyo. It is expected to touch down within the hour. Our reports indicate the winds exceed 130 mph, making the hurricane on the verge of a category four."

Keyes grumbled, understanding the gravity of the situation. He picked up his coffee cup, took a long sip, and nodded for James to continue.

"The hurricane is expected to tear through Japan. Then the remnants will cross the Sea of Japan and touch down in South Korean."

"What types of winds will hit the Korean shore?" Keyes sought information about the readiness of the American fleet, located in Japan and South Korea. He didn't like what he was hearing so far.

"Not exactly sure," Commander James said. "But it will likely be a category one, or a severe tropical storm."

Keyes shook his head. More undefined intelligence that made planning difficult. Nobody seemed to want to take a position on anything these days for fear of being relieved of command. Whatever area of the military he dealt with in trying to make tough decisions, everything was couched with qualifications nowadays. You couldn't pin people down. He wasn't looking to hang someone from a yardarm, but rather needed their best hunch.

"Why can't I get a simple answer out of anyone?" Keyes snapped.

"That's the best we've got from the weather bureau right now."

"Understood. You're giving me what you've been told," Keyes barked. "I'm not putting the blame on you. You're a sailor like me and are just reporting the information, but I need better intelligence all around, considering what we may be facing."

Keyes pounded his fist on the coffee table. Cups and saucers rattled. He glanced at the diplomatic attaché and wondered when the man planned to cut into the conversation and interfere with Navy operations.

The suit obviously mistook the eye contact as a welcomed opportunity to speak.

"Admiral Keyes," Mr. Hopkins said. "If you don't mind me saying… we've got far more important things to attend to than a small-scale SEAL operation and the weather."

Keyes wanted to thrash the bastard. This paper-pushing weasel had no clue about what's involved in commanding a Pacific fleet. The pressure was building and Keyes needed to relieve it. He wanted to get up and kick a trashcan or pound the table again. Instead, he ground his teeth together, and his consternation and intensity wasn't lost on the suit.

The man sat back and waited for Keyes to reply.

"We're in the process of taking in much-needed intelligence." Keyes looked directly at the suit. "You have to obtain and consider all of the details, even the minutiae, before making major decisions."

"Understood, sir," Mr. Hopkins replied. "Not trying to step on your toes. Just can't see what the weather has to do with *our* problem."

"You can't see it... because you haven't a clue!" Keyes bellowed. He pounded the table and a cup tipped out of the saucer, spilling coffee all over. Lieutenant Commander Williams reached for a napkin and started to clean up.

Commander James leaned forward and helped her tidy things. He glanced up at Keyes with a twinkle in his eye, as though amused at the lashing Keyes handed out to the suit. Keyes took a deep breath and leaned back in the sofa.

"Now, I might not have gone to George Washington University... like XO, James here, or Annapolis like Lieutenant Commander Williams, or Harvard like you, sir—"

"Actually, I went to Bates College," Mr. Hopkins corrected. "Harvard is where I got my Masters in Government, but please continue..."

This guy really is an ass, Keyes thought.

"What is the status of our forces in Japan?" Keyes said to James. He'd quit trying to explain strategy to a man who didn't have a clue how things worked in the field.

"All of the ships that aren't at sea as part of this task force," Commander James said, "are secured at deep-water docks."

"What about flight capabilities?"

"Everything is grounded."

"South Korea?"

"Same."

Keyes pondered the situation. "How about Okinawa?"

"Everything is shut down and fairly secure there. However, the base is outside the severe storm center and won't get hit as hard."

Keyes turned to Williams, the intelligence officer. "What is the status of Japan's Self-Defense Forces?"

"The Maritime Self-Defense Force and Air-Self Defense Force are shut down, pretty much the same as our forces."

"And the Ground Self-Defense Force?"

"They have been mobilized as a force in ready to address the storm... in a disaster relief role. Their Ground Forces are not currently mobilized for combat."

"The Seawolf remains off the coast of North Korea?"

"Yes, sir," Williams responded.

"Anything else you want to add to your report?"

"Despite the storm," Williams said, "we have a landing helicopter platform moving through the straight... between South Korea and Japan. The ship has a full contingency of 2,000 Marines, tanks, amphibious personnel carriers, and several helicopters below deck."

"The LHP is on the wrong side of Japan." Keyes shook his head. "Any fighters aboard?"

"Unfortunately, the ship was being used for a helicopter training exercise and got packed without jets."

"Have we had any direct communications with Japan's Self-Defense Forces about the situation he described?" Keyes said to her, while pointing at the suit.

"We got an informal report of the activity, but haven't been able to confirm."

"Why the hell not?" Keyes bellowed.

"There is a problem with their communications system."

"We're the United States Navy..." Keyes grew weary from the insufficient reporting. "You can keep tabs on a couple of SEALs below water, but cannot speak to commanders on a major land mass."

"The communication problem is not with us..."

Keyes felt better that the incompetence lay elsewhere. But he wasn't entirely relieved. The Japanese forces had always been highly professional, reliable, and dependable. He couldn't imagine they'd allow communications to falter for any period of time, unless they had a serious issue brewing.

An ominous feeling gripped him. Keyes looked towards the suit and figured something momentous was about to happen, or had already begun.

FIVE

Penton drove his Jeep toward the senior barracks. Rain blew across the road, whipping sideways from the heavy wind. An ominous malaise crept over him. The usual comfort from pattering of raindrops on the soft-top evaded him. A thunderous deluge pelted the hood, and monsoon conditions swirled around him.

He thought about how bad it might get. The most recent weather report wasn't merely an upgrade from a tropical storm to a category one, a change from 55 mph winds to 75 mph, but rather an extreme shift in storm conditions. This hurricane was going to reach a category three or four, with winds exceeding 130 mph and severe flooding caused by storm surges.

Penton pulled up to the barracks, hopped out of the Jeep, and ran towards his quarters, occupying the last unit. Reaching the door, he was already drenched. Penton worried the wind might tip the Jeep over during the night.

Stepping inside, he wondered if the Harriers left on the flight line would get damaged. Then, he thought about who'd get the blame. *Maybe we should have brought all the jets inside and left a few Ospreys on the flight line.*

The carbon-based fuselage of the Harriers made them weigh half as much as the Osprey, coming in at about 15,000 pounds, compared to over 30,000. Someone's head would role for any damage. But the commanding officers of the permanently assigned squadrons wouldn't have stood for it. Either way, it was a losing proposition.

Penton walked into the kitchen area and tossed his cover on the table. He removed the shirt to his utilities and draped it over a chair. The term blouse had never resonated with him. His quarters were comprised of a living area with a puffy leather sofa, and a kitchenette and dining area, adjacent to the living room. He also had a private bath and bedroom down a short hallway.

He sat down in a leather chair matching the sofa. Penton pulled out his cellphone and stared at the floor, contemplating whether to call his daughter. The time difference with her in North

Carolina was thirteen hours. Late afternoon in Okinawa would be the crack of dawn the next day in Wilmington. Wind rattled his window and the lights flickered.

"Oh, what the hell…" He decided to make the call. If she didn't answer, he'd just leave a message.

The phone range only twice. "Hello?"

Penton paused not responding, surprised she'd even answered. It had been a month since they had spoken.

"Dad?" Caitlin said, nervously. "Why the silence? You've got me worried, here."

"Nothing to worry about, honey…" He paused, lost for words. "Just surprised you're up so early, that's all."

"Well, you know me," said Caitlin. "Up in the morning with the rising sun."

He chuckled at her reference to a Marine Corps marching cadence. "Must not have been easy—" he finally said, morose.

"What?" she said, clearly unsure of his meaning.

"Growing up with a Marine."

"Had its good points, too."

"Like what?" he pondered aloud.

"Kids at college spend too much effort trying to have a good time…"

Penton sat up waiting to hear what she'd say next.

"I'm up at the crack of dawn, going for a run, keeping in shape, staying healthy. And I'm getting straight A's in school."

He smiled proudly. Caitlin's accomplishments were one of the few things giving him comfort in life. "Must not have been easy on your mother, either." He finally broached the subject.

"She handled it fine." Her voice crackled, trying to hold it together.

"Not sure that was the case. Maybe I dragged her into it…"

"My mother was a bright woman," Caitlin protested. "I know in my heart that she made her own decision to join you in the Marines. And she decided on her own to stay with you. Nobody forced her to do anything that she didn't want to do."

Penton sat quiet, brooding. He mulled the comment over. Having both grown up in the suburbs of Chicago, the couple naturally met at Chicago State University. He'd quit college after their freshman year to join the Marine Corps. Penton went through boot camp at Parris Island and finished his initial training, then ended up based at Okinawa for a year. He circulated back to the states when she'd completed her sophomore year. Penton asked her to marry him and she accepted. Then, he spent most of his career at New River Air Station in coastal North Carolina. She finished her degree in Sociology at Eastern Carolina University.

"The accident wasn't your fault," Caitlin said, breaking the silence.

"Maybe not the collision itself." He exhaled. "But she'd still be here today, if it wasn't for me. We'd been arguing… she left the house because of me."

"But… Dad," Caitlin pled. "The police did a thorough investigation. Mom wasn't speeding or driving erratically. She wasn't doing anything wrong at all. The guy that hit her ran a red light after he'd been in a bar all afternoon."

Penton knew the story all too well. But he was never quite convinced that his wife's agitated state of mind didn't contribute to the accident somehow. A drunk driver hits the wife of a highly decorated Marine. Of course, the Jacksonville, North Carolina police would pin everything on a drunken nobody. "Should've treated her better," he muttered, regret stirring up sorrow he desperately tried to keep locked away. A tear ran down his cheek.

"Dad?" Caitlin said and paused.

"Go ahead." He leaned his head back, and tried to regain composure.

"Please don't get upset with me—"

"I'm not going to get upset with you, honey."

"Well, I've got something to say about all of this," she continued, "and I'm not sure that it will sit well with you… how I feel about it, that is."

"Say what you like," he encouraged her.

"You have a lot of grief to deal with," she said. "And there are regrets. Don't take this the wrong way."

"I'm not—"

"You haven't heard it yet."

"Go on."

"When you go on about your regrets," she said. "It takes away from my memories. The time that I spent with Mom... our life... I don't regret any of it. Regret... regret only cheapens my memories, and it's all I have left of her." She sobbed. "Can't we just be happy for the time we had together?"

Penton breathed heavily. The comment was a dose of reality. *Out of the mouths of babes*, he thought. "Perhaps, I've been a little selfish," he finally said.

"I don't want you to feel bad about this. Time to move forward."

"How do you mean?" He wondered where she was going.

"Your entire life has been about us," Caitlin said. "Our family and the Marines have been your entire existence. Mom has been gone for five years, now. And you'll be retiring soon... Maybe you should get out there."

"Get out there?"

"Date."

Penton hadn't dated in decades, not since college, before he'd met his wife. Couldn't even respond to the comment. "I'll be moving back to North Carolina, soon enough. Just up the coast from your school."

"Dad, I graduate in two years," Caitlin said, taking a deep breath.

"Not sure that I follow." He sat forward in the chair.

"Well, after I graduate... I'll be moving along."

"How so?"

Another long pause.

Penton sat back, wishing he'd poured a Scotch. His head throbbed from the blow on the flight line. A drink and a couple aspirin would help.

Still no comment.

He glanced at the Marine Corps flag hanging on the wall. Underneath the flag was a drink cart. Penton contemplating getting up, fixing a Rusty Nail, but didn't want to interrupt her thought process.

"I'm pretty sure that I'll be moving away from the coast."

"Never expected you to stay in coastal North Carolina, forever." He forced a laugh. "Thought that you were going to get a graduate degree, though."

"I am going to graduate school... but I haven't decided where."

"You'll have to do what's right for you," he said, trying to sound supportive.

"Chapel Hill has six courses of study for a Ph.D. in psychology, and we only have one here."

"Not trying to persuade you one way or another. But they started that program at your school with a practitioner's focus, with the hope that graduates would stick around and serve the southeastern community."

"Sure, that's what I wanted to do when I began my degree," Caitlin said. "But once you get into the higher-level courses, you start to track towards a certain path. Haven't decided which way I ultimately want to go, but I'd like to keep my options open... and consider a few graduate programs."

"I'm sure that you'll make the right choice."

"Thanks, Dad." She sounded uplifted. "That means a lot."

"Glad we had the chance to talk."

Even as the words came out of his mouth, Penton felt depressed. The thought of his daughter moving off was a dismal prospect. He'd come to expect that she'd get her advanced degree nearby and open a practice in coastal North Carolina. Penton pictured himself stopping by her house for cookouts, drinking a beer, having a normal life, like regular people.

"Guess, we'll just have to wait and see." She projected a reassuring tone.

"Yeah, sure," he said, not convinced. "This is something to take one step at a time."

A lull fell over the conversation, as if the discussion had run its course. The storm raged outside his unit, battering the brick structure.

"Dad?" she finally said.

"What is it?"

"Why did you call me?"

"Maybe just to chat…" He searched for the right answer. "Catch up a bit."

"So early in the morning?"

"We've got a hell of a storm kicking up," he explained. "It reminded me of one that hit us in New River before you were born. Hurricane Hugo."

"Yeah, I remember hearing about that storm. Tore through the state like there's no tomorrow."

"I guess the storm got me thinking of North Carolina… missing you."

"Bad weather can remind us of our mortality," Caitlin said. "Lots of people died in that storm."

"Well, I have concerns about this one. Probably why I called."

Rapid knocking at the door caught his attention.

Penton got up to check it out. A young lance corporal stood on the stoop as rain pounded on him. The kid pulled his trench coat tight, but rain poured on his head, soaking his cover, and ran down his neck.

Opening the door, Penton looked into the young Marine's eyes. Something had gone terribly wrong. Penton gave a quick goodbye to Caitlin. Then, he ended the call and got dressed to leave.

****

Penton dashed outside to a white Chrysler van. Black inscription on the driver's side door revealed staff officer insignia. Someone high up had sent for him. As the driver climbed behind the wheel, Penton slid the rear door open and hopped onto a bench seat.

Glancing around the back of the van, he noticed it was spotless. The van belonged to the commanding officer of the base. Penton knew it the moment he slid inside. Most of the vehicles around base were not kept up to Marine Corps standards due to busy schedules, but the immaculate condition of this vehicle gave it away.

An unsteady feeling overcame him as the van headed down a stormy street.

"What's this all about?" Penton shifted on the seat and dug the driver for information.

"Not sure, Master Gunnery Sergeant."

"You must have some idea."

The driver shook his head. "Way beyond my paygrade, Master Gunnery Sergeant, Penton. All I know is that I have instructions to pick you up."

"And take me where?" Penton insisted.

"Not at liberty to say."

Penton noticed a few palm trees strewn along the roadside. One of them had fallen into the street. The driver veered around it and momentum leaned Penton into the door. Wind drove the rain sideways and shook the van.

Penton figured the impromptu meeting pertained to storm damage on base.

"You're taking me to the base command center," Penton said, thinking the likely place for meeting about storm control.

"You're the one who said it, Master Gunny," the driver replied. "Not me."

Penton's throat suddenly grew dry. He was on the verge of wrapping up a thirty-year career and found himself bracing for an ass-chewing. A Harrier broke loose, or something flew into one of them and caused significant damage.

He shook his head. If he'd brought the Harriers inside, one of the squadron commanding officers permanently stationed at the base would have complained. The training and deployed unit had been the path of least resistance. A move that no Marine should ever take. The hard way was always the better course of action.

They took a right turn and Penton swayed into the door again. He righted himself and glanced out the window, confused. "If we're heading to the command center," Penton said. "Then, you're going the wrong way."

SIX

General Yoshi still couldn't believe what had appeared on the screen. The Ground-Self Defense Force set up a command center at a facility on the outskirts of Tokyo. As head of the Eastern Army, he'd planned for relief concerning the tropical storm. Then the storm was upgraded to a serious hurricane.

He'd immediately made plans to increase the response for disaster relief. When an odd image appeared on a Maritime Self-Defense Force sonar screen, General Yoshi took precautionary measures and disbursed tank crews to the industrial area near the harbor, along with mobile missile crews. And he'd prepared a contingency squadron of F-2 fighters. The North Koreans always had him on edge, and he never totally trusted the Chinese. Then, he stood in the command center watching an incoming video communication.

A massive Kaiju appeared on screen, having surfaced in the harbor.

The beast lunged out of the water and sent a wave surging toward shore. A flood of water washed around the heavy armored vehicles, knocking a few of them over, and then sluiced towards the city.

Defense forces had not readied themselves for an attack. Lorries were packed with potable water and food supplies, rather than ammunition and weapons. Only a handful of soldiers had been issued weapons and ammunition, merely for deterring looters. A problem more readily found in other countries during a disaster.

The creature had destroyed a fishing trawler and a few smaller boats. Yoshi took note of the Kaiju's size. It stood over sixty feet tall and lingered near a pier, which tethered a few large oil tankers.

Zamera could cause immediate harm to the nation's valued waterway. And Yoshi felt helpless.

"Get me Major Hira and Colonel Sasaki on the line," Yoshi commanded.

"The communications link is down," a sergeant first class responded.

"How can that be?" Yoshi pointed at the screen.

"We've got incoming visual, but no outgoing capabilities right now."

Yoshi shook his head in disgust. "This couldn't have come at a worse time," Yoshi griped, derisively.

"The storm has interfered with our network."

"We're supposed to be ready for a catastrophe, or war."

"The system should be back on-line within an hour. We're also taking steps to enable the backup radios."

"How long will it be before the radios are functioning?"

"We expect fifteen to twenty minutes."

The response time was much faster than Yoshi had anticipated, but he glanced at the screen and wondered if the delay would make it too late. He hoped his subordinates were prepared to make tough decisions without him.

"That will have to do," Yoshi finally said. "We'll contact them once you are ready."

"There's just one thing…" the sergeant first class said.

"What is it?"

"They have to understand the system is down, and step up their radios to accept our communications."

Yoshi couldn't believe it. We live in a time when everyone took vacations in remote areas and carried on conversations with cellphones. "Wait!"

"What is it, sir?"

"Get me Major Hira's cellphone number."

"That may take a moment."

A moment was a lot faster than fifteen or twenty minutes. In fact, a moment was all they had judging by the scene unfolding on the screen before him.

****

Major Hira poked through the hatch of a battle tank. Rain pelted him and obscured his vision. He couldn't get through to General Yoshi, but Hira had gone ahead and assembled a line of Type 90 battle tanks along the hillside overlooking the harbor.

He'd also deployed a few missile carriers. Mitsubishi trucks loaded with six tubes that shot land-launched missiles were situated on a knoll above the line of tanks. The conventional warheads on the missiles, and the 120mm smoothbore cannon rounds fired from the tanks, would be enough to kill anything alive.

Hira peered through his binoculars at the Kaiju ravaging the harbor. Waves pounded into its legs without the slightest indication it might falter. The beast had sunken a few vessels and feasted upon the castaways. Now, the creature turned its attention to the dock jutting from the shoreline. Large oil tankers bobbed in the violent water. Hira knew he had to move forward, but hadn't received a communication from General Yoshi. Surely, the command center would be aware of these developments.

He pressed his communications link and couldn't get through. But the radios between tanks were operational. Hira ordered a younger officer to make radio contact with the command center. Just as he gave the order, Hira's cellphone vibrated in his pocket. He'd brought the phone along as backup.

"Major Hira," he answered.

"This is General Yoshi."

"We've got a Kaiju in the harbor, sir."

"I know all about it. This is the go-ahead to attack."

"You are aware of the oil tankers?"

"We understand all of the risks," Yoshi replied.

"Consider it done."

Hira ended the call and gave the order to commence an attack. All the tanks raised cannons and crew members targeted the beast. The missile crews tilted their launch-pods upward getting ready to fire.

The creature moved toward the dock, apparently taking interest in a few stragglers running along the pier. Skeleton crews remained on deck of the massive cargo vessels.

Each giant foot surged from the water and plunged back down as the beast moved toward the pier. Stepping closer, the Kaiju's tail whipped back and forth, cutting into the ten-foot waves. Seawater crashed into the shore as wave after wave battered the coast.

Hira couldn't comprehend how the creature managed to stay upright in the swirling currents.

"Fire!" Major Hira commanded the tank crews.

Cannon muzzles blared as ordnance exploded from the thanks. The rounds sailed through the air, following a trajectory toward the immense creature.

The tanks bucked back, and then nudged forward.

Hira's head whipped back and forth.

A few of the 120mm rounds lobbed into the water as the Kaiju thundered toward the dock, landing in the tempestuous surf with a splash. Other rounds hit the creature and dug into its plated scales.

The direct hits had little impact on the beast.

Hira ordered another volley, and the tank crews hustled to reload. His own crew below were hard at work. A spent shell casing clanged on the deck. He gave the order and the tanks erupted with another salvo of cannon fire. The barrage of 120mm rounds found purchase in the creature's hide.

A few of them sunk through the protective armor, and the beast turned to the firing line and wailed in pain.

The shrill cry was followed by an intense, angry roar.

Then, the creature advanced on the dock. Giant claws scraped the wood decking, splintering parts of the pier to bits. People stumbled into the water and the Kaiju scooped them up, chomping them down by the mouthful.

Hira watched in awe as the creature grabbed hold of the tanker's hull and shook it madly. The Kaiju bit into the control center above the ship's deck. Glass shattered and metal crumpled in the beast's huge teeth. It slipped a claw beneath the stern and tipped the nose of the vessel toward the harbor.

Oil spilled into the water and meandered over the surface in rough waves.

"Tank commanders," Major Hira called into the communications link, "prepare to fire again."

Everyone responded in unison, affirming the order.

"Missiles, prepare to fire."

Hira waited a moment for the creature to steady itself. Then, he gave the order to fire all cannons and missiles at once. A fusillade of ordnance exploded from the hillside. Missiles flew through the air, whistling along toward target, as rain and wind offered feeble resistance.

The missiles exploded in the side of the creature and flames billowed from the impact.

Hira couldn't discern whether the weapons had any effect. The Kaiju roared, but this time, the horrific sound appeared as though it was driven by fury alone.

Another volley of rounds drilled into the creature's hide. This time, the Kaiju shrieked in pain. Hira surmised that some of the rounds hit home, where prior hits had dug holes into the armor-plating, weakening the protective cover. The smaller rounds were more surgical, but still didn't deter the creature.

The beast continued lifting the ship's stern, pile-driving the bow toward the ocean floor. Flames from the missiles cascaded down the Kaiju's scales, fluttering into the oil slick below. Metal creaked and bent like a girder giving way under tremendous pressure.

Then, the oil tanker snapped in half, and its cargo holds spilled into the harbor, gushing black petroleum over the raging sea.

All the oil caught fire and the conflagration lit up the overcast haze.

Fire spread to the dock and set it ablaze. Hira shook his head in dismay, then he ordered the crews to reload and ready for another assault.

Hira belayed the order when F-2 fighters ripped through the sky. General Yoshi must have gotten through to the Air Self-Defense Force. The planes fought the heavy wind as they buzzed through the air.

Fighter jets whizzed by the beast and distracted it from the destruction at hand. The creature dropped the tanker, and it sunk to the bottom in two pieces, as flames whirled around the Kaiju.

The beast turned to face the oncoming planes. Its tail smacked into the dock, snapping a piling. An inferno blazed along the surface of the water, and the pier burned as wood and oil fueled the fire.

Jets closed in on the creature and released their missiles simultaneously.

As the fighters soared upward, Hira gave an order to issue another volley of rounds and missiles from the ground.

Ordnance homed in on the monster all at once.

This final attack and the fire erupting on the water would certainly bring about the demise of any known living creature.

SEVEN

Captain Kate Able returned to her dilapidated barracks after an early release due to the storm. She'd already gone to the gym to lift weights and run on a treadmill, and then headed to the chow hall. When she got back to her room, she went into the head to take a quick shower.

Warm water poured over her lithe body. Her life in the Marine Corps as a Harrier pilot offered little comfort. She learned to appreciate the small things in life. Kate wore her brunette hair at shoulder-length and pulled it back while on duty. She'd always had her share of boyfriends in high school and college, but her stellar career in the Marines hadn't allowed much opportunity for relationships, despite her lean figure and muscularity.

As the water cascaded over her chest, both nipples on her perky breasts turned hard. She lathered up and permitted herself a slight tease, gently caressing herself as she washed off.

The open shower bay didn't afford an opportunity to do anything more than brief contact. A moment later, a lieutenant her age stepped into the showers.

Kate nodded to her, and then rinsed off and headed to a sink.

She looked into the mirror and noticed slight bags around her crystal-blue eyes. The tour of duty on the rocky island was beginning to take its toll. Toweling off quickly, she freshened up and headed back to her room.

Her flight suit lay on the top bunk. A metal rack housed bunk beds with thin mattresses, white sheets, and olive-drab wool blankets. Each bed had one pillow. Rough canvas with blue ticking stripes, the pillows were stuffed with down feathers, and the course fabric and pointed quills scratched her face at night.

She grabbed the flight suit and hung it in the storage locker, which held all her possessions for the six-month swing through Okinawa. She pulled on a green T-shirt, and then slid on the cargo pants to her utilities, tightening the web-belt around her thin waist.

Then, she plopped on the rack and started reading a science fiction magazine on her Kindle. Someone gently knocked on her door.

"Who is it?" she said, wondering if it were the duty sergeant.

A slight pause before the person answered. She looked at the beer cans on her windowsill and contemplated hopping off the rack to toss them into the trash. But the duty sergeant wouldn't hesitate to announce himself.

Another light knock on the door.

"Come in," she said.

The door swung open and First Lieutenant Tim Baker stepped into the room. A wiry pilot, he stood in the threshold still wearing his flight suit. He looked at her meekly.

"What is it?" she asked.

"Just wanted to see if you've been to chow…"

"Already went to lunch and the gym."

"That's right," Baker said, nodding. "Forgot you cut out early."

"Rank has its privileges." Kate smirked.

"Maybe I'll catch you in a few hours for dinner, then."

"Sure," she said. "Probably will be a tenacious downpour tonight."

"Already doing it now," Baker responded. He looked at the beer cans on her shelf in awe. "You drink all of those yourself?"

Kate laughed and nodded. "Yup."

"The six-month tour is supposed to be a blast for the first few months. And hit you hard the last three."

She shrugged.

"Seems like it starts taking its toll a lot sooner."

"We'll manage just fine. Ninety days and a wake up, and this place will be behind us. An important tour of duty to have under your belt, though."

"Yeah, and if you're lucky… you won't have to come back here again."

"Everyone has to come here at least once in their career," she said, finally sitting up on the bunk. "And if you plan full retirement, you should expect to come back."

"Not sure how anyone can do thirty years," said Baker.

Kate canted her head at him, confused.

"Sorry," he said. "Forgot your family lives for this shit."

"Dad and Uncle are career Navy men. Grandpa, too."

"I know," Baker replied. "Everyone knows… which makes it more embarrassing that I forgot."

"No big deal." She laughed. "The military is a way of life for us."

"Why did you select the Marines, when you had the advantage of such a prominent Navy family?"

"Wanted to make it on my own," Kate said. "But I guess something kept me from venturing too far astray."

They both laughed at the comment. Baker turned to leave.

Kate glanced at the beer cans on the windowsill. "Guess, I'd better clean that up. Should be setting the example."

"That's a fine example," Baker said.

Wind and rain battered the windows. Kate shrugged in dismay. "Quite a mess out there for a tropical storm."

Baker shook his head.

"What?"

"Storm's been upgraded to a severe hurricane. We'll be locked in the barracks for hours, with only emergency power before this thing is over."

"Our birds are tied to the flight deck—"

A hurried knock rapped on the partly open door, breaking off her thought. Kate peeked out the hatch. A young lance corporal stood in the hallway with a dire look on his face.

Kate understood immediately that she had to go with him.

****

Penton waited in the van for the driver to return. He sat back and watched rain cascade over the windshield, and thought about the discussion with his daughter. She'd clearly given him the go ahead to move on. Caitlin had actually suggested that he start dating again.

He shook his head, unsettled by the prospect. Penton would rather hang out the side of a helicopter taking fire than go on a blind date.

The van had stopped outside of the dilapidated barracks the air base used for Marines rotating through while training and deployed. Penton glanced at the building and wondered who they were picking up.

"Be back in a minute," the driver had said, climbing out of the van.

"Take your time," Penton replied, but he really didn't want to wait long.

"Plan on making this quick." The driver had bolted through the rain and entered the front door of the barracks. A moment later, he spoke with a Marine, who stood behind a podium wearing a duty-belt, green webbing with a brass buckle, like drill instructors wear. The duty Marine seemed to question the driver, sent to fetch someone on short notice without papers.

The duty Marine glanced through the plate-glass doors at the staff van. He eye-balled Penton, and then nodded to the driver, giving the go-ahead. Then, the driver headed down a hallway and slipped out of sight.

Wind shook the van hard, reminding Penton of the storm. Despite the dismal thought of retirement, having nothing to do, and no troops to command, he welcomed the prospect of putting the pressure and politics behind him. Thoughts of damaged Harriers weighed heavy on him. Everyone had let him make the decisions, knowing there wasn't enough room in the hangars for all the aircraft. And they knew full well that he was retiring soon and would make a good scapegoat if anything went wrong.

Penton wondered if a mishap could affect his pension. He doubted it.

Then, the side door whipped open, and rain gusted into the van. A young captain motioned for him to slide over. She hopped inside and shut the door with authority. Turning, she looked over at Penton and smiled, almost flirtatiously. He seemed to attract the attention of young female Marines. Penton wore his sandy blond hair at a maximum regulation length, and he'd stayed lean and muscular with a square jaw.

A fit, crusty Marine standing slightly over six feet tall, he tended to garner interest. Yet, the Marines had a strict fraternization policy. Another reason why he kept to his duties and avoided romantic interests.

"Captain Kate Able," she said after a moment.

"Master Gunnery Sergeant Penton." He shook her hand.

She smiled again, and he couldn't understand why.

Captain Able had a firm handshake and a confident aura about her. He'd seen her in the gym a few times. The driver slammed his door and shifted the van into drive. The windshield fogged over from body heat. He put on the defogger; it hummed so loud the noise should have dissuaded further conversation.

"You seem familiar," she said over the blaring fan.

"Well, maybe I've seen you at the gym."

"That's it..." She smiled coolly, as though knowing it all along.

"So, you're here TAD?" Penton said.

"Yes, I'm with VMM-214."

"The Black Sheep Squadron."

"You know your stuff."

"I'm the ordnance chief. So, I've got to know everything."

She nodded and smiled again.

Penton wasn't comfortable with the interaction. She was very fit and highly attractive, intelligent, and confident. Not the sort of combination that made for good boundaries. He looked out the window and tried to let the trip take its course.

More palm trees were down. A few trunks lay across the road, so the driver had to maneuver into the oncoming lane. Traffic was light, so Penton didn't fear a collision, but vision was obscured by the heavy rain. He grew concerned the young driver might crash the van.

"Where do you think we're headed?" Kate said after a moment.

"Beats the hell out of me," Penton responded without taking his eyes away from the window.

"So, you have no idea?" She didn't sound convinced.

"The command center," Penton finally said. "But you didn't hear it from me."

The driver chuckled up front, and Penton allowed himself a smile.

"An inside joke?" Kate said.

Penton turned to her and nodded. Her blue eyes sparkled, and he gulped, taken aback by the dynamic young woman.

Kate smiled again, revealing perfect teeth. She suddenly seemed very familiar, a resemblance to someone from the past. "You're not Tom Able's daughter?"

She chuckled and nodded an affirmative. "Get that all the time."

"Well, I knew your father years ago. He was a hell of a pilot."

"That's what everyone always says."

"What is he up to now?"

"Just took mandatory retirement. Before that, he was commander of a flight training squadron at NAS Fallon."

Penton nodded, understanding the significance of her comment. After the Marine Corps took control over Miramar, the Navy moved Topgun out to Fallon, Nevada. The girl sitting next to him had surpassed all her peers and was the first one in her class to make captain. Her name had been kicked around about becoming a Blue Angel.

"You act like something just jarred a memory," Kate said.

"Well, I have to say that you're very observant." Penton shrugged. "I was just thinking that I'd heard about you before."

"Really?" She canted her head. "How so?"

Penton didn't think she sounded insincere. The young captain was so proper, maybe even a little naïve. She probably hadn't realized that her family name would cause her to be the talk of the rather small Navy and Marine Corps Aviation community. "Hear that you were being considered for the Blue Angels," Penton finally said.

Kate pressed back in the seat. "How could you've heard that?"

Penton grinned and lifted his eyebrows. "People talk."

"But I haven't even heard that yet. Not even sure it's true."

"That's not surprising." Penton laughed.

"You can't put a lot of stock in rumors. I'm just glad for all that's happened so far."

"They aren't rumors." Penton shrugged and patted his chevrons. "You're under consideration."

She looked at him wide-eyed, obviously registering from his tone and demeanor that the comment was truthful. A stellar career and Penton figured she'd earned every bit of it. He liked the fact she had the spunk to go with the Marines rather than the Navy. "You didn't hear it from me, though."

Kate grinned and glanced out the window.

He could tell she was ecstatic about the news, a challenge. But the look on her face reflected maturity, understanding the pressure of stepping up to take on a highly visible role. She demonstrated wisdom far beyond her years.

****

Later, the van rolled through the heavy storm and pulled up to a squat brick building. Penton noticed several cars in the parking lot. Rain cascaded on the pavement and the brick steps leading to a set of double doors. A haze of wind and deluge made the building shimmer ominously in the night.

"This is it," the driver said, opening his door.

"Guess we've got to run," Penton said to Kate and grinned.

She nodded and slid the door open.

They hopped down to the macadam and rain danced around their boots. Kate slammed the door shut, and then they dashed toward the building. Kate pulled ahead of Penton. Wind gusted into him, impeding progress. He plied his way through the stormy conditions and heard the driver stomping after him.

Entering the building, Kate smiled at Penton. She didn't seem to gloat about making it inside first, likely expected it. Rather, she seemed impressed that he'd beaten the younger Marine to the door.

Turning, he found a Marine on duty behind a podium. A young corporal wore utilities and had a sidearm strapped to his side. The driver nodded to the corporal and walked right past him. Penton figure they both worked for the commanding officer of the base.

They know more about what's going on than me, he thought.

The driver moved at a brisk pace, leading them down the hallway. Kate hurried after him and Penton followed a few steps behind her. He couldn't help but notice how well her muscular build filled out her uniform.

Rounding a corner, the driver stepped to a metal door and opened it. Kate caught hold of the door as the driver rushed down a flight of stairs. Penton followed them to a lower level and soon entered a conference room.

A large table encompassed most of the room. Every squadron commanding officer sat circled around the table. The base Commanding Officer, Colonel Tomkins, sat at the head of the table with a notepad in front of him.

The three new arrivals stood idly in the doorway, waiting for Colonel Tomkins to pause and take notice of them.

The command center had a large flat-screen hanging on the wall, and someone had turned the volume up. Rear Admiral Keyes appeared on the monitor. His body pitched occasionally, indicating he'd tuned in from aboard ship. "Do we have everybody, here?" Admiral Keyes said.

"Master Gunnery Sergeant Penton and Captain Able just walked in," Colonel Tomkins replied.

"Good," Admiral Keyes said. "Now we can get started."

"That'll be all," Colonel Tomkins said to the driver.

The lance corporal left the room and closed the door. Most of the seats were taken at the table. Colonel Tomkins motioned for Penton and Kate to step closer so they could gain a better view of the screen. Admiral Keyes sat on a posh sofa. They weren't offered a seat at the table with the higher-level Brass. The base sergeant major sat at the opposite end of the table from Colonel Tomkins, though. Perhaps a privilege of serving in the main administration building down the hall from the commanding officer.

Penton moved closer and stared up at the screen. Keyes had a dire look of concern on his face, revealing this meeting didn't have anything to do with damaged aircraft on a flight deck.

"This isn't going to come across easy," Keyes said after a moment.

"We're all ears." Colonel Tompkins smiled kindly.

"We've got a serious situation developing in Tokyo as we speak," Admiral Keyes continued. "The storm is hitting hard and the city is basically under siege."

Penton felt his stomach turn. He figured North Korea or China had mobilized.

Keyes seemed to sense the reaction of the Marines in the room. He shook his head. "This is not what you're thinking…" he said. "Maybe it's a whole lot worse."

EIGHT

Hardy steered the SDV through the choppy waters of a small cove. Then, he directed the craft toward a pebbled shore. The nose touched ground and the SEALs disembarked, kicking off their flippers and taking to the beach while scanning for hostiles.

They checked the brush and listened intently for foot soldiers.

Nothing. Rain poured down on the forest and waves chopped at the shoreline.

A quiet landing, just like Navy Intelligence had predicted.

They busied themselves moving the SDV into a concealed location, and then the SEALs worked to camouflage the vehicle with netting and leafy branches.

Once the SDV was secure, they got their equipment together and plotted a course for the missile location. Hardy decided to keep communications to a minimum, so they operated by hand signals.

A path led from the cove into the woods. They followed the trail, being careful to watch for approaching soldiers. Hardy noticed bootprints in the soil and figured the area was heavily patrolled.

He couldn't understand why the North Koreans would place such an emphasis on the remote area, not far from the Russian border. Miles of coastal lands and dense woods made the area of little value given today's modern intelligence and technology. Large troop movements, mobile tanks, and personnel carriers could be detected by satellite.

They traveled a little further inland, and Stiles checked the ground with interest. Hardy moved closer to him. Stiles lifted his chin toward the latest boot imprints.

"What has got you so concerned?" said Hardy.

"There's too much foot traffic." Stiles shook his head.

"I was thinking the exact same thing."

"What do you think?"

"Not sure. But let's move off the trail. We'll plot a course through the woods."

"That will cost us some time," Stiles reminded him.

"Maybe, but saving a few minutes isn't worth risking the entire mission."

"Roger that." Stiles nodded in agreement.

Hardy stepped off the path and headed into the woods with Stiles trailing a little behind him. They trudged along at a brisk pace, going up and down hills, and covered a mile in slightly over 15 minutes.

Growing up in New Hampshire, he'd learned how to shoot a rifle, hunt, and track game. And Hardy lived near the ocean, so he spent summers sailing and scuba diving. His parents wanted him to go to college, but he needed to get away. The Navy had been a natural choice for military service. What started as a short hitch before going to college had turned into a lifelong career. He wondered sometimes about civilian life, what it would be like to have a regular job, a family. But the thought of going to an office every day was unsettling.

Nearing the halfway point to the target, vehicle traffic reverberated from a nearby road and brought Hardy out of his thoughts. They crouched and listened intently. Sounds came from the northwest, rumbling. Hardy crept ahead and moved into a prone position, while Stiles hung back and protected the rear.

Hardy crawled over the wet forest floor and came upon the roadway. Rain pelted the tar and obscured his vision.

A moment later, three lorries rolled past, jam-packed with troops.

He crawled toward Stiles, and then the unmistakable sound of tracked vehicles echoed through the valley. Hardy waited to see what headed their way. Then, tanks came rolling along the road, with cannons bobbing up and down, and the tracks chewing asphalt.

A crew member rode with his head sticking out a hatch. The young man looked in Hardy's direction as though the soldier had made direct eye contact.

Hardy flicked off the safety of his MP-5 and slowly reached for a concussion grenade. If the tank stopped, he planned to shoot the soldier protruding from the hatch, climb onto the turret, and lob the MK3-A1 inside.

His heart raced. All senses kicked into overdrive at the anticipation of a conflict. A surge of adrenaline drove up his spine.

The tank slowed, and he prepared to shoot the man sticking out the top. Then it lurched forward and continued rolling down the street. Hardy breathed a sigh of relief.

He shook his head in disbelief. *Why hadn't Intelligence picked up on this level of troop activity in the area?*

A scrambling on the woodland floor caught his attention.

Stiles moved towards the road. Hardy held up the sign for him to halt, and then pointed to the roadway and signaled troop movement. His teammate flipped off the safety of his rifle and checked his combat knife.

Hardy hoped they wouldn't need either until reaching the missile location. Then, screeching brakes, and the metallic whine of a large truck coming to an abrupt stop, echoed through the surrounding forest.

Boots smacked the ground as infantryman alighted from the back of a transport. Soldiers headed directly to the tree line with a senior non-commissioned officer commanding them. He instructed the troops to fan out and press into the woods.

Stiles and Hardy exchanged glances. The opportunity to flee was utterly lost.

Twelve soldiers assembled at the senior non-commissioned officer's direction, fanning out around the truck.

Hardy shouldered his rifle.

He took aim.

And squeezed the trigger.

A bullet tore a hole in the leader's head. He dropped to the pavement with a thud as blood gushed from the wound. Rain poured down and quickly diluted the crimson stream.

Hardy's rifle was equipped with a silencer so the younger soldiers stood around, dumbfounded, confused as to where the shot had come from.

Stiles got into a kneeling position and fired two rounds, quickly knocking down soldiers with each shot. Hardy followed suit and took out a couple of infantrymen. The rest of them caught on and dropped to the ground, shooting wildly into the woods.

Bullets from AK-47s ripped through the forest, cutting up leaves and snapping tree branches.

Hardy and Stiles moved into prone positions in depressions in the ground. The North Koreans had the advantage, firing from an elevated position, and the sheer numbers of soldiers firing were bound to find a target.

The operation was planned to approach by stealth, but the automatic rifle fire from the AK-47s lit up the forest and likely echoed for miles. Hardy pulled the pin on his grenade and lobbed it onto the street.

An explosion tore through the soldiers, ripping a few of them apart with shrapnel.

Others were stunned by the concussion blast. Hardy stood up and ran diagonally toward the enemy position. He fired his rifle on semi-automatic, spitting shell casings as he closed the distance. Hardy hit each of the prostrate soldiers as he neared their position until his rifle ran out of ammunition.

Then, he swung the piece out of the way and drew his sidearm.

An enemy soldier at the end of the line sat up and took aim. Hardy hadn't transitioned weapons when the muzzle of the AK-47 flashed.

He took a bullet in the chest and toppled over.

Footsteps stomped through the wet ground behind him, and Stiles opened fire on the remaining North Korean soldiers. The man that shot Hardy took a bullet in the torso and one in the head. Stiles cleared the area as he'd been trained, then turned his attention to the driver of the truck. Hardy reloaded and raised his rifle but didn't have a shot, so he traced Stiles' movements closely.

The troop transport rumbled to life and started down the road.

Stiles hopped on a footboard and reached for his sidearm. His rifle hung on a sling that looped over his shoulder. He fired the 9mm Berretta into the driver's shoulder. The wounded driver braked, trying to bring the truck to a halt.

The transport swerved to the edge of the road and stopped before rolling off the roadside down an embankment. Hardy got to his feet.

Stiles finished the job with a kill shot to the head. Blood and bone fragments splattered the opposite window. He hopped to the ground, holstered the pistol, and Hardy checked the back of the truck for more troops. Empty.

Grabbing his rifle and running at port arms, Stiles double-timed back to the scene and checked the bodies strewn alongside the roadway. Every one of them was dead, so he trotted over to Hardy to see how he was doing.

Hardy waved him off and took a deep breath. The bullet hit him square in the chest where body armor covered his torso.

"That gear saved your life," Stiles said, chuckling.

"Wouldn't have pulled that stunt if I hadn't been wearing it."

"What's next, Chief?"

"Get the road clear of those bodies, ASAP."

Stiles nodded in agreement.

"No telling when another truck will come along."

They tossed the dead soldiers into the woods, making sure the corpses weren't discernible from the road.

After the soldiers were hidden from view, Hardy jogged up the road to the truck. He pulled the driver from the cab and dragged him to the woods, leaving the door open so the heavy rain would wash some of the carnage away.

Then, he tore a piece of cloth off the driver's jacket and headed back to the truck.

"What are you doing?" Stiles asked, curiously.

"Cleaning off the truck," Hardy said. "What's it look like I'm doing?"

"Just wondering the game plan, that's all."

Hardy shook his head, disappointed Stiles couldn't keep up.

"I mean... why do you care if the truck is clean?"

"Because we're going to drive it right to the missile site."

Stiles looked at him wide-eyed. Maybe the prospect seemed over-the-top risky. Hardy shrugged. "You got a better idea?"

"Not really," Stiles said, shaking his head.

They climbed into the cab with Stiles behind the wheel. Hardy checked his MP-5 and looked over the rest of his weapons.

The slug to the chest hurt like hell. He wondered if the bullet cracked a rib.

****

As the truck eased away from the battle scene, Hardy glanced in the rearview mirror on the door. There wasn't much of a sign that a conflict had taken place. He figured they were good to go for a while.

"So, what happened back there?" Stiles finally said.

"A crew member in the tank spotted me in the woods," Hardy replied. "Just dumb luck, but he likely wasn't sure what he'd seen. I bet they called in and some Brass decided to have infantry soldiers check it out."

"Makes sense," Stiles said. "A bad break, though."

"Yeah, and we're out here in the middle of nowhere surrounded by a sizeable force." Hardy inhaled deeply. "Those soldiers didn't seem to know exactly what they were looking for when we hit them."

"So, what are you saying?" Stiles pressed.

"Communications were spread by the North Koreans about us," Hardy explained. "But they clearly do not know much."

"That's good," Stiles said. "But they're going to get suspicious when the infantry soldiers don't report in."

Stiles had a point.

Hardy glanced at the radio on the dashboard, and he considered if one of them should respond to the next communication from the North Koreans. Both SEALs spoke the local language, so a communications barrier wouldn't be an issue. He wondered if the North Koreans used code words for a basic operation like this, or if they addressed soldiers by name.

"Thinking about faking it?" Stiles said, as though reading his mind.

"Might buy us some time, if we can pull it off." Hardy shrugged. "But it could also bring the whole North Korean army down on our heads if we slip up."

"How much time do you think we have… if we don't respond?"

"They will know something is up immediately. Might already suspect it when they don't hear from the senior NCO who got tapped right away."

"So… what do you think?" Stiles repeated.

"I think we've got five minutes to get to the missile site, and reinforcements will head right there if someone doesn't hear from this truck soon." Hardy scratched his chin, contemplating. "Maybe gives us fifteen to twenty minutes to get there, take out the guards, and dismantle the missile."

"That fast?" Stiles questioned.

"Yup. Intel dropped the ball on this one."

"How so?"

"All of this troop activity isn't an exercise… it's meant as a safety measure for the missile."

Stiles gulped, and then pressed on the accelerator.

NINE

Major Hira remained in position. Fighters buzzed past the creature's head and swooped around to attack. The planes shook violently in the heavy wind. Closing in on the Kaiju, the jets simultaneously released their missiles. At the same time, a contingency of tanks fired their cannons, and land missile crews let their ordnance rip.

The creature stood in a blaze of flames, as oil streamed from the broken vessel into the harbor catching fire. Hira watched the carnage in awe. The beast turned toward the bursts of weapon-fire igniting from the hillside. Then, the Kaiju let out a deafening roar, which carried a guttural sound along with the raging wind.

Everything exploded at once, as the missiles and 120mm rounds pounded into the creature. Smoke and haze intermingled with flames rising from the ocean. Waves crashed toward shore as the storm raged on.

The scene grew obscured by the attack, and Hira wasn't sure whether the creature remained standing. He ordered all the teams to reload, expecting the jets to make another pass, and riddle the creature with machinegun fire. Lifting his binoculars, Hira checked for the result of the attack.

Flames and smoke wafted through the rain, continuing to conceal the battle scene from view. Hira wiped the lenses on his binoculars and tried again. Still, he couldn't make anything out.

"Report on the target!" Hira yelled into the communications link.

"Target hit," crew leaders responded in unison.

"What is the target's condition?" Hira demanded.

A moment passed without a response from any of them.

"Target condition?" Hira repeated.

"Can't make out the target through the hazy conditions," a tank commander said. Others followed suit with similar reports.

Major Hira shook his head. He tried his binoculars again and looked toward the harbor. Flames raged as the jets buzzed in for another pass. "Hold your fire," Hira commanded the ground crews. "Let air support take another crack."

The jets closed in on the spot where a volley of ordnance had exploded. Wind blew hard into the fuselages, shifting a few of the planes off course. Hira hoped for a precautionary volley of machinegun fire, strafing a fallen and severely wounded creature. After all, the thing was merely a giant lizard. Nothing could survive such a violent attack.

Something shimmered in the haze. The Kaiju staggered and plodded toward the shore.

Hira wanted to give the order to fire, but the fighters were on course for the target. Fighter jets swooped in front of the creature and rattled off machinegun fire. Rounds pelted its thick hide. A menacing roar thundered louder than the jet engines. The creature shook its head, more annoyed than injured. Turning to mark the path of an approaching jet, the creature swatted the plane from the sky.

The fighter spiraled into the ocean and exploded upon impact with rough waves. Hira couldn't tell if the pilot had ejected. A few other planes soared high above the Kaiju, and then moved in for another pass.

Machinegun fire erupted from the planes as they stippled the armored-plated hide with lead. The creature wailed in agony, and then lifted a claw into the path of an oncoming plane. The jet flew into its palm, like hitting a brick wall. The plane exploded on impact, and the Kaiju barely registered a blow, tipping slightly on its right leg.

Another plane buzzed by at a safe distance and emptied its munitions into the creature. Rounds whizzed by its head while a few found purchase. The remaining fighters zipped off into the distance.

Hira surmised the fighters had run out of ammunition. The planes were battered by the weather, jostling through the sky, and then flew out of eyeshot.

"Fire!" Hira ordered when the area cleared.

"Yes, sir," the tank commanders said.

"Roger," the missile crew commanders replied.

The hillside erupted with another volley of rounds and missiles directed at the creature. Hira wiped the binoculars dry and peered through the torrential rain. The Kaiju waded toward shore, moving at a steady pace.

Missiles sailed past the creature and detonated in the rough waves, while others struck the beast in the belly and chest. Explosions lit up the dreary sky.

Then, several 120mm rounds pounded into the creature, digging holes into its heavily plated hide. The Kaiju roared in pain, and then stepped onto shore, uninhibited by the attack. Heavy footsteps thundered into the ground. Another roar, but this one in rage.

Hira contemplated the next order, struggling between getting off another volley of ordnance, or retreating to regroup.

The Kaiju closed the distance fast, taking prodigious steps towards the line of tanks. A trail of flames scattered across the ground behind him. Bits of burning oil cast off its legs and shed from the long tail, as it whipped back and forth.

Small fenced-in industrial areas with outbuildings and parked cars lay between the approaching monster and the line of defense. Hira ordered another assault on the creature. The tank commanders followed his order and instructed their crews to load the cannons. All the missile crews readied for another launch.

"This time… fire every missile you have loaded on the carriers," Hira said.

The missile crew commanders responded in the affirmative.

"Tank commanders…" Hira called into the comm-link. "Fire when ready."

A volley of 120mm cannons erupted, hurling rounds at the creature. The barrage was followed by intermittent bursts, as various cannons were loaded and fired at different speeds. Round after round found purchase burrowing into the thick hide.

The Kaiju stopped in its tracks and bellowed in agony. A round or two had passed through to the creature's underbelly.

Hira realized the beast was vulnerable. It swung its head from side to side, trying to shake off the pain. A shrill yowl carried toward the defensive line, along with the howling wind, sending pinpricks through Hira's ears.

"Fire all missiles!" Hira yelled.

The tubes erupted from the hillside, shooting missiles at the creature.

"Reload and fire all cannons," Major Hira commanded.

"Shouldn't we evacuate?" said a crew commander.

"Missile crews retreat," Hira said. "Tank crews remain steady."

"Understood, sir," tank commanders replied, but many sounded unsteady.

The task at hand wasn't something they'd ever trained to do in combat. Hira expected them to lose confidence. But not much stood before the advancing beast and the city. "Fire when ready!" Major Hira barked.

Soon after he'd given the command, tanks rocked back and forth, as the cannons erupted with rounds homed in on the creature.

The Kaiju charged on the perimeter as the latest volley struck home. Another wail of pain emitted from the Kaiju's muzzle while it writhed about in suffering.

This time, the creature did not falter. Monstrous steps marched it closer.

Sharp claws protruded from each foot, measuring the size of a dump truck, digging into the earth to stabilize the creature. Each step brought the Kaiju nearer to the fortified position, crushing fences and cars, and igniting the outbuildings that didn't get crushed into matchsticks.

Everything around the Kaiju lit up in a blaze of fire. Smoke and billowing flames wafted through the deluge. And detritus of mass destruction trailed in its wake.

"Retreat!" Hira screamed in panic.

"Retreat! Retreat!" the tank commanders echoed.

Hira slipped inside his tank and sealed the hatch. "Move out!" he yelled to his tank commander, even though the operator was already in motion.

The creature pounded up the hillside and stepped on a tank. Armor-plated metal caved in like a tin can. Screams flooded the cabin and transmitted over the communications link. Hira pictured his troopers being crushed to death, as the weight of a building pressed on the tank, bones snapping and lungs pushed in, asphyxiating the soldiers.

Hira tried to shake off the ghastly image as his operator maneuvered their tank. Another tank was decimated under the monster's footstep. Horrific cries of agony spread over the communications network.

Operators of various tanks attempted flight at the same time. Some of them backed up, while others turned into the path of oncoming tanks. Hira watched through the viewing scope in awe. The panicked maneuvers caused them to collide with each other. Metal clanging into grinding tracks echoed across the battle scene.

Tanks piled up everywhere. A disastrous sight, the retreat was anything but organized. Hira realized they'd never been trained for this sort of contingency, and the disorganization lead to unnecessary deaths.

The creature stomped after them mercilessly. A giant foot came down hard and caved in three tanks caught up on each other. Flames whisked into the grey sky.

The clamor of soldiers being crushed resonated across the communications system.

The pileup kept them all from dying at once. Distorted metal and the Kaiju moving after other victims left crew members in tanks with hope. Then, a patch of fire caught on a broken diesel fuel line and erupted in a ball of flames.

An explosion shook Hira's tank, followed by the horrific screams of soldiers burning alive.

He glanced into the viewfinder and immense scales came into view.

"Move!" Hira screamed. "The Kaiju is directly upon us."

"Roger," the operator grunted.

Hira felt the tank speed up. It collided with another tank, bouncing off, but kept rolling. Their tank pulled away from the creature, gaining distance. He breathed easier, but then realized the Kaiju had focused on their tank.

Attracted to the tank's flight, the beast stomped after them in pursuit.

TEN

Penton stared at the video screen in disbelief. He couldn't accept what he'd watched was real. All his instincts told him it was true, though. The concern on Admiral Keyes' face, and the Brass sitting around the table. Everything suggested a dire situation.

The admiral came back on screen. "Figured a picture was worth a thousand words," Keyes said, shaking his head.

Colonel Tomkins took a deep breath and smirked. He appeared skeptical and spoke first. "Rear Admiral Keyes... have you been able to verify the film footage we've just seen?"

"No, gentlemen and ladies, we have not." Keyes shrugged.

"Well, have you made direct contact with Japan's Self-Defense Forces?"

"As I reported to you earlier," Keyes said. "We have not been able to make direct verbal communications with the Self-Defense Forces. However, we did track a large mass headed toward Tokyo earlier today."

"Why didn't anyone do anything about it?" Colonel Tomkins said.

"The creature was picked up as a whale on the sonar."

"Understandable," Colonel Tomkins said. "But are we sure it's even real?"

Admiral Keyes clenched his teeth and paused, obviously tired of being questioned. The entire room sensed his frustration. No one dared speak another word. Keyes sat back in a posh leather sofa. Aboard a massive warship in the middle of the Pacific Ocean during a hurricane, he wasn't a paper pusher. Everyone knew he had come up the hard way, starting as an enlisted sailor. And everyone in the command center at MCAS Futenma waited for him to settle down.

Penton wondered when the gamesmanship would pass, so they could get to the plan and explain why he was there.

"We've had to fall back on communications through a cellphone," Admiral Keyes finally said. "But I've spoken with General Yoshi. And he assures me that Tokyo is in grave danger."

"Might be so," Colonel Tomkins pressed. "But from what?"

"That fucking creature tearing up the harbor. What else?"

"What the hell is that thing supposed to be?"

"We don't have a clue," Keyes admitted. "The creature appears to be indestructible and has taken everything that's been thrown at it."

"Seems to have suffered a few good blows, though." This from Lieutenant Colonel Jeb Brady, commanding officer of the Flying Tigers.

Keyes nodded in agreement. He smiled, apparently glad to have some support. "We expect to be able to take the thing down... before it does too much damage."

"How are Japan's Self-Defense Forces capabilities?" said Colonel Tomkins.

"The creature rolled through them like they were standing still," Keyes replied. "Just like you saw in the video."

Penton watched Colonel Tomkins shake his head and chuckle.

"What are their backup capabilities?" Lieutenant Colonel Brady asked.

Now Admiral Keyes was shaking his head.

"That good?" Colonel Tomkins said.

"As you saw, the creature walked right over their tank and missile crews. The Japan Air Self-Defense wasn't successful, and we don't expect too much more from them."

"Why not?" Colonel Tomkins said. "Is there a lack of readiness on their part?"

"The storm has made takeoff and operation of their jets standing ready for an emergency almost non-operational."

Colonel Tomkins nodded, understanding.

"We've got an LHP off the coast of South Korea," Lieutenant Colonel Brady said. "She's got full amphibious force readiness. Two thousand Marines and fighting vehicles, plus a squadron of attack helicopters for close-combat support."

Admiral Keyes shook his head. "The ship will take too long to maneuver around Japan and get into place. Plus, the type of approach you suggest isn't the most effective."

"What's the plan?" Colonel Tomkins snapped at beating around the bush.

"The plan is to send a contingency of Harriers from Okinawa… fully loaded with the best and most appropriate ordnance."

Penton finally got the picture why he and Captain Able were in the room.

****

After the meeting, Penton and Kate headed upstairs and stepped outside into the pouring rain. The driver sat in the van waiting for them. Dashing across the pavement, Kate slid the door open, and they climbed in back.

Penton noticed the concerned look on Kate's face. He reached for her hand to provide reassurance. Kate didn't pull away. Instead, she massaged his fingers, a tender touch, when she was the one facing a crisis. Kate had just watched the creature take down two jets.

"Harriers are more stable in storms like this…" Penton offered.

She nodded, but didn't seem convinced.

Harriers are capable of vertical-lift takeoffs and landings. They do not require a runway, similar to helicopters. Penton figured the Brass wanted to use Harriers in the event a sudden landing was required, either due to the storm, or the monster.

"You'll do just fine," Penton said. "You're one of the best pilots in the world."

"Never flown in winds like this before." She shook her head.

"The Japanese Air Self-Defense jets handled the winds. They just misjudged the creature, and they didn't have the best ordnance."

"I'm sure you'll take care of that." Kate forced a laugh.

"We'll make sure your squad is well-equipped."

"So, what's the plan?"

"Drop her off at the barracks," Penton said to the driver.

"What then?" the driver said.

"Take me to my place, so I can get my Jeep. Then swing back over and pick her up."

"Sure thing," the driver said.

"By the time you're ready," Penton said to Kate, "I'll be at the MALS-36 hangar."

Kate nodded, getting the picture. Then, he glanced out the window and noticed the storm had picked up. Gusting winds blew stronger than before.

An ominous feeling overcame him. Penton wondered what they were really up against.

****

The driver dropped Penton off at the staff non-commissioned officer barracks. Penton ran inside and grabbed his keys and a Marine Corps-issue poncho. He tossed his cover on the dining room table, then donned the poncho and headed outside.

Wind pounded hard, and he fought to reach the Jeep. It started right up and he shifted the manual transmission into gear and then headed toward the hangar. His lightweight vehicle swayed from the heavy gusts and teetered a couple of times.

Penton wondered how a jet could stay in the air. The thought of losing Kate due to the weather concerned him and he didn't know why.

Arriving at the hangar, he found the ordnance shop shutting down. Penton spotted the corporal who'd transported the injured Marine to Navy Hospital. Alvarez sat behind a metal desk scribbling on a form. Dedicated, she was the last Marine left in her unit. Everyone had gone home to weather out the storm.

"We've got a serious situation on our hands," Penton said to her.

"What do you need?" She grinned at him.

"Call Top Anderson. And get your five best ordnance personnel assembled here pronto. This is a high-priority mission that just came down."

"Will do!" She reached for the phone. "What are you going to do now?"

"I'll be up at the ordnance dump, starting to get things ready." Penton turned to leave the shop. "I'll call in from there… once your people are mustered."

Alvarez smiled and picked up the phone, calling in unit members.

Penton headed back to his office and fetched the keys for the build-up area. He pulled them out of his desk drawer and then headed out the rear hatch into the rain. He trotted over the gravel parking area as rain battered the hood of his poncho. Penton couldn't hear anything but the storm.

He climbed into his Jeep and shut the door. Penton pulled from the parking lot and headed to the ordnance dump.

A moment of relief slipped over him after climbing in the vehicle, out of the elements. Penton thought about how Marines spent countless hours training in horrible weather, and many battles were fought in severe conditions.

There wasn't any use in complaining or wishing for better weather. *Suffer in silence*, he thought.

He drove down the stormy roads and rolled up to the fenced-in compound. The guard shack was empty and the gate chained shut. He looked around but didn't see the private on duty. Penton shook his head and glanced uphill. The slick-sleever was nowhere to be seen.

A narrow driveway led up a slight hillside and then wound into a covered overhang. Storage lockers lined both sides of the area, like pulling up to a gas station. Penton suspected the guard had taken cover under the truck-port, but the storage lockers concealed the young Marine from view.

Penton unlocked the gates and swung them open. He drove through slowly, putting on his headlights to alert the guard. The last thing he needed was to get shot by a jumpy boot.

He eased around until the Jeep approached the concrete landing. A silhouette stood up from a palette of inert rocket warheads.

The private shouldered his M-16 and aimed at the approaching vehicle.

Penton shut off the headlights and turned on his parking lights, hoping the young Marine would recognize the Jeep. Aviation Ordnance wings served as the front license plate.

But the Marine held the rifle ready to fire. He slowly walked diagonally across the front of the vehicle with the barrel trained on the driver. Penton pulled back his poncho hood and the private stared at him wide-eyed.

"You can lower the fucking rifle, now," Penton said.

"Sorry, Master Gunnery Sergeant," the private replied, meekly. "I had no idea it was you."

Penton shook his head and pulled forward under the protective cover. "You could have figured that out at the guard shack, if you'd been down by the gate." Penton pulled up and maneuvered close to a stanchion. He hopped out of the Jeep.

"Well, I was just walking the premises," the private continued.

Penton flicked a switch and powerful lights flooded the covered area.

"Sergeant Morales told us… to make a pass through the lot a few times a day."

"Don't doubt he instructed you that way."

"Sure did," the private affirmed.

Penton quickly headed to a storage locker. "But it didn't look to me like you were walking the grounds. Looked as though you were sleeping on post."

"Just up here checking on things…"

"Save it."

Penton twisted a key in the padlock.

"But—"

Penton waved him off. "We don't have time for this nonsense right now. Get over here and help me lift this box to the ground."

The private set down his rifle and walked over to the storage locker. Penton swung the door wide-open and reached inside. He slid the box to the edge of a shelf. A wooden crate, it weighed a great deal.

"Be careful not to drop it," Penton said, as the private strained to lift it.

They maneuvered the box a short distance, and then set it down on the concrete. A thud reverberated across the build-up area as the crate smacked the ground. Penton pulled a face, then cracked the lid open.

He peered inside at the green warheads. The inert warheads used for training were blue and solid inside. Penton reached into the box and pulled out a warhead. He felt the contents shift inside. All the active warheads had explosive material cased inside the metal head. Pointed at the nose, and threaded on the end, so it could be screwed into a rocket-motor tube.

Penton planned to load each fighter with two rocket pods, capable of housing up to seven rockets each. The squadron would send five planes, so he needed enough to fill ten pods. "We'll need seventy warheads."

The private nodded, understanding. But he had a concerned look on his face. "What's this all about?"

"Can't get into it now," Penton said. "We've got too much to do."

"Okay, sure." But the kid looked worried, like he knew a conflict would break out.

"We'll need all of the boxes in that locker."

They lowered each box to the ground and lined them up. A truck would roll up and the team of Marines from Top Anderson's unit would load them.

Penton fished around the storage locker and snagged a bunch of cartridge activating devices. He carefully placed them into a crate. The CADs were round, metallic rocket components, about the size of a silver dollar and a half-inch deep.

CADs get inserted into the rear of the rocket and rub against a metal fin inside the pod. When the pilot fires a rocket, electric current travels from the aircraft to the pod and sends a current into the fin. Then, the fin electrically charges the CAD, which explodes and causes a combustible propellant within the rocket tube to burn, launching the rocket into flight.

The pods were stacked in another part of the build-up area. Penton reached for a phone attached to the stanchion that housed the light switch. He called the ordnance shop and instructed them to get a truck and head out to meet him.

Then he turned toward the private. "Come with me," Penton said. "We're going to bring the pods up here so they're ready to load when they get here."

"Can't we load them where they are?" the private griped. "It would take the same amount of time."

Penton wanted to punch him. "You're a Marine!" He shook his head. "Now, get moving. We don't have a second to spare."

They headed out into the rain and the growing darkness and double-timed over to the storage area where the LAU-68 rocket pods were located. The pods were stacked on rows of lumber to keep them off the ground, but nothing else protected them from the elements. Rain cascaded over the pods and harsh winds bandied them.

"I'll take the front and you grab the rear," Penton said.

"Sure thing." The private moved into position without further comment.

Penton figured he'd make it easier on the kid. Each pod was shaped into a cylinder about five feet long, with a honeycomb opening at the front where seven rockets could slide inside. Two rockets on top, three in the middle, and two more fit into the bottom.

Penton placed his back against a pod on the top of the pile and slid his hands behind him, grabbing hold of the top shafts with his fingers. An awkward position. The private stood on the other side and easily grabbed hold of his end.

They trudged uphill, straining to carry the pod. But they reached the covered area quickly.

Setting the pod down, Penton trotted back to the pile with the private in tow. They repeated the maneuver nine more times, getting drenched in the process. When they'd hauled the last rocket pod up to the concrete pad, the private was worn out. His shoulders drooped, and he dragged his boots on the ground.

Penton had to pull him along and the kid stumbled a couple of times.

As they set the pod down, a truck rumbled into the build-up area. Penton directed it under the protected covering. The truck pulled alongside the pods and warheads, and then four Marines piled out from the cab.

Penton pointed to the crates and the rocket pods. "These need to get loaded ASAP," he said.

Fresh from the barracks, they moved into action without saying a word. The truck bed stood four feet above the ground. The private stepped over to help but had difficulty lifting the pods into the back. Penton helped him get them over the threshold.

A Marine climbed up and slid the LAU-68 rocket pods toward the cab. They all worked together to load each crate. It took four of them to lift each one onto the truck. But they had the truck loaded in no time.

Then a Marine turned toward Penton. "What's next?"

Penton tossed him the keys to his Jeep. "We'll get the rest of it," he said, climbing into the cab of a truck. "You take my Jeep back to the hangar."

ELEVEN

Maki stood frozen and watched as the tidal wave crashed onto city streets. Pouring a flood of water, the wave disbursed everywhere in torrents.

People turned and fled. Water streamed down streets and sidewalks. It spilled down stairwells leading to the subway. Her family had planned to take the tube back to their apartment. Now, the transit system was not an option.

Fireworks showered the sky and boomed from the nearby harbor. Maki couldn't understand why anyone would celebrate in such a disastrous storm. The sounds grew in intensity until the noise resembled explosions.

The storm caused a tsunami and damaged buildings by the harbor, she thought. Maki figured everything would settle down, and then work crews would come out like any storm and fix everything. Except the roar and the large silhouette had her on edge.

She couldn't fully comprehend the situation. Maki shivered.

Her father stood beside Maki's mother, glancing back and forth. He seemed confused. Water undulated toward them.

"We need to go!" Maki cried.

"The subway is dangerous," her father said.

"Momma, let's run like the others."

But her mother remained silent, deferring to Father like always in a technical situation. Mother didn't bow down to him in the home, and often stood her ground, moving against tradition. When circumstances such as this occurred, her mother relied upon his engineering and problem-solving skills to get them out of a situation.

He studied the approaching water carefully, then grabbed his wife's arm and hurried toward a narrow alley.

Maki trailed behind them. Her mother grasped her little hand so tightly it hurt. Dread grew in the pit of her stomach. The alley seemed like the wrong choice. Everyone else ran down the main street, fleeing for their lives.

Reaching the end of the alley, her father stopped and turned. He pointed toward where they had come from. A surge of water coursed down the main street. People screamed for help, and then the cries became muffled, eventually fading out.

"We would have been killed," her father asserted.

Her mother nodded in agreement.

Maki felt for the people who didn't make it. "Maybe they can hold their breath and swim," she offered.

Her father shook his head; a realist, he wouldn't let her cling to false notions.

Water bashed off the corner of the building near the mouth of the alley. A stream poured into the corridor. The water pressed towards them, running over the concrete and creeping to four feet deep out near the street.

Her father scanned the back of the alley. A narrow passageway led to a door. He looked at the approaching flood and back at the passageway. "No good," he said, shaking his head. "We could get trapped down there."

"What do we do?" Mother sounded frantic.

"Check the doors," father insisted.

Mother let go of Maki's hand. She rattled doors on one side of the alley, and Father tried some on the other side. A trickle of water sloshed around Maki's rain boots. Only a few inches deep, but it crept higher and higher the longer she stood there. Within a moment, the water had risen to a foot deep.

"Here!" her father said, cracking a door.

"Oh, my!" Mother stepped over to help him.

Father struggled with the door, unable to pry it completely open.

Maki trundled in the water toward her parents, ready to slip through the doorway when she was told.

Her mother grabbed onto the door, and both of her parents pulled and strained to open it. Father placed a foot on the wall for leverage. Still, the door didn't budge.

The current pulled at Maki's rain boots. She felt as though the flooding might topple her. Looking back toward the main street, she noticed water coming into the alley had risen to six feet at the corner of the building.

Her heart raced in panic. The water would quickly submerge her entire family, unless they could get the door open. They cracked the door ajar.

"Maki!" her father yelled. "Get inside."

She scooted beneath their arms and slipped past Father's leg. Maki shimmied into the doorway, feeling the door and the weight of all the water pressing against her. Maki's forward progress became impeded when she got partially inside the building.

The door pushed against her so hard that she couldn't move ahead. Her lungs felt compressed. She had difficulty breathing.

"You go," he said to her mother.

Mother dipped a shoulder into the opening and brushed against Maki. Then, a force jolted Maki inside the building. Maki landed on the floor of a storage room. Water trickled into the room, puddling on the concrete around her.

Her mother squeezed partway inside. The door pressed her violently into the jamb, as though life might compress out of her at any moment.

A shoulder collided into mother's side and tossed her forward.

She toppled to the floor. And the metal door slammed shut with a clang. Then her mother screamed in agony.

TWELVE

Hardy jostled in the front seat of the troop transport as it bounced over a desolate road. Each jolt sent pain shooting through his chest. Reaching into a cargo pocket, he grabbed two pain capsules, downing them without any water.

They closed in on the target area fast, and were just minutes away. Hardy checked over his weapons, getting ready for a fight.

Stiles looked at him. "How do you want to handle this?"

"Running it through my mind," Hardy said, grinning.

"Figured you'd say something like that."

Hardy shrugged, and then returned his attention to his weapons check.

"Well, we're almost there…"

"Understood."

Hardy glanced out the windshield.

Stiles turned his attention back to the road. He clearly had concerns about the way the mission had unraveled. Hardy wondered if getting seen in the woods had been a boot mistake, rather than a chance stroke of luck for the enemy.

A long, wooded drive led off the main road. The North Koreans occupied a warehouse at the end of the dirt driveway, situated about a quarter mile away. Options were to stop the truck and approach quietly by foot, or roll right up and charge in. Both plans had advantages. He just wasn't sure what exactly the North Koreans knew.

"Have it figured out yet?" Stiles said.

"Yup," Hardy replied, straightening up. He felt an adrenaline rush kick into gear. The strategy was the best option given the circumstances.

Stiles shook his head upon hearing the plan.

A moment later, Stiles eased up the driveway and brought the truck to a stop. The two SEALs climbed down from the cab and walked toward the warehouse. Their target was less than five meters away, and no doubt anyone inside the building heard the truck. Probably heard the firefight down the road, too.

The building had two large sliding doors, which rolled on tracks like a barn. A wooden door was cut into one of the sliding doors. Hardy approached the small door and checked the rusty knob. Locked.

He rapped on the door, and then stepped to the side.

Each SEAL held a concussion grenade.

A soldier opened the door and peered outside. He looked directly ahead toward the truck, and apparently didn't see them tucked to the side. A perplexed look crossed his face, turning to shock when Hardy stepped forward with a SOG SEAL fighting knife in hand.

Hardy lunged forward and pulled the soldier outside. Wrapping a hand around the man's mouth, he cut the soldier's throat with the razor-sharp knife. He waited a moment and eased the dead man to the earth. Blood gushed out the slit in his throat, and gurgling emanated from the open wound.

The SEALs entered the building single file. A large land-launched missile sat on a trailer in the middle of the room. Hardy tossed a grenade into the back right-hand corner of the warehouse, and Stiles lobbed his partway down the left side of the building.

A few soldiers stood around the missile holding AK-47s. Catwalks ran along each side of the vaulted ceiling, suspended by cables attached to support beams. The guards shouldered their weapons.

The grenades exploded, knocking a few of the soldiers to the deck, while others stumbled off-balance. Hardy trained his MP-5 on a soldier perched on the catwalk to the right.

Hardy fired his rifle.

A bullet smacked the sentry's forehead.

The soldier teetered off the catwalk.

He dropped to the concrete floor with a heavy thud, and then machinegun fire erupted from the middle of the room.

Stiles stood oblique to Hardy's left, a partial wedge-shaped formation. A blast flared from his rifle barrel; multiple shots ripped into a soldier standing by the missile.

Hardy shot two men on the other catwalk, and then pressed forward into the center of the room. Automatic weapons erupted from the rear of the trailer. Hardy rolled underneath the trailer and popped up on the other side.

He took aim, squeezed the trigger, and capped one of them in the cheek.

The soldier spun around in a death dance, while squeezing his trigger. Stiles fired at the other soldier, and hit the man only after his comrade riddled him with bullets.

Hardy moved around the rear of the trailer. Two men lay on the floor from the concussion grenades. One of them writhed in agony, riddled with shrapnel. The other scrambled for his rifle.

He shot the one reaching for a weapon. Two bullets rang out of the MP-5, striking the soldier in the chest and head.

Stiles checked the other fallen soldier for weapons.

And Hardy swept through the rest of the warehouse, clearing the expansive room. He didn't encounter any other enemy soldiers.

Nothing.

He shook his head, thinking it was too easy.

All casualties totaled only eight, which was in line with the information he'd been given by Navy Intelligence, but it seemed light for such an important detail.

"I'm going to check out back," Hardy said, jogging toward the rear doors.

"Sure." Stiles crouched by a wounded soldier.

"Be extra careful with him," Hardy warned.

"Yeah, wouldn't surprise me if he's willing to die."

"He's as good as dead for blowing this assignment," Hardy replied, stepping out a back door. He scanned the area. An open gravel driveway circled to the back, so vehicles could pull through the warehouse.

Hardy looked beyond the parking area into the woods.

No sign of troop activity.

If any North Koreans heard the gunfire, they'd hightail it toward the warehouse. Hardy searched the wood line more carefully. Still, no sign of movement anywhere.

He scanned back and forth with the same result.

"Headed around front," he spoke into the communications link.

"Roger, let me know the result."

Sweeping around front, Hardy hugged close to the building. He performed a hasty scan near the building, and then scouted the area in front of the truck. Nothing.

Hardy trod away from the building and approached the transport. He walked along the driver's side, keeping close to the massive wheels. Then, he knelt and peeked underneath. No soldiers hid beneath the truck.

He stood up and walked around back. Nobody lingered behind the truck, and the transport was empty. Hardy peeked around the other side of the truck but didn't find anyone there. Shaking his head, he wondered how the North Korean's managed to leave the area unsecure. He remembered the military convoy from earlier in the day.

Listening intently, he tried to hear any commotion from the road. Everything remained still, until the unmistakable sound of a diesel engine echoed through the countryside, along with tracks grinding into pavement.

Armored infantry swiftly approached the warehouse.

THIRTEEN

Penton rode shotgun out to the magazines where ordnance was stored in bunkers. An afternoon grey sky began slipping into dusk. He alighted from the truck and walked up to a guard shack. Rain pelted his poncho and danced off the macadam. Two young Marines watched him closely. A guard walked from the hut into the storm and slowly approached the gate.

"What can we do for you?" the guard barked.

"Open the gate, now!" Penton pulled back the hood on his poncho.

"Sorry, Master Gunnery Sergeant… didn't know it was you."

"Let's just get a move on it."

Penton crossed his arms, while the young Marine fiddled with the lock. He pondered whether security measures were lackadaisical. Anyone could slip onto the base in a secluded area, hotwire a truck, then roll in and cap the guards and abscond with ordnance. Sentries didn't take threats seriously.

He shook his head thinking about it. When the lock popped open, he didn't wait for the guard to remove the chain. Penton grabbed a few links and yanked it through, handing the chain over to the young Marine.

Then, he shoved the gates open and waved to the driver of the truck. Windshield wipers flapping back and forth obscured the driver from view. Penton couldn't tell if the Marine got his signal. Then the truck grumbled and lunged forward, and Penton climbed inside.

He directed the driver toward the Magazine Area where a road wound past bunkers with armor-plated doors. Short driveways led up to each magazine, which housed bombs, missiles, and rocket motors.

Penton scanned the area and pointed to a magazine near the end of the line. The driver backed the truck up to the doors and cut the engine. Everyone hopped out and headed toward the ordnance dump. Penton unlocked the doors and swung them wide-open.

He stepped inside and flipped on a light. Stacks of thick wooden crates were piled in neat rows on top of pallets. All the boxes were four feet long and a foot wide. Each box was a foot deep, and ropes protruded from both ends, serving as handles to carry them.

"We need seventy MK-40 rocket motors," Penton said to the Marines.

"Yes, sir," they replied in unison.

"Don't call me, sir," Penton said. "I work for a living."

A few of them smirked at the comment, and then went full-steam into loading the truck with enough boxes to handle the payload. Marine recruits are trained to call their drill instructors 'sir.' But when they get into the fleet, only officers are afforded that title. Sometimes when pressure mounts, young Marines fall back on calling their seniors 'sir.'

They finished the task and climbed back into the truck, while Penton closed the magazine doors. He locked them and clambered into the truck.

The driver turned to him: "What's next?"

"Right there." Penton pointed to a magazine down the roadway.

The driver repeated the operation, backing up to the doors. Penton hustled through the rain and unlocked them. Marines lined up behind him. Opening the doors, a bunker of cluster bombs filled the space.

"We're going to need six," Penton said.

"Aye, sir," they sounded off again.

Penton smiled. *Never get Marine Corps boot camp out of their heads*, he thought.

Each CBU weighed five hundred pounds. The detail of Marines marched into the magazine and grabbed two steel poles. One of them was threaded at the end, and the other was smooth.

They twisted the threaded end into the nose of the bomb then slid the smooth end of the other pole into a slot by the fins. A ridge on the smooth rod brought the insertion to a halt. Then, two Marines grabbed hold of each pole, and all four of them heaved the bomb from the floor. They shuffled forward, carrying it to the truck.

Penton helped them lift the CBU onto the truck bed.

Rain pelted the ordnance in the back of the truck. Penton thought about how troops tend to handle ordnance delicately. Yet once it gets loaded onto aircraft, the bombs and rockets are exposed to the elements, and shake around during takeoff. Ordnance gets bumped and jostled in flight, especially during combat.

He stepped around to the cab and slid onto the bench seat. "One more stop," Penton said to the driver.

"Figured there'd be another." The kid grinned and shifted into drive.

"Need everything those birds can hold."

"Who are we striking against?"

Penton shook his head. "You know better than to ask that question. Besides, you'll know soon enough."

The driver mashed the gas pedal and sped the truck toward the next magazine. Penton bounced down from the truck and trotted over to the doors. He opened them wide and directed the Marines to a few munitions crates.

Ammo cans held belts of ammunition for the GAU-12 Equalizer. A five-barrel 25 mm rotary Gatling-type aircraft machinegun. The weapons were stored in the cage back at the ordnance shop.

"Grab as many of those as we can fit in the truck," Penton instructed.

"Yes, Master Gunnery Sergeant," they barked.

"Let me give you a hand." Penton grabbed a can and felt the heft.

They loaded the truck and locked the bunker up behind them. Then, the driver raced back toward the MALS-36 hangar. He rounded turns fast, causing Penton to sway in his seat.

"Slow down a bit," Penton said.

"Sorry, thought we were in a rush."

"Yeah, but we need to get there in one piece. Spill all this ordnance on the road and we'd drop behind schedule..." Penton shook his head. "And somebody would have my ass."

"Roger..." The driver stifled a laugh.

When the truck wheeled onto the flight deck, it stopped at the Combat Aircraft Loading Area. Captain Able had reported with four other pilots. They stood ready in the hangar doorway, wearing flight suits and holding their helmets with flashy emblems. Their support teams had already unfastened the Harriers and moved them near the loading area.

Top Anderson had a crew of ordnance technicians loading the GAU-12 Equalizers onto the Harriers. Penton's truck wheeled into the loading area, and then he climbed down from the cab.

Wind gusted across the tarmac and whipped the rain into a frenzy. A field workspace was already assembled, and Marines went about preparing to load the aircraft, while fuel trucks filled the planes.

They set the rocket motors on the table and screwed in warheads, and then each rocket had a cartridge activating device inserted in the rear by the fins. Other Marines loaded the rocket pods onto the Harriers. Then the rockets were slid into the honeycomb openings in the front of each pod, one at a time.

The cluster bombs were loaded on the planes, utilizing similar poles to those in the magazines. Lifting the heavy ordnance into place, they hooked the bombs to the bottom of the planes and removed the poles. Technicians wired the bombs to the planes, so the pilots could flip a switch and send a current down to each bomb and release it.

After the GAU-12 Equalizers were mounted to the birds, technicians loaded them with cartridge belts. The rotating machineguns were capable of firing 1,800 to 4,200 rounds per minute. Penton walked around each Harrier, checking the rocket pods, bombs, and machineguns. He made sure the ordnance and weaponry were properly affixed to the planes, and that the electrical lines were attached correctly and secure.

Penton finished his check and headed into the hangar. He met with Kate and the rest of her squadron. He explained all the ordnance in detail, even though Kate had flown enough hours to have a comprehensive understanding.

The discussion included a review of current Action Orders and Bulletins issued by Fleet Command on a regular basis. They pertained to safety items. Kate took in all the information and studied him seriously.

When he finished briefing them, she forced a smile and looked him directly in the eye. Her demeanor appeared slightly morose. Penton reached out to shake her hand, but she stepped forward and embraced him.

The hug lasted longer than he expected. Kate squeezed him hard, almost refusing to let go. She leaned back and swiped a strand of hair from her face. Then, she took a deep breath and smiled confidently. "Thanks for all your help, James," Kate said.

"Just doing my job," Penton replied.

"Your commitment and underappreciation for your efforts are the stuff my family always talked about." Kate shrugged. "My father was always impressed with the way Marines get things done… without complaining or seeking recognition."

"Suffer in silence," Penton muttered the motto.

Kate nodded, understanding the creed. "That's why I selected the Corps."

"You made the right choice for yourself."

"Now, I've got a job to do."

She smiled one last time and put on her flight helmet. Kate stepped out of the hangar and into the harsh wind. Rain pounded down at an angle as she walked towards her fighter. The rest of her crew followed her lead, stoic and proud.

****

Penton watched the Harriers fire up. They shot straight into the air, one at a time, and then blasted off toward Tokyo. He felt disheartened at seeing Kate fly away into the dreary evening sky. Rain pelted down. The storm was hazardous enough to keep them from reaching their target. Never mind what peril lay ahead from the menacing creature.

A moment later, Penton walked over to the Combat Aircraft Loading Area. Marines busied themselves boxing up tools and stowing munitions. Top Anderson stood in the pouring rain without a poncho. The deluge poured over him, soaking his utilities, but he didn't seem to mind.

"Come to see how it's done?" Top Anderson laughed.

Penton grinned. "Suppose our work on this mission is over."

"Maybe…" Top Anderson shook his head, doubtfully.

"What?" Penton insisted.

"Just a hunch… we're not out of this yet."

A young private first class snatched up a few cartridge activating devices, then shoved them into a cargo pocket. Penton jogged over to the Marine. "Wait!"

"What?" the private first class muttered.

"Take those out of your pocket," Penton demanded.

"Sure…" The private first class fished the CADs out of his utilities.

"You've got a dangerous situation there."

The kid stared back at Penton, dumbfounded.

"A report came out from the fleet in the last month," Penton explained. "There was an incident involving a young Marine like yourself. Put a handful of CADs in his pocket, then started walking across the flight line—"

"Yeah?" the youngster mumbled.

"Well, static electricity activated the CADs," Penton said, reproachfully. "Blew his damn leg clean off."

The private first class stared at him wide-eyed. "Damn!" He handed over the CADs. Penton put them in a crate filled with ordnance. Marines hauled the wooden box to the truck, and then loaded it into the back, filled with items for return to the build-up area.

Penton climbed into the cab of the truck. He instructed the driver to take him over to the command center. Top Anderson waved as the truck rumbled to life. Penton dipped his chin in response, and the driver pulled the rig off the flight deck.

They headed across base and rain pelted the steel roof. Penton thought about Kate, soaring through the sky in horrific weather conditions. He wondered if she'd make it. A pang of regret unsettled him, but he didn't fully understand why.

He'd only just met Kate, but the thought of losing her was devastating.

FOURTEEN

General Yoshi stared at the screen. He didn't quite comprehend what he'd just seen. Japan's Self-Defense Forces had thrown everything they had at the Kaiju and it withstood the attack unscathed.

Now, the beast plied its way toward the city with nothing to stand in the way.

"How are we coming with communications?" Yoshi snapped.

"We're about thirty minutes from reconnecting," the sergeant first class replied.

"That's not fast enough," Yoshi stammered in dismay.

"Our people have cut the time in half already."

General Yoshi shook his head. He groped around for a cellphone and dialed the number he had for Major Hira. The phone rang, but then dropped into voicemail.

Yoshi shook his head again. He put the phone down and wondered if Hira's tank had been destroyed. They had lost so many soldiers in the fight.

A vibration snapped him out of thought. Yoshi looked down. The phone rang, vibrating on the console. He picked it up and answered. "General Yoshi, here."

"This is Major Hira... you called?"

"Just trying to get a status from the field."

"Our line has failed." Major Hira sounded dejected.

"We saw the Kaiju attack. Our command center has video from monitors around the city, even down by the harbor. You did your best."

"We're retreating now," Hira said, anxiously.

"Any chance to reassemble... create a fallback line?" Yoshi pressed.

"Our tank communications are operable," Hira said. "So, I'll check in with the commanders and get right back to you."

"Much appreciated," Yoshi said. "I know it's tough out there."

"The creature is chasing after my tank now," Hira huffed for air. "Not even sure we'll be part of the new defensive line..."

General Yoshi swallowed. He gasped for breath, as if the air went out of the room. The defensive line was broken, and the fighter jets had failed. Now, his company commander on the ground was in peril. "Get yourself free of it!" Yoshi insisted.

"We're trying to do our best…"

"Break away from that thing, and circle around," Yoshi stammered. "Set up the new line further back, so your tank commanders have time to get into position."

"We'll do all we can," Hira replied. "Got to go."

"Take care, Major. You're a credit to Japan."

A muddled replied came over the phone, fuzzy and distorted. Yoshi thought it sounded like appreciation, but the call dropped before he could expound further.

****

Major Hira looked through the scope and saw the Kaiju closing in fast. The creature didn't move quickly, but each stride sent it across large tracks of land.

"Move!" Hira screamed to his operator.

"Can't go any faster," the tank operator replied.

Hira shook his head. The tank bobbed along at 60 kilometers per hour, slowed down by the urban terrain. He patted the gunner on the shoulder. "Load the cannon," Hira said. "And turn the turret around toward the creature."

"Yes, sir!" the gunner replied, moving into action.

"Maybe we can slow the thing down."

Then, Hira spun the scope around and peered into it. City streets and tall buildings lay ahead. The tank moved from the industrial area towards downtown. Other tanks were doing the same, fleeing for the protection of tall buildings and the maze of narrow streets.

"Fire when ready," Hira told the gunner.

A mechanical sound echoed through the tank, as a 120mm round chambered in the big gun. The gunner fired and a boom reverberated through the cabin. Hira checked the trajectory. The large round dug into the creature's ankle.

The Kaiju let out a deafening roar. A chill ran down Hira's spine; the creature was close behind them.

Hira jostled in his command seat, as the tracks grumbled over a city street, chewing up pavement. Tall buildings towered overhead.

"Swing down a side street," Hira instructed the driver.

"Got it," the driver replied.

Then, the driver slowed and shifted the controls. The tank pivoted toward a side street, and Hira whipped back as the tank accelerated. He checked the scope again. The Kaiju continued meandering down the main street. Huge feet stomped past the side street. Massive claws crimped into the tar, breaking the street to bits.

A moment later, the long tail snaked by them, whipping into the buildings. Glass shattered and stone façades cracked. Hira sighed in relief. Then, he clicked on the comm-link and instructed the surviving tank commanders to regroup.

He told them to assemble a defense line along a greenery near Tokyo Tower.

****

Admiral Keyes still couldn't believe that he didn't have a direct line with the head of Japan's Self-Defense Forces. Nobody could explain how the communications systems were malfunctioning. But he suspected the creature had disrupted cables and towers. He watched the video feed from various locations around the city in awe.

The grim scene looked real enough, and distress signals had gone out. Keyes understood why some military leaders might have their doubts. A giant monster washing up on shore and stomping around was far-fetched.

He studied the screen carefully. Members of his command team stood by, idle, probably wondering what he was doing. The suit fidgeted but kept quiet.

Keyes wanted to check for signs of a hoax. The severing of communications and the destruction occurring in Japan was reportedly tied to the creature seen on the video. But he couldn't rule out interference from China or North Korea. Either nation could have interrupted the communications lines and fed manufactured video to cover an invasion.

"Get me an image of the mass that appeared on our sonar before the attack," Keyes barked at Williams, the intelligence officer.

"Yes, sir," Lieutenant Commander Williams said, rising from her seat.

"Also, link us with a satellite view of Tokyo Harbor at the start of the attack."

"Will do." Williams stepped from the room.

"You don't think this is real?" said the Executive Officer Maxwell James.

"We have to respond like it's really happening."

"Agreed. But shouldn't we form a contingency plan in case the Marine pilots find a pack of soldiers storming Tokyo, rather than the monster in the video?"

Keyes glanced back at the screen. His gut instinct told him the destruction was real enough. A seasoned war veteran, he knew the difference between Hollywood and the real thing. Many officers were eager for a fight and likely took the situation as a hostile aggression from China or North Korea. They'd need to get the LHP headed around the island of Japan.

"We *are* going to need a contingency plan for the Harriers," Keyes finally said. He scratched his chin, nodding in agreement. "Either way, we'll need a backup plan."

FIFTEEN

Maki stared at the metal door while her mother writhed on the floor and screamed in anguish. No sounds emanated from the other side. No yelling or pounding. Father hadn't even cried out when the door shut.

"Maybe he's out there trying to get in?" Maki hoped.

Mother shook her head, convinced otherwise.

"We don't know!" Maki insisted.

She looked at her mother strewn on the floor, distraught. "I'm going to help Father," Maki finally said.

Then, she got up and walked over to the door. Maki tried to push it open. The door wouldn't budge. Her mother's screams of desperation turned to sobbing.

Maki stood close to the door and listened for her father. She didn't hear any cries for help. No pounding or scratches at the door. Nothing. She tried the door again with the same result: futility. Maki turned to her mother. "Would you please help me?"

Her mother rose from the floor, shaking her head and crying.

"We need to try," Maki pressed.

"When he shoved me inside…" her mother said, weeping. "I saw the look on his face. And I knew that he wouldn't make it… because he knew he wouldn't make it."

"Let's try anyway." Maki grabbed the doorknob.

Mother wiped her tears with the back of a hand, and then moved toward the door. She shoved a shoulder into the solid metal. Maki pushed with both hands, straining her tiny legs.

The door cracked open. Water rushed inside, but her father wasn't there.

Maki couldn't see him, and she did not hear him. Only the sound of rushing water filtered through the aperture. Mother shook her head, defeated. Then, she let go of the door and it slammed shut, pushing Maki's hands back.

"Maybe he went around the corner to the little alley," Maki offered.

"The water rushed into the alley. He couldn't stand, never mind run for safety."

"Well, it's worth checking," Maki insisted, stomping a foot.

"What do you want to do?" Mother glanced at her compassionately.

"This way," Maki said, pointing.

They headed through the storage room and stepped into a hallway. Maki led the way as they meandered through the building toward the back. Eventually, they reached the rear of the building. She found a window overlooking the alley they had contemplated running down.

Maki peered out the window, but only saw a flood of water battering the door her father had questioned. The current flowed strong, and the door held steady. *It was probably locked*, she thought.

"We'd all be dead if we had gone that route," her mother said.

"You're right," Maki replied, nodding her head.

She stared out the window at the water rising in the alley. "Where is Father?"

"Must have been swept away." Mother shook her head, despondent.

Maki pouted, then pointed out the window. "Look, the water is not deep enough to cover his head. He wouldn't have drowned… not yet."

"I'm not sure what we can do."

Maki pressed against the widow with both hands, moving about frantically. She desperately tried to find a latch or mechanism to open the window. *Maybe he could swim into the alley and climb in through a window*, she hoped.

"You can't open that window."

"Why not?"

"It's an office building."

"So?"

"The windows don't open."

Maki scowled, thinking about how could people spend all day indoors without being able to open a window and breathe fresh air. A trickle of water ran across the floor and caught her attention. Mother looked down.

"Come on," her mother finally said. "We need to get to higher ground. The water is seeping into the building."

****

Maki's mother led her through the dark building to a stairwell. All the power had gone out. A few emergency lights cast a slight glow, reminding Maki of losing electricity at school a few times.

They trampled up the stairs, with Maki's rain boots slapping on the concrete steps. After traversing a couple of landings, she wondered why her mother kept pressing upward.

"Why are we going higher and higher?" said Maki.

"So, we can get a better view of the city."

"Hope we get there soon. I could use a rest."

"Just a little further," Mother reassured her.

Yet, they climbed more and more stairs. Maki's legs grew tired and numb, weary; she wondered if they were headed to the top of the building.

They slowed at a landing and Maki was glad for the rest. Then, her mother reached for the handle and opened the door. Nothing but darkness lay beyond the threshold. Maki didn't like the interior hallway.

Her mother tugged her hand, pulling her forward.

Maki planted her feet, resisting.

The hallway was dark and disturbingly silent. Dread crept up Maki's spine, like a chill on a brisk night. She shook her head, afraid to press forward.

"It will only take a few seconds for our eyes to adjust."

"The place is creepy," Maki said, defiantly.

"Come on," Mother pled. "We can't stand here all day."

Mother pushed the door open wider and stepped through. It seemed as though she planned to leave Maki in the stairwell alone.

"Wait!" Maki scurried after her mother, boots pattering on the carpet.

They walked down the hallway and entered a larger room. An emergency light flooded the area. Empty cubicles filled the space along with office machines. Maki had seen it all before when visiting her father at work.

Her mother walked over toward the glassed-in offices on the outside wall. Grey light reflected through the windows. Some of the buildings nearby still had power. Maki looked around and didn't see anyone.

"Where did all the people go?" Maki asked.

"They probably left the building and went outside."

"Maybe they went to see the fireworks?"

Mother shook her head, sadly. "I don't think those were fireworks."

"What do you think they were, then?"

Her mother didn't respond, not right away.

Maki looked her in the eye, earnestly. "Please tell me what is going on?

A tear ran down her mother's check. "Wish I knew what was happening. But I think those sounds we heard… well, I think it was the military."

Maki didn't understand. "Why would the military be making so much noise?"

Her mother shrugged, bewildered.

Mother started crying and tears poured down her face. Maki stepped closer and hugged her. And her mother squeezed her back, tightly. "I don't know what we're going to do." Mother shook her head, confused, and sobbed.

Then, her mother clasped a hand over her mouth in shock.

Maki turned to see what had caught her mother's attention. A massive scaly creature trundled past the window, standing nearly as tall as the building. The enormous body cast a shadow over the office. Maki shuddered.

She stood in the grey darkness, staring into a menacing yellow eye.

✸✸✸✸

Outside the tall buildings, Major Hira's tank churned up the pavement of a side street while traversing to higher ground. He sat in his command chair, trying to assess the unit's capabilities. Many tank commanders had reported in with details of the damage.

Dusk began to blanket the devastated city. Hira surmised a third of the tanks had been lost. All the missile transports were intact, but they'd fired their ordnance and offered little support. He shook his head. The Self-Defense Forces had never planned for such a disaster, despite warnings from aging citizens.

Old-timers recounted folk legends of giant creatures from the past. They referred to the monsters as Kaiju. Beasts had risen up from the depths of the ocean, stomping on the ancient shores and soaring through the skies, fighting each other and rampaging villages.

Hira's grandfather mentioned tales of a similar attack that happened back in 1965. A lone Kaiju had surfaced on the coast of Japan and stomped onto shore, decimating power lines and crushing cars and buildings. The Self-Defense Forces lured it away from the mainland and cornered it on a deserted island. With the help of American naval forces, a small nuclear missile issued through the humid tropical air and detonated on the atoll. The mushroom cloud dissipated and a month later, scientists and military personnel combed the island wearing protective suits. Geiger counters registered Strontium-90, but the search party didn't find any of the creature's remains. Reports issued that the Kaiju had sunk to the bottom of the sea to die.

Many villagers feared the creature hadn't died in the blast but merely returned to a deep sleep, as the Kaiju were known to do through legends. They named the monster that had ravaged Tokyo, calling it Zamera. And they feared it would return one day to exact revenge.

The tank struck a curb and jostled Hira from thought. He checked the scope and confirmed the driver had them on course toward Tokyo Tower. Other tank commanders checked in through the communications link. Now, the estimate of remaining tanks totaled just two-thirds of the original contingency.

"Commanders, report on your firing capacity," Major Hira spoke into the communications network.

"Five rounds," a commander replied.

"Four rounds," another said.

"We have five."

"Four."

"Down to three."

The reports continued to come over the comm-link. Hira determined that most of the tanks had four to five rounds. His own tank was down to three after firing at the beast during its pursuit.

"We've got enough to make a final stand," Hira concluded.

"Orders?" said a tank commander.

"Head to Tokyo Tower and form a defensive line."

"What if the Kaiju doesn't wander in that direction?" a commander broke in.

"My tank will create a diversion," Hira responded.

"A diversion?"

"We'll lead it to you."

"Understood," tank commanders replied in unison.

Hira heard his driver gulp.

"We're down to three rounds." This from Hira's gunner.

"We've outmaneuvered it before," Hira reasoned. "So, our tank has the most experience and best chance of pulling it off."

"But we cannot stop the thing," the driver stammered.

"We've got to hold it back… delay its incursion while General Yoshi develops and implements a plan."

The cabin fell silent.

"Until then," Hira continued, "we are Japan's only hope."

"Yes, sir!" the soldiers bellowed.

Hira glanced into the scope. Checking the road ahead, he glanced down side streets in search of the creature. Then, the distinctive scales came into view as the beast's tail whipped down a parallel street.

The spectacle made Hira's hand tremble, causing the image in the scope to become obscure. He let go of the viewfinder.

He took a deep breath and looked back into the scope. A tip of the tail slithered out of sight. The Kaiju pressed ahead, making it difficult for the tank to cut in front of the monster. Hira's tank needed to race to intercept the creature.

"Faster!" Hira yelled. "We need to get in front of it."

"Difficult on these streets," the driver said. "But we'll give it a try."

"Load the cannon," Hira ordered.

A casing clanked into place.

"Done," the gunner replied.

The tank lunged ahead, picking up to 70 kilometers an hour. It tore up the city street. Bits of tar flew off the tracks and dinged parked cars and windows.

Encountering a dip in the road, the tank veered to the right and collided with an automobile. Armor-plating scraped against sheet metal and a cacophony of grating steel echoed outside the tank. Muffled scrapes penetrated the cabin. Then, a roar ensued, as though the collision attracted the Kaiju's attention.

Hira flipped open the hatch and popped his head out of the tank.

"Strike another car," Hira told the driver.

"Understood, sir," the driver said meekly.

Another squeal reverberated down the narrow corridor. Zamera roared again. Hira climbed back into the tank and shut the hatch. "He's right behind us," Hira said, sliding into the command seat.

"Can't go any faster," the driver said.

"We're going to lose our lead when we cut over to the street that it's on," Hira said, shaking his head. "And we'll run right into it."

"Maybe something will attract its attention," the gunner broke in.

Hira shook his head. "The area seems fairly cleared out."

"I'll do the best that I can," the driver said.

Rumbling down the street, Hira knew they would have to cut over to a side street and whip in front of the creature. They'd lose speed. Making both turns quickly would put them in front of the Kaiju's path.

Any mistake and they'd collide into the creature.

Hira looked into the scope and pegged the tower at a kilometer away.

"We're going to have to make the turn now."

"Need a little more time to clear the angle," the driver said.

"If we wait much longer, the creature will move left of the tower. Our defensive line will be of no use."

"We run into that thing, and the plan's a failure," the driver said.

A side street appeared in the viewer. "Turn now!" Hira ordered.

The tank jerked forward, slowing down fast. Hira shifted in the command seat as the armored vehicle pivoted left and then accelerated, throwing Hira and the gunner backward. Diesel engine stressing, gears whined and the motor groaned. The intersection ahead remained clear of the beast.

A moment later, the tank neared the corner and decelerated. Hira jerked forward and back as the tank rounded the corner and sped up. He checked the viewfinder and spotted a clawed foot about fifteen meters behind them. Its long tail slid on the ground behind the creature.

Hira looked for the other foot and didn't see it.

Then, a rumbled noise emanated from the right, and the ground trembled, sending reverberations under the tank. The tank swerved to the right, as the shockwave undulated over the roadway.

Hira couldn't make out what was happening in the viewer.

Flipping open the hatch, he stuck his head out. The other monstrous foot was right beside them, planted in the street. And the trailing foot began to move forward. It would possibly knock the tank over with the swipe of a claw, or step on the armored vehicle and crush it altogether.

"Move!" Hira screamed. "We're right beneath it."

"You got it!" the driver yelled.

Engine groaning, diesel exhaust wafted into the cabin. Hira felt the tank snap forward with acceleration. They pulled past the creature's stationary left foot. Hira swallowed, and then stepped down into the cabin.

He reached for the hatch and caught the grimace of the creature staring down at him. Saliva dripped from the immense, crooked fangs.

And the creature's fierce yellow eyes seemed pleased at the sight of its prey.

SIXTEEN

Crosswinds shook Kate Able's fighter in the darkening sky. She led her squadron over the vast Pacific Ocean, while the other pilots trailed behind in a typical wedge formation. They spaced their planes further apart than usual due to the storm. She appreciated the decision upon encountering severe conditions.

Her jet had lifted off the tarmac in Okinawa, rising vertically without much resistance from the tropical storm winds. Then, she catapulted into the sky with the other pilots following suit. One after another, the Harriers plied through dense rain toward the main island, ready to confront the enemy.

They flew without incident leaving the air base. Kate thought about her career choice during the flight. Valedictorian of her high school class, she went on to attend Annapolis and excelled. Long before graduation, Kate made up her mind to go with the Marines. Her older brothers had gone with the Navy, one a pilot and the other selected Navy Intelligence due to poor vision. No one in her immediate family tried to change her decision. They left it to her uncle, who pressed the issue at every turn. She was part of a legacy and should embrace it.

When the squadron got closer to the hurricane, Kate increased altitude, so they navigated above the worst of the storm. She excelled in flight school and got her first pick of an assignment, the Black Sheep Squadron of Pappy Boyington fame. Based out of MCAS Yuma, Arizona, the unit was now comprised of AV-8B Harriers and stationed alongside the Marine Corps elite MAWTS-1, Marine Aviation Weapons Tactics Squadron. And so, she'd been exposed to advanced fighter training, soaring over the desert skies, and grew into one of the finest young pilots in the world.

Now, they closed in on their target and would descend toward Tokyo. Kate wondered how much the training actually prepared a pilot for the real thing. She inhaled and tried to shake off doubt. *Do or die*, she thought.

She activated the communications link with the command center. "We're about twenty minutes out from the target."

"Things are getting pretty hairy on the ground," Colonel Tomkins said.

"My squadron has to begin descent, soon."

"Understood." Colonel Tomkins sounded miffed.

"We'll need coordinates for the target…" Kate said, "in order to map out the drop-in altitude."

"Afraid you'll be facing a moving target." This from Admiral Keyes.

"Admiral, I wasn't aware you were patched in," Kate said, apologetically.

"Perfectly fine," Keyes replied. "Just take care of your squadron up there. We'll patch you in with the best coordinates we can provide."

"Roger." Kate exhaled. "We'll need them soon."

"Have them for you within five minutes—"

The connection went fuzzy. Static.

"You should route toward Tokyo Tower," Keyes finally said. "We've just resumed contact with General Yoshi, head of the Self-Defense Forces. Apparently, he's got a plan in progress that we can piggyback on."

"Understood," Kate said. "I'll await further instructions."

Communication with the command center broke off. Kate wasn't sure if the transmission had been interrupted or the line just ended abruptly. She relayed the initial coordinates to her squadron.

She began the descent into the storm, wondering what was in store for them.

****

Keyes stared into the monitor in disbelief. General Yoshi glanced back at him appearing frantic. Yoshi had lost his composure. The Self-Defense Forces were coming apart at the seams. Everyone in the background appeared to move around frantically and without purpose. Their command center was in disarray, paralyzed from the top down.

"We've got a desperate situation here," Yoshi eventually said, shaking his head, distraught.

"Understood, General," Keyes replied, trying to placate him.

"The entire city is in danger," Yoshi stammered. "Perhaps the entire nation."

Keyes frowned. "We've got a squadron of fighters on the way. Things will be under control in good time."

"Our jet fighters already attacked the monster and failed—"

"We're loaded for bear, though."

"Please do not take offense, Admiral," Yoshi stammered. "But I'm not certain you understand what we're up against. The creature has withstood missiles, 120mm rounds, rockets, machinegun fire, and an explosion of flames from burning oil."

"We've packed something onboard that should do the trick," Keyes replied, sounding less confident. He thought about all the sorties the United States have flown in wars over the last fifty years, and the airstrikes aimed at punishing threats. All of them went off as tactical achievements with few missteps. But this was something entirely different.

Yoshi brought up images on the screen. A war scene flooded before Keyes with a small picture of General Yoshi in the left-hand corner. The creature moved from the harbor, doused in flaming oil, as rounds and missiles pounded into it with minor impact. Then, the beast pressed inland and crushed tanks, while a trail of fire burned in its wake.

"This situation calls for a backup plan," Yoshi said.

Keyes nodded in agreement. "We have some options. But how do we draw the thing away from the city in order to truly destroy it?"

General Yoshi smiled kindly. "I might just have the answer."

After listening to Yoshi's thoughts, Keyes signed off and got up from the sofa. He didn't like the situation one bit. And he didn't enjoy having a suit in his command center. Keyes stretched his legs, cracked his neck, and got himself a coffee. This time, he ignored the fine china and poured it into a mug with the logo of the Gipper on the front.

He took a long sip, and then glanced at his intelligence officer.

"We need to get in touch with the Seawolf," Keyes said. "And get me the captain of the ship patrolling in the Straight of Japan on the horn."

SEVENTEEN

Hardy checked the area for hostiles. Finding it clear, he trotted through the rain, and headed back into the musty warehouse. He caught up with Stiles, disabling the Tochka missile. Dead soldiers lay strewn about the rough, cement floor.

"We've got company," Hardy said.

"I need more time." Stiles didn't look up, busy at work.

"There isn't enough time to clean this place up." Hardy glanced around at the bloodstained floor.

"You'll have to start on them, while I finish up here."

Hardy nodded in agreement. Then, he turned and headed to the wooden door. "Lock this behind me."

Stiles nodded, but didn't budge from his task.

Hardy smiled, knowing Stiles wouldn't leave his post to secure the door. He headed outside into a heavy downpour and scanned the area. Nobody had arrived yet. He trucked off into the woods, setting up a position to flank arriving troop transports. Pungent decayed vegetable matter drifted from the damp forest floor. The spot he'd chosen was slightly to the rear of where trucks might unload.

He nestled down in the dirt and waited, patiently.

A few minutes later, a troop transport rumbled down the driveway. The truck approached at speed, headlights cutting through the grey evening. The North Koreans understood an assault had unfolded, but they might not expect a high-level threat. *Probably think the commotion relates to rural thugs*, Hardy thought.

The transport wound down the wooded drive and halted behind the vehicle the SEALs had commandeered. Hardy thought the move amateurish. He regretted not taking a moment to booby-trap the damn thing.

When the truck stopped, soldiers alighted from the rear, boots smacking gravel. They fanned around both sides of the transport.

Hardy lay in a prone position.

Aiming the MP-5, he slowly squeezed the trigger.

His shot struck an infantryman in the head.

The soldier dropped to the ground with a thud. Blood gushed out the hole in his head. His comrades looked at the wound aghast, and then scanned the woods, trying to figure out where the shot had come from. Hardy's silencer helped conceal his position.

He popped off two more shots. A couple more soldiers fell to the ground. The rest of them dropped to prone positions and opened fire, wildly blasting into the woods without any sense of a target. Enemy bullets ripped through the forest to Hardy's left. He'd smartly chosen to set a position further away, expecting two trucks to arrive.

Squeezing off a round, Hardy dropped yet another soldier. Reinforcements from the far side of the truck circled to a forward position. They set up under the truck and alongside their comrades. A cacophony of communications emanated from the vehicle. Twilight settling in began to obscure the enemy. Hardy squinted.

Then, the soldiers returned heavy fire toward Hardy's location. Bullets tore into the forest, and rifle fire cracked repeatedly from a perimeter around the truck.

Hardy bawled up behind a tree and waited for a break in the offensive.

Rain danced through the tree tops. They'd narrowed in on his position, but he didn't think anyone had seen his muzzle flash. Spent gunpowder drifted through the air. He had an opportunity to take a couple more out before they zeroed in on him.

Hardy squirmed to his right and nestled into a depression. A fallen tree gave him protective cover. He peered at the enemy, locating three soldiers lying on the driveway to the side of the truck, exposed more than the others.

When the enemy fire let up, Hardy squeezed off two head shots. Both riflemen twisted upon impact and kicked at dirt in the throes of death. The movement gradually subsided until they lay limp.

Fire erupted from all around the transport, a volley directed at Hardy's position.

The enemy had him pegged. Rounds dug into the fallen tree and hit the soil all around him. Hardy couldn't get a look at them. Raising his head would result in a fatal wound. He rolled further to the right, trying to gain a vantage point. He needed to observe enemy troop movement.

Hardy crawled to a stump and peered at them. The assault let up. But none of the North Korean soldiers advanced on him.

Keeping an eye on them, he reached into a cargo pocket for a grenade.

Then, a bullet shattered glass, and the transport driver flopped against the door window. Blood pumped from his skull. *Stiles had joined the party*, Hardy thought.

More bullets riddled the ground, striking a few of the soldiers lying under the truck in prone positions. Infantrymen took hits in the legs and back, and the firing pattern indicated Stiles broke toward the rear of the truck.

Soldiers flailed on the ground, disoriented. Hardy rose to a kneeling position and capped another one. Then, he pulled the pin on the M67 and lobbed it toward the truck.

The fragmentation grenade exploded in front of the transport, and soldiers writhed and cried out in agony from the shrapnel.

Stiles blasted away from the other side of the truck. All his semi-automatic rifle fire marked shots from an angle, avoiding dangerous crossfire.

Hardy stood and ran toward the back of the truck, firing his MP-5 while seeking cover from the damaged vehicle.

Flames blazed from the hand grenade blast. A soldier crawled out from under the truck to avoid further burns. Hardy shot the man in the chest as he tried to roll in a puddle. The soldier's AK-46 erupted, wildly firing in every direction.

A bullet struck Hardy's chest.

Pain spiked through his rib cage.

He tumbled to the ground.

Hardy rolled behind the rear wheel, caught his breath, then popped under the truck and fired away. He shot furiously.

Bodies jounced, as he riddled soldiers beneath the transport.

A couple of soldiers had wormed along the perimeter. Now, they scrambled to their feet and dashed toward the rear of the vehicle. Boots pounded the ground as they closed on Hardy with rifles ready to fire.

Hardy heard a click, a distinctive sound of the MP-5 being out of ammo.

Dropping the rifle, he reached for his sidearm, as the soldiers rounded the back of the truck. They turned the corner, rifles ablaze.

He squeezed the trigger on his 9mm, dropping the lead soldier.

The next soldier kept firing and struck Hardy in the thigh and chest. He fell to the ground clutching his P226, Sig Sauer.

Hardy rolled under the truck. He squeezed off another shot. The soldier flew backward as a round penetrated his cheek. Flesh tore and blood spurted, as the trooper dropped dead. Stiles trotted up and grabbed Hardy's vest, dragging him out from under the truck.

He dropped a knee and looked at Hardy's leg.

"How bad is it?" Hardy said.

Stiles smiled. "Looks like a through and through." He chuckled and reached for his web-belt. Then, he fastened it to Hardy's leg to prevent a bleed out. With the wound secured, Stiles circled the truck and checked the bodies.

A moment later, Hardy removed the belt and set it on the ground. Then, he pulled a first-aid kit from his commando utilities. He cut open the pant leg, exposing the bullet holes. Rainfall washed blood away in a crimson stream.

Cleansing the wounds, he breathed a sigh of relief. The bullet had passed through a muscle without hitting a major artery. He bandaged his leg, then grabbed the steel bumper on the truck and pulled himself up.

"All clear," Stiles said, stepping from around truck.

"Well, that's a relief." Hardy shook his head, as adrenaline wound down.

"You going to be alright?"

"Let's see."

Hardy stepped over to his rifle gingerly. He picked up the MP-5 and ejected the magazine, then loaded a fresh clip. Slinging the rifle over a shoulder, he snatched up his P226 and reloaded it with two more rounds. Both weapons glistened from the drizzle.

"Seem to walk okay…" Hardy finally said.

"Yeah, but can you run?" Stiles picked his belt off the ground.

"My chest hurts a hell of a lot more than the leg. The leg just burns."

Stiles shook his head. "Three shots in the chest in one short mission. Must really hurt. You're going to be bruised all over."

"Probably have a couple broken ribs." Hardy laughed and it hurt.

He grabbed his chest. The joking sent pain spiking through his upper torso. "Might hurt to run, though," Hardy confessed.

Stiles shook his head. "You're a mess."

"How far you get with the missile?"

"Almost there."

They headed back to the warehouse with Stiles in the lead. Hardy trailed behind, limping. Both lungs constricted from the blunt trauma, and his leg throbbed from the bullet holes. A twinge of pain radiated through his thigh, causing him to hobble along.

As Stiles opened the warehouse door, Hardy heard something. He stopped and tried to listen through the rain. "Did you hear that?"

"Hear what?" Stiles replied.

"Stop walking and I'll tell you."

"Okay." Stiles halted.

"That…"

An unmistakable sound of diesel engines on the country road rumbled in the distance. The noise was fainter this time. "We've got about five to ten minutes," Hardy said.

"Should only take me five. Maybe you better start into the woods."

Hardy shook his head. "Never leave a man behind, ever."

"You're not leaving me behind, just getting a head start."

"Can't take the chance," Hardy said, checking his rifle. "They could arrive sooner than expected. You get back to work on the missile, and I'll watch your back."

"Sure thing." Stiles started for the door.

"Besides," Hardy continued. "My adrenaline will kick in… if we have to move out. We'll do just fine."

The door shut behind Stiles.

Hardy glanced around, checking for infantrymen headed through the forest. No sign of movement anywhere. But he figured it would be the longest five minutes of his life.

EIGHTEEN

Kate obtained coordinates for the target, then her squadron descended through the storm toward Tokyo. Wind and rain pounded her windshield and shook the plane. She fought to control the joystick, and worked the pedals and levers to steady her rudder and flaps.

A downpour pelted her Harrier. She knew things would only get worse.

Crosswinds shifted the small fighter without notice, but the squadron was spaced far enough apart, so the wingtips didn't collide. The deluge and impending darkness impaired visibility. Kate couldn't see the planes at the farthest ends of the formation.

"Captain Able to squadron," she finally said. "We're closing in on target."

"Roger," a few pilots replied, flatly.

She took the response as aviators being focused on the task at hand. "All pilots confirm your status," Kate demanded. "And check on your wingman."

"Rocking steady," Lieutenant Baker said. "Wingman looks fine."

"Same here," Lieutenant Merrill replied.

"All set here," Lieutenant Stanley said.

"Roger that," said Captain Wecker.

The jets ripped through the sky and dropped out of the clouds. Kate's plane shook violently as her fighter descended toward the city.

Tokyo Harbor came into view. A macabre war scene lay before them, and the water was covered in a slick of smoldering flames. The pier was engulfed in an inferno, and the fire spread onto shore in a trail of havoc.

Buildings were smashed apart and ablaze, while power lines lay on the ground, ripped from poles snapped like matchsticks. Automobiles and tanks alike had been trampled and crushed. Metal parts were bent, twisted, and askew.

A trail of destruction led from the harbor inland. Everything was saturated as though a tidal wave had splashed down.

Kate spotted Tokyo Tower in the distance and traced the path of mayhem toward it.

Then, a powerful crosswind shot her plane sideways. Wingtips touched and her jet went into a spiral. Kate spun with the force, rather than fight it. The Harrier rolled, but she spun until the momentum ebbed and then righted the aircraft.

The plane continued to pull. Kate let the jet roll around again. As she twirled back into position, the force eased and she steadied the fighter.

She looked to her right and Baker appeared fine. His wingman further right fought to control his plane. The effort made the jet unstable, but he'd made it through the worst of it. Looking to her left, Wecker flew steady, but his wingman spiraled out of control. Merrill couldn't steady his plane.

"Loop along with it," Kate said into the communications link.

"Can't get a handle on her," Merrill gasped, desperately.

"He's caught a backdraft," Wecker said.

The wind compounded the problem with the jet blast. "You have to roll with it," Kate repeated.

"He's too far gone…" Wecker said. "Dizzy and disoriented."

"Steady your flaps!" Kate snapped. "And hold your stick firm."

"*Trying*," Merrill responded frantically.

The plane finally leveled off and he moved back into formation.

"That was close," Merrill muttered.

"Don't fight the wind so much."

"Easier said than done." This from Lieutenant Baker. "Unless you're an Able."

Kate clenched her teeth at the derisive comment. Sure, her family's military experience gave her an edge over others. But flying skills weren't handed down through the blood stream. She worked extremely hard for every accomplishment.

Her squadron buzzed over the harbor and headed toward the city.

Kate directed them to fly a few hundred meters over the office buildings. Tokyo Tower jutted into the skyline in the distance.

The creature stomped down the city streets below, meandering toward the tower.

All the carnage resembled a military invasion. The sheer size of the beast alarmed her, with its jagged head and snarling fangs. As the creature trundled along, it filled the width of a main street. It stood almost as tall as the largest buildings. Large feet stomped on the ground, splitting the pavement and vibrating parked cars. And a massive tail dragged behind it, whipping from side to side.

Thick scales covered the creature, as though armored-plates hung all over its hide. Kate shook her head, wondering how they could defeat such a thing.

****

Hira clamped the hatch shut and hoped his driver could pull ahead of the creature.

The Kaiju straddled their tank and could easily crush them to death. Just thinking of the beast lingering above them, and the potential of impending doom at any moment, Hira grew claustrophobic. All sides of the tank seemed to close in, and it became difficult to breathe.

Rumbling over the city street, the tracks chipped into the tar and the diesel engine groaned. But the tank had picked up speed. Hira glanced through the viewer and both prodigious feet trailed behind them.

Judging from the size of the creature and the distance they'd moved away from its feet, Hira expected the head and snapping jaws were lingering above the tank. Sharp, jagged teeth, dripping with saliva stuck in his mind. The beast longed for red meat.

The tank swerved into a parked car and scraping metal echoed along the corridor of vacant office buildings. The Kaiju let out another menacing roar.

"He doesn't like noise," Hira said to the driver.

"That seems to be the case."

"Try to keep to the middle of the street." Hira looked into the viewer.

"Doing the best possible," the driver said, shaking his head.

The driver didn't speak again; he focused on operating the tank. Hira placed them at a similar distance as the last time he checked. Somehow the immense, awkward creature kept pace. *It's pursuing us*, Hira thought.

He turned to the gunner. "Are you ready?"

"Yes, sir," the gunner replied.

"Wanted to get further away—"

"Understood."

"We've got to take the risk and fire now." Hira shifted in his seat. "Maybe we'll get lucky and penetrate its scales, hit a spot that has already been shot."

"The creature might slow up if we do."

"Or it could topple on us."

The gunner nodded, perceiving the gravity of the situation. "I'll do my best," he said to Hira.

Hira looked into the viewfinder to help guide the gunner.

A drop of saliva or snot from the beast's nostrils dripped onto the tank. The lens on the scope blurred. Hira rose from the command chair and worked the hatch open. He popped his head out and marked their position.

"Fire!" Major Hira bellowed down into the cabin.

"Yes, sir!" said the gunner.

The turret recoiled as the round blasted from the cannon. Only a few meters away from the Kaiju when the gunner fired, the round sailed through the air.

A wail of agony howled through the night, as the round dug into the creature's lower leg. The beast lost stride, and the tank pulled away. "We did it!" Hira yelled, as he climbed back into the cabin and sealed the hatch.

The gunner and driver cheered as they widened the distance.

Hira got onto the communications link with General Yoshi. "We're making progress toward Tokyo Tower with the creature in pursuit."

"I knew that you could do it," Yoshi replied.

"We just gave the creature a blow. Apparently, it takes firing at close range to really make an impact on its scales."

"I'll get word to the Joint Task Force."

"Thank you, General. I've got to get back to my post."

"You take care," said Yoshi.

Hira cut off the conversation and directed the driver to maneuver toward the tower. The tank slowed and pivoted to the right, turning onto a street headed in the direction of the defense line.

The creature stomped after the tank, vibrating the ground behind them.

Checking the viewer, Hira made out a distorted image. He placed the creature ten meters behind them. It gained on them when they turned the corner. The Kaiju moved slowly, but kept up with giant strides.

"Commanders, this is Major Hira."

"We hear you," came a unanimous response.

"Have you gotten the word about trajectory?"

"A closer shot makes more of an impact," a commander said.

"That's exactly right." Hira checked his viewfinder. "We need to plan three volleys as the creature approaches the defensive line. One from a distance, a second from fifty meters, then a third from ten meters or less."

Nobody responded to the dreadful instructions.

"Did you hear me?" Hira snapped into the communications link.

"We heard," the same commander said flatly.

"So, the instructions are clear?"

"Ten meters is a suicide mission."

Hira considered the comment. The only means to slow the creature was to lure it toward the tanks and fire at close range. Everything else was futile. "Abandon your tanks after the last volley," Major Hira said. "You'll have better luck fleeing on foot."

"Understood, sir," the tank commanders sounded at once.

Hira checked the scope and saw the tower three hundred meters ahead. "Steer toward the left flank to avoid getting hit by friendly fire," Hira told the driver.

His driver nodded, understanding.

Then, Hira glanced into the viewer to check on the monster and found it right on top of them. "Faster!" Hira yelled.

Panic resonated through the cabin. The driver worked the controls and the tank jerked ahead. Grinding emanated from underneath, as the engine whined from strain. "Not sure it will hold out," the driver said, sweating.

Suddenly, jets swooped in from out of the sky and launched rockets at the Kaiju. The creature wailed as ordnance exploded into its side. It shook off the blows and kept after the tank. Harriers buzzed by and circled around for another pass.

Hira exhaled, daunted by the proximity of the beast.

As the Kaiju closed in on them, it let out a vicious roar, sending a shockwave at the tank. The tank vibrated from the soundwave. Hira's driver pressed the tank harder, then a loud clang registered from the guts of the vehicle. Smoke billowed into the cabin and Hira gagged. But the tank kept pressing ahead, losing only a little steam.

They closed within two hundred yards of the defensive line.

Hira got on the communications link. "Fire!"

All the tank cannons erupted with a volley of 120mm rounds. Then Harriers swooped in for a sortie. Each plane released rockets from pods on both wings, sending them sailing toward the beast.

Rockets exploded as the 120mm rounds dug into the creature's hide. But the attack had the opposite effect than they'd anticipated. Stomping madly, the creature picked up speed and charged the defensive line.

Another roar pierced through the city, as the Kaiju trounced on top of Hira's tank.

Metal caved and the roof collapsed. Steel pressed on Hira in the command seat. His arm got wedged in mangled plates. The tank bounced over a curb and collided with a building, then ground to a halt as concrete and steel collapsed on them.

Hira's driver was crushed from the impact. Blood dripped from his cracked skull. The gunner scrambled about the tank, alive. Fuel spilled from a broken line and ignited. The cabin burst into flames. And Hira could hardly breathe, asphyxiated from lack of oxygen.

Pulling him by the shoulders, the gunner tried to work Hira loose from the twisted metal. A heavy stomp reverberated through the tank. "The creature is above us!" Hira yelled.

The gunner looked toward the hatch in awe. He reached for the twisted lever, but the lid was wedged shut. Another stomp and the tank rolled over. All the occupants were tossed about the compartment. Hira's arm tore at the socket, popping the shoulder out of joint. He screamed in pain. Then, the Kaiju nosed the tank again, rolling the vehicle onto its side. Hira tumbled around with an arm pinned, straining ligaments.

Frustrated, the creature couldn't get to the meaty crew. It bellowed an irate squeal, then stepped on the tank with its full weight. The gunner cried out in fear, a desperate shriek, as the armor-plating bent and creaked inward.

The gunner dropped to the deck, peering upward in fear. Terrorized.

Hira couldn't scramble to a safe pocket in the cabin. The turret and roof caved in, pressing on his chest. Pinned down, he gasped for air, as oxygen left his lungs. Squirming to free himself with futility, Hira kicked and choked while desperately trying to replenish his oxygen supply. His lungs and throat began to burn.

He couldn't breathe. Reverberations jostled on the street as the creature boomed away. The pressing ceased before the roof crushed his chest. Hira slowly suffocated, as flames inside the tank began to scorch the crew.

Charred flesh wafted through the cabin, and the gunner's screams resounded the final sensations before Hira slipped into a horrible death.

NINETEEN

Penton stared at television monitors in the command center on MCAS Futenma. A screen relayed the battle scene in Tokyo from a satellite, and another broadcasted video feed from Japan's Self-Defense Forces. Admiral Keyes narrated the latest intelligence to senior officers patched into a video conference.

The ghastly scene was more horrific than Penton had anticipated. A path of destruction led from the harbor into the city with a trail of flames in its wake. Harriers soared through the sky combating the massive creature, while a row of tanks lined up in front of Tokyo Tower, firing in futility at the angry beast. General Yoshi participated in the conference, and he didn't reflect any optimism.

Yoshi muttered that the creature couldn't be stopped. He claimed it was hell bent on revenge. They had encountered it during ancient times and as recently as the mid-nineteen sixties. Zamera was the name the people had given to the creature. A joint-task force blew it into the ocean depths, and now it had arisen and sought to destroy all of Japan for attacking it.

Penton surmised the defense forces couldn't slow the creature down, never mind stop it, or destroy the monster. He wondered what the next step might be, and expected it would be drastic.

"We're not making any headway against the creature," Admiral Keyes agreed.

"You cannot harm it with conventional weapons," Yoshi insisted.

"The creature hasn't faced all that we have, though."

"Zamera won't be slowed by any of it."

Keyes appeared in the corner of a screen, shaking his head. "What are you suggesting?"

"This is going to take similar measures as used in 1965."

"We've got peace treaties calling for total abolishment of nuclear weapons," Keyes reminded him. "Not only are they unauthorized to use, we aren't even *supposed* to have any in the area."

Even Penton knew that the United Nations had recently enacted a treaty in which all members agreed not to use nuclear weapons and to take them all off-line altogether. He pondered what Yoshi was suggesting.

"Your words betray you," General Yoshi admonished.

"Even if your suspicions were correct..." Keyes replied. "Nuclear fallout, even from a small missile, would cause more harm than the monster."

"We need to divert the creature," Yoshi said. "Lead it away from the city toward the coast... direct it north toward Chiba Prefecture."

"How we going to do that?" Admiral Keyes crossed his arms.

"We've got a general plan, but we need to determine a way to execute."

Keyes raised his eyebrows. "There might be something we can do, but I'll need to have a better understanding of your plan for a diversion. Let's talk directly and try to work out a solution."

The images wavered, and then the battle scene came back on the screen. Penton watched the creature take all the firepower the joint defense force had and press forward unscathed. Admiral Keyes was no longer in the upper left corner of the screen. Communications with Fleet Command severed, entirely.

"They only tell us what we need to know," Colonel Tomkins said after a moment.

"Right you are," a couple officers muttered, laughing.

"We're like mushrooms," said a major.

"*What?*" Lieutenant Colonel Brady snapped.

"We grow best in the dark..." The major chuckled.

Brady shook his head. "This isn't the time to take things lightly. I get the sense they're really talking about using nukes in a densely populated civilian city."

"They want to lure the creature away from the city," Colonel Tomkins interjected. "Then, we'll fire a small nuke at the beast in the countryside."

"A small nuke?" Brady repeated, skeptically.

The colonel leaned back in his chair and put his hands behind his head. Penton figured the man would relish a cigar about now.

"There's a submarine in the Sea of Japan…" Colonel Tomkins told them.

"And?" said Lieutenant Colonel Brady, insisting.

"Well, I suspect the submarine has nuclear capacity."

"What makes you say that?"

"Just a hunch," Colonel Tomkins said.

"A *hunch*?" Brady shook his head in dismay.

"Yup." Colonel Tomkins leaned forward and put his elbows on the table. He glanced around at everyone. "And I bet I know what it is…"

"A Tomahawk armed with a W80 warhead," a major said.

Colonel Tomkins nodded. "A Tomahawk armed with a W80 warhead."

"Big enough to take out a creature that size," Lieutenant Colonel Brady said. "But not so big that the nuclear fallout cannot be contained."

"Or at least minimalized," Colonel Tomkins reasoned.

Their words hung in the air for a moment, as though the gravity of the situation had dawned on everyone at once. Actually putting a nuclear weapon to use for the third time in history was an ominous proposition. Worse, the situation involved the exact same countries as the last two times.

Penton's throat grew dry as he contemplated the prospect. He stepped out of the room to find a water fountain. Mutterings filtered from the conference room into the hallway.

None of the Brass had a clue what would happen next.

TWENTY

Kate dove toward the beast and launched her rockets. The creature stood with a foot on top of a tank, crushing it like a tin can. Flames billowed out the sides, and the chance of survivors was minimal.

Another pilot from her squadron followed suit. Then, the others flew toward the monster and released several rockets. Her fighter thrust upward, and she caught sight of the explosions out of the corner of her eye. Rockets pounded into the creature's chest and side but seemed to have minimal effect on it.

The beast let out a menacing roar then stomped toward the defensive line.

Flying around to make another pass, Kate noticed the tanks sitting idle while the creature moved closer and closer to them.

She patched into the communications link. "This is Captain Able. Why aren't the tanks firing at the creature?"

"We've just learned from General Yoshi… you have to fire at close range in order to impact the monster's armor. We recommend that you do the same."

"Who is this?" Kate said, trying to confirm the order.

"Sorry, this is Commander James. I'm here with Admiral Keyes."

"Just so we're clear. You want us to fire at close range."

"Captain Able, this is Admiral Keyes… We want you to get as close to the creature's belly as possible, and fire away."

"Understood, but the tactic can put my pilots at risk."

"This is a desperate situation," Keyes said. "We know you'll do your best."

Kate instructed her squadron with the new orders, then flew toward the creature, increasing speed the closer she got to him. When she reached the beast, she fired two rockets at its belly, and pulled up hard.

The jet rumbled as it shot straight into the air. She looked down and saw explosions lighting up the night. A yowling shriek of pain wailed from the creature below.

Her comrades followed suit, but didn't get as close to the creature when firing their rockets. Circling around for another pass, Kate saw their rockets didn't have the same impact as hers.

The beast swatted at the planes in futility. Another angry roar emanated from the creature. It hissed, and then trundled at the tanks.

Kate made a wide pass, then instructed her squadron to increase altitude. They flew high into the air, while Kate ascertained the creature's approach toward the defensive line. She factored its speed and distance.

They circled around and approached the creature head on.

"Release CBUs," Kate ordered.

"Aye, ma'am," two of the pilots said.

Three planes dropped their bombs and flew high into the sky. All the bombs snapped open, like jaws on a giant fish, and hundreds of small missiles rained down on the beast, carpet-bombing the hell out of him.

Projectiles dropped from the sky with sharp needle-like points stemming from the nose of each miniature bomb. They whizzed through the air and penetrated the beast's thick armor, causing it to howl in agony.

The other two fighters swooped in and fired more rockets.

Explosions burst all over the monster, as the fighters cut to the sides of the creature, with one pulling to the right and the other veering off to the left. The beast roared, but the blasts didn't harm it a bit. Neither fighter had gotten in as close as Kate, but they had fired at closer proximity than previous attempts.

She shook her head, discouraged. The creature was impervious to serious harm.

Carpet-bombing had wounded the creature, but didn't slow it down. Kate pressed the communications link. "We've got to get in tighter before firing."

"Roger, but that pass was a hell of a lot closer than before," said Captain Wecker.

"Not close enough," Kate replied. "Pull in close like I just did."

"You're a daredevil, Able," Wecker said.

"Just get in there and do some damage."

"We're coming around and will double-team its chest." This from Lieutenant Baker, meaning him and Merrill would come around together.

Kate pulled her joystick to the right and flew around to come in behind them. A double-punch, she hoped to topple the creature. *Maybe if the thing falls over, it won't be able to get up*, she thought.

The jets powered in directly at the creature's chest. Moving in tight, they hadn't released their rockets yet. Another moment and they were still closing in fast. Kate trailed behind them, far enough away to avoid their jet blasts. Finally, Merrill fired his rockets and pulled left. The ordnance exploded, wafting out toward his wingtip.

The creature squealed and batted at Merrill's plane. But the beast swatted air.

Baker pressed forward, accelerating toward the creature.

"Fire!" Kate yelled at him.

His rocket motors ignited and burst from the pods. Baker dumped his entire load at the beast. Rockets pounded into the creature's chest, erupting in explosions and billowing flames.

The creature flailed from the blasts. Flames undulated beneath the creature's thick scales. It howled from the burning pain.

Baker cut right and hit the throttle. His fighter shot forward just as the beast raised an enormous claw. His jet plowed into the beast's paw and exploded on impact. The collision barely shifted the creature's stance.

Kate flew in behind Baker, as tears blurred her vision. She moved in close and fired all her rockets, then opened fire with the GAU-12 Equalizer, riddling the beast with 25 mm rounds. And then she pulled hard, upward.

Her jet pointed nose to the clouds. Kate shifted in her seat, as the cockpit moved from horizontal with the ground to a vertical position.

The engines thundered as she increased speed. Swatting with both arms, the creature thrashed at her exhaust fumes, useless to impede her extrication. Kate marked its claws in the corners of her eyes, keeping track of its movements to ensure she didn't suffer a repeat of Baker's plight.

Then, she heard a clunk on the nose of her plane, and her fighter spun out of control.

Kate couldn't get the Harrier to level off.

The control stick locked up on her, and a jet engine fizzled out. Merely a short distance from the ground, her plane would surely crash.

"Mayday, Mayday!" Kate broadcasted widely. "I'm going down."

****

Maki had stood frozen until the creature passed by the window. Then, she ran up to the glass and watched it slink down the road, each step thundering into the ground, cracking pavement, as its giant tail whipped back and forth.

The creature stood as tall as the buildings, but somehow moved its enormous body with ease. She watched the beast suddenly look down. A tank whipped in front of it and the creature picked up its pace. An explosion erupted from the street; the creature yowled in pain.

"They're attacking the Kaiju," Maki said to her mother.

"I think they've been fighting it most of the day. Probably the reason for the distress call."

Another roar and the creature stopped in its tracks.

"He's got them," Maki said. "I just know it."

Then planes flew out of the clouds and zipped toward the creature. Maki noted the strange-looking planes with markings like she'd seen on television.

"The Americans have come to help," Mother said.

They pressed against the glass and watched a battle unfold. Fighters swooped toward the creature and fired rockets. Explosions echoed through the corridor of tall office buildings. Maki's ears rang from the loud noise.

She pulled her mother's arm. "We must leave here."

"Why?" her mother said. "This is safe."

"No, it's not," Maki insisted.

"What makes you say such a thing?"

"The military thinks these buildings are empty." Maki canted her head. "Planes are firing rockets at the Kaiju right near offices just like this."

Her mother nodded in agreement. She took Maki's hand and headed for the stairs. "They could easily head this way and attack the Kaiju without knowing we are here."

They headed back to the stairwell and descended quickly.

"What about the water?" Maki said.

"Hopefully, it has receded."

"What if it hasn't?"

"We'll have to deal with it, then."

Somehow, the stairwell seemed darker than beforehand. Maki's rain boots slapped the concrete steps as she tried to keep up. Mother kept a tight grip on her hand, and a few times it felt as though she'd pull Maki over.

We're going too fast, Maki thought. But she didn't want to trouble Mother.

Maki moved her legs faster and faster, letting the motion increase to a sprint down the stairs. Soon, they neared the bottom. They rounded the landing for the second floor and Maki glanced down at the first floor.

A man stood in the shadows with a heinous grin on his face.

"Wait!" Maki cried, pulling Mother's hand.

"What is it?" Mother almost tripped on the stairs.

Maki pointed at the man, speechless.

Her mother looked where Maki pointed, then an alarmed look crossed her face. Maki nodded, reflecting concern about the danger.

The man shook his head, and continued to smile.

Mother paused for a moment, as though trying to assess if a threat were real. The man wore filthy clothes. He stepped forward with his palms turned up, suggesting he didn't mean any harm. A mouthful of yellowed teeth, and a sardonic gleam in his eyes reflected otherwise.

Maki's heart raced with fear. *He can't be trusted.*

The man took another step forward. Maki's mother reached for the door leading to the second level. She flung it open and dashed into the hallway with Maki in tow.

The man started up the stairs in pursuit.

Maki plodded after her mother, wondering if her stubby legs could outpace the deranged man.

"He doesn't belong in this building," her mother muttered.

"No, he's a scavenger," Maki said, worried Mother might stop.

"This way." Mother pulled her around a corner.

Maki glanced back as she rounded the turn. The man panted after them, holding something in his right hand. A hint of steel reflected in the emergency lighting. "He's got a knife!" Maki gasped.

Her mother picked up the pace, then cut down a dark hallway.

Maki knew her mother would never trust the man now. She took a few breaths, then heard the patter of the man's work boots in pursuit behind them.

A moment later, and her mother took another turn.

They ran into a spacious room filled with cubicles. And conference rooms spanned the outside walls. Mother swung an exit door open, and let it slam shut, hard. Then, she pulled Maki into the middle of the office and ducked under a desk.

Mother pulled a chair in front of them. Wedged in-between the cubical wall and a filing cabinet, Maki could see through the shadows into the wide aisle.

Her pulse quickened, and she heaved for air, almost convulsing.

"Breath slowly through your nose," Mother whispered.

Maki nodded, understanding the need for silence, but the running expended all the air from her lungs. And fear had her panic-stricken.

The man's pursuit slowed to a pitter-patter, as he neared the door leading to another stairwell. A creak resounded through the office when the man opened the steel door. He stepped onto the landing, and the soles of his boots squeaked on the tile. The door didn't close shut. He merely lingered there, trying to listen for footsteps on the stairs. Then, the door slammed shut, but Maki couldn't tell if he'd gone into the stairwell.

She listened for the echo of footsteps emanating from the stairs, but didn't hear anything. Heart pounding at her chest, Maki worried her anxiety might give them away. The man hadn't gone down the stairs. She felt certain his steps could have been heard from their hiding place.

Everything remained still, and she began to think he'd gone down the stairs quietly. Mother stirred, as though planning to check if he was there. Grabbing mother's arm, Maki shook her head, suggesting they wait.

A moment passed, then she heard the distinctive sound of footsteps on the industrial carpet. The man moved slowly about the office, trying to go undetected.

Maki pointed toward the sound. Mother nodded, understanding.

The man stalked through the office, trying to stir them into flight. He eased down the aisle, peeking into cubicles. Maki saw him slip past their safe harbor and continue along in the darkness. His footsteps got lighter the further he moved away from them, until eventually, she couldn't hear him any longer.

They hid under the desk space for a while. Maki grew sore from the cramped quarters and hard floor. She wondered if the man had given up and moved along to another room. He had entered the building to pilfer and take advantage of the commotion. Surely, he'd want to get back to the task at hand and leave them alone.

Maki's mother must have had a similar notion in mind. She looked at Maki and nodded; then, she pointed up, indicating a plan to look around.

Her mother gently slid the chair forward.

Then, a stomp reverberated from the aisle, and the chair whisked away, colliding with a nearby cubicle. The man leaned into the office space and jeered at them with his tortured grin. A sardonic jeer of a deviant emanated through the dark room.

They were trapped.

His stench permeated the air. Vile.

Drool pooled in his open mouth.

A bulge protruded from his pants, grotesque. Maki understood his intentions, and why he'd been sidetracked from his looting. The degenerate repulsed her.

He held the knife in one hand, and reached for her mother's ankle with the other.

She resisted, pulling her foot back. He leaned back, pulling and heaving Mother's leg. Yanking the outstretched leg, he dragged her from under the desk. Mother squirmed to roll onto her belly and scramble to her feet.

The man pounced on top of her. He pinned her arms back, and saliva dripped on her face. His knife lodged between their hands.

Mother thrashed and jammed a knee into his groin.

He arched back and bellowed in pain.

She grabbed computer wires in a desperate attempt to get to her feet. A printer skittered off the desk and cracked him in the head. The man slumped forward, while she shifted trying to get out from underneath him.

Maki climbed out from under the desk, as the man regained composure. She grabbed a stapler and whacked him in the head. He slumped over, tangling his limbs around her mother.

Mother flailed and beat him wildly, then clambered on top of him.

The man groaned in pain and turned his head, disoriented.

Maki helped her mother stand, and they ran toward the stairwell with her mother trailing behind, slowly recouping her equanimity. They ran down the stairs and crossed through the storage room in the back. Mother found a door, and it opened into an alley. Water had already begun to recede.

They stepped outside into the cool evening air. Maki pulled ahead of her mother, trying to find a passageway leading to where they'd entered the building. She desperately wanted to find her father.

Maki ran down the alley. Her rain boots pattered in rivulets of water. She found the door and worked the latch, then she flung it open. Water streamed over the threshold. Mother ran up from behind and peered over her shoulder. They paused and looked inside.

Nothing.

She pulled away from her mother.

Maki ran down the alley.

She turned a corner and abruptly stopped. Dread choked her breath.

A body lay partway around the corner. Bloated and pale from drowning, the corpse was strewn on the sidewalk as water trickled around it.

The dead man wore professional clothes and a trench coat. His bald pate faced away from them. Maki rushed to his side and looked at his face. A pair of eyes bulged from the dead man's head, cast in permanent shock.

Death had distorted the man's visage. Maki clapped a hand over her mouth and began to cry. Her mother stepped alongside her and caressed a shoulder. "Maki, it's not him."

Maki moved closer and registered the discrepancies. He had a bigger nose and a fleshy chin. Still, the sight of the man made her sob. Father had suffered a similar fate. Maki pictured him tossed aside by the current.

"It's not fair!" Maki bellowed.

"He saved us…" Mother said. "Always put us first."

"Why?" Maki cried. "Why did he have to die?"

"We must go now. No time to mourn."

She grabbed Maki's hand and led her away from the dead man. They stepped out of the alley. Father had led them out of harm's way. Maki knew it for certain. Anyone on the main street would have been swept away by the water.

When they ambled down the sidewalk, Maki checked left and right, looking for her father. She didn't like the idea of him lying in a gutter swirling with rain water. The Kaiju had gone up the street to the right.

"Maybe we should go in a different direction from the monster," Maki said.

Mother nodded, agreeing with her. "We go this way," Mother said, pointing toward the left.

Maki followed after her. "Hopefully, the military will make the city safe."

"We need to stay out of the way and avoid the fighting."

"Do you think the Kaiju is out for revenge?"

"What makes you say that?"

"Grandpapa told stories about it."

"He's a foolish old man."

"Apparently, he's not."

Maki glanced up at her mother and noticed the comment sinking in. Younger generations had written off the Kaiju as mere folk legend. Elders weren't revered nearly as much as in the past, and many of their stories were considered mere nonsense.

Now, the older generation seemed more open-minded and in tune with the past. The Kaiju had been here decades ago, and came back to rampage the city. Maki heard more explosions, then the creature roared.

A dreadful sound that echoed through the tall buildings.

She looked over her shoulder and saw a burst of flames rising in the air. Tokyo had erupted into a city of chaos.

"We must run," Mother said, pulling her along.

"But the Kaiju is back there fighting with the military…"

"The danger is too close. We have to get away."

Mother dragged her down the street toward the harbor, while Maki desperately searched for her father. They didn't encounter anyone along the way.

A tsunami had cleared them a path.

They got a little further down the street and ran into standing water. Layers of oil skimmed the surface. Her mother shook her head.

"We can't go this way," Mother said. "The water is too deep."

"The ground is dry over there." Maki pointed.

"Come."

Running along the edge of the murky water, the two of them plied their way toward higher ground. Maki stumbled a couple of times and glanced at the street.

All the tar had been churned up, making the pavement uneven. Tanks had come this way.

****

Kate's fighter spun out of control. The cockpit intermittently pointed at the ground and the sky. Ejecting from the plane might launch her directly at the earth without time for the parachute to open.

She timed the circumlocutions, then hit the eject button.

The cockpit glass whipped off and shot behind the plane, as the jet continued to descend toward the city below. Her ejection-seat burst into the air, and a popping sound emanated from beneath it. The fighter careened away as her parachute billowed open.

Jet engines roared toward the city below. Kate dropped fast in a wake of exhaust. She glanced up to see if the chute had fully expanded.

Nylon ruffled in the wind, then a gust caught under the fabric. The chute snapped wide-open and the ejection-seat shot upward violently. Then, the seat settled and drifted gently toward the ground. She glanced down at the battle scene.

Tanks rolled ahead from the defensive line, aggressively approaching the creature. Closing the distance, the tanks fired one after another. Rounds dug into the beast's thick scales. The creature bellowed in pain and stomped toward the tanks. Another volley of rounds erupted from the large cannons.

A few rounds struck the creature in its lower right leg. The beast lost its gait and stumbled into a nearby building. Glass shattered and stone panels split apart. Debris pelted the street below.

The creature let out a roar, then righted itself, and pressed ahead.

All the tanks moved toward the creature in a makeshift line, firing sporadically. Distance between the opposing forces narrowed rapidly. The creature plodded into the oncoming tanks and stomped one in its tracks.

Smoke and flames billowed out from the turret. Through the commotion of grinding metal and explosions, faint screams of agony lingered in the air. Another tank rolled into the creature's path.

A menacing foot with sharp claws squashed the tank.

Still, other tanks circled around to engage the creature. Cannons fired round after round, until the fusillades slowly diminished in capacity. Streets were crammed with the wreckage of destroyed tanks. And the surviving tanks had clearly run low on ammunition.

Rattling machinegun fire replaced the explosive cannons.

Tanks broke away from the battle and fled for the protective cover of city streets and tall buildings. The creature roared at the tracked vehicles creaking away from the scene. It canted its head from side to side, then followed after a few of them.

Kate's parachute slowed her descent. Her plane had flown high enough to allow the chute to fully engage. Winds carried her toward a high-rise building.

She dropped below the level of the rooftop and glided toward the side of the building. Her ejection seat bumped against the glass and jolted her. The safety belts kept her buckled in place. Something bumped again. And she stopped moving.

The chute flapped against the building. Kate glanced upward. A portion of the canopy had snagged on a piece of metal protruding from the parapet.

Nylon fabric tore.

The chute collapsed.

More tearing.

Weight from the ejection seat pulled on the parachute. The material wouldn't hold for long, and she'd plummet to the sidewalk below. Kate released the safety harness and scrambled on top of the seat.

Reaching for her survival knife, she entwined her left arm in shroud lines, then cut the belts attaching the chute to the seat.

The ejection seat dropped away, eventually striking the ground with a resounding thud.

She sheathed the knife and climbed up the chute, wrapping a leg around a bundle of lines and pinching it off with her flight boots, like climbing a rope back at Annapolis. Kate grabbed onto the fabric and inched her way up.

Nylon tore from her effort and she dropped back down a foot.

Kate took a moment to gather herself, breathing deeply and keeping still. The parachute held when she didn't move.

Hanging suspended from the parachute, Kate spied tanks approaching from down the street. The creature barged after them, colliding into buildings, shattering glass and breaking concrete loose.

Her heart raced in trepidation. She started up the chute moving swiftly.

The canopy continued to rip, causing her to drop as much as she'd progressed. Kate remained virtually in the same place, scared the material would give way, and petrified she'd fall to the ground.

The pavement below rumbled from the creature's aggravated stomps.

She gave it another go and felt the chute tighten. A few shroud lines had caught on the parapet. Kate scrambled upward as easily as climbing a rope. Then, she heaved herself onto the rooftop.

Looking down, three tanks rumbled past, churning up the asphalt. The creature took massive strides, keeping pace with the tanks, as diesel engines whined and groaned.

Then, the stamping feet came to an abrupt halt, leaving only the sounds of the tanks creaking off into the distance. A prodigious snout slowly rose above the edge of the rooftop. The creature took prolonged sniffs of the air. Moist nostrils heaved in and out, as if sampling a delicacy.

The nose dropped out of view, then a footstep below shook the ground, reverberating into the building. Kate wavered from the tremor.

A high-pitched roar pierced the evening air, and then the creature smashed into the side off the building. The parapet along the rooftop crumpled, glass broke, and girders creaked from bending under stress.

Kate bolted for the rooftop access door.

Another roar and shuffled footfalls shook the building. Then the creature crashed head-long into the side of the tower. The poured-cement roof broke apart and bits of concrete hurled to the street below, while chunks dropped into the lower floors, opened wide from the mighty attack.

Just as Kate reached the door, the floor beneath her feet gave way. And she plunged downward.

TWENTY-ONE

Penton stared at the screen in disbelief for the second time in one day. Bursting flames from Baker's plane still fresh in his mind, he watched as Captain Able's fighter crashed to the earth and exploded.

The attack hadn't been a success. It was an utter failure, and the creature pressed ahead and decimated the remaining tanks. He'd watched the Kaiju scoop up tank crew members as they fled the scene, gnawing on flesh and bones with massive teeth. Penton could imagine the ear-splitting wails of pain from the soldiers.

Now, the damn thing was destroying a building. Kate's parachute dangled from the rooftop. Penton clenched his fists, anger spurned by helplessness. He wanted desperately to get out there and do something.

"Let me fly out there in an Osprey," Penton said to the colonel.

Colonel Tomkins raised an eyebrow, then glanced around the room as though requesting feedback.

"The storm is winding past its peak," said Lieutenant Colonel Brady.

Tomkins nodded in agreement. "You can get out there with a rescue team. But just remember, the admiral is fixing to launch a nuclear missile at the damn thing."

"Understood, sir." Penton snapped to attention, then clicked his heels together. He marched out of the conference room and headed up the steps. A fighting Marine, he'd already spent more than enough time in the committee room.

Penton grabbed his poncho, draped in a corner of the small entrance area, and then he headed toward the door. He bid adieu to the duty Marine and pushed the hatch open. Wind and rain whipped into the building.

Outside, he jogged over to the truck he'd commandeered earlier in the day and slid behind the wheel. The keys were in the ignition. Penton fired up the truck and headed back toward the MALS-36 hangar.

He reached into a pocket for his cellphone. And took a deep breath before hitting the call button. "Top," he said. "Penton here."

"Jesus… what the hell is going on now?"

"We've got a situation on the ground in Tokyo."

"Yeah," Top Anderson said, befuddled.

"We're going to need to send a rescue team over there."

"The Ospreys from the Fighting Tigers. Got it."

Penton rumbled through the storm and dodged around fallen palm trees. Windshield wipers squeaked back and forth. "Appreciate it."

"Knew we needed to keep a couple of birds on reserve."

"Can you get it in motion?" Penton said. "I've got to swing by my place and grab my gear."

"You're going with them?" Top Anderson questioned.

"Yeah," Penton replied. "And we're only going to need one aircraft."

"Roger," Anderson said. "We'll load her with an M2 machinegun."

"Much appreciated." Penton hung up the phone.

He wheeled the truck up to his barracks, and found his Jeep parked safely in front. Penton shook his head and smiled at the diligence of his Marines. Climbing from the truck, he dashed for the door.

Penton stepped inside. He recalled how only hours earlier he'd been on the phone with his daughter, hunkering out a storm. Now, the world was turned upside down, and a giant creature he never knew existed had gone berserk in Tokyo.

He cut on a light and walked down the hallway.

A small closet was located right outside his bedroom. Penton opened the door and reached inside for his seabag. He went into the bedroom and tossed it on the floor. A deployment bag, he kept it packed for emergency alert readiness, but he didn't need some of the items inside. Penton changed into his flight suit and boots.

Then, he dumped the contents of the seabag onto his bed, and fished around for his Colt .45 officer's Model 1911. A smaller barrel and shorter handle, the weapon was the perfect size for small operations. He chambered a round and holstered the pistol.

Then, he grabbed a first-aid kit and compass and headed back out to the truck.

He drove through the storm to the armory and checked out his M16-A4 rifle. Then, he hauled ass over to the hangar and pulled the truck onto the flight line. Top Anderson stood in the rain, directing Marines hustling in action. A support tractor hauled the aircraft out of the hangar, while everyone scrambled to get the bird ready for flight. Penton ran over to chat with Top.

The fuel truck rolled up as two pilots sauntered to the hangar doors. They wore flight suits and carried flashy helmets. An enlisted man trailed behind them. He wore a flight suit as well, and Penton pegged him for the crew chief immediately.

"Let's head over," Penton said to Anderson, motioning toward the flight crew.

"Fly boys already here?" Top Anderson chuckled.

Penton smirked at the comment and jogged over to the hangar. Top Anderson thumped along behind him. Penton reached the flight crew and popped a quick salute to the officers. They responded in unison.

"Captain Simmons," the older pilot said, reaching for a handshake.

"Master Gunnery Sergeant Penton." They shook hands.

"First Lieutenant Johnson."

Penton offered his hand.

"And this is our crew chief, Staff Sergeant Blakely," Simmons said, pointing.

"Blakely…" Penton grinned. "Thought I recognized you."

"How you doing, Master Guns?"

"Could be better." Penton grinned.

"So, what is the story?" Simmons asked.

"We're assigned to carry out a rescue mission," Penton replied. "We've got a downed Harrier and need to secure the pilot."

Everyone on the flight crew nodded, understanding.

"There's more…" Penton looked them over in earnest.

"What's a Harrier doing out in a storm like this, anyway?" Simmons questioned.

"A squadron of Harriers were assigned to fly over Tokyo."

"Tokyo?" Simmons said. "Why on earth—"

"We've got a major crisis."

They all looked at him, concern registering on their faces. "What is it?" Simmons said. "China or North Korea?"

Penton shook his head. "Afraid it's much different from that."

He explained the situation and Simmons snickered. "You're pulling my leg," Simmons said, as his co-pilot laughed.

Penton stood with his hands on his hips. And Top Anderson had his arms crossed with a stern look on his face. The pilots looked the senior enlisted Marines over, and the smiles slipped from both of their faces.

"We don't have time for this horseshit," Penton scolded them.

Top Anderson grinned as Master Guns rebuked the younger officers. "Let's get that bird in the air and get me to Tokyo," Penton said, turning away. He walked out into the rain and supervised the Marines preparing the armament for the Osprey.

When the aircraft finally took off, a gust of wind shook the Osprey, causing it to dip toward the tarmac. Penton wondered whether the Brass would end up having to dispatch a rescue team to pick them out of the ocean.

****

Admiral Keyes watched the screen in awe. The giant creature repeatedly smashed its upper torso into a dark office building. Keyes could really go for a Scotch and water about now. He licked his lips and got up to pour himself another cup of coffee.

"What would make something do a thing like that?" Keyes said.

"Maybe the thing is part of some secret Chinese experiment..." a younger officer suggested.

"A first strike weapon?" said Executive Officer James.

"I'm saying..." Keyes snapped. "Why would it stop and bang up a building when it had been chasing those tanks?"

"Perhaps the thing is losing its mind, going crazy," James offered.

"Yeah, it seems like a pretty bizarre thing to be doing."

"Maybe it's after something in the building," said Williams, the intelligence officer.

"What?" Executive Officer James griped and shook his head.

Williams rose and walked over to the screen. She pointed at the parachute snagged to the corner of the building. Everyone's mouths dropped wide open. "This thing is a meat eater," she said. "We've already got reports of it devouring people down at the harbor."

Keyes took a swig of his coffee. "Ain't going to be any end to this havoc until that thing is plumb dead." He spoke in a southern drawl and shook his head.

"The creature might be prehistoric..." Williams said.

"And?" James quipped.

"It could be the only one of its kind..."

"That goes without saying." James chuckled.

"This could be the only one in existence, living, fossil, or otherwise."

"We still have to kill the damn thing," Keyes said, pointing at the screen. "Look what it's doing out there."

The beast stopped pounding the building. It stood beside an opening with both claws crimped to the crumbled façade. Nose sniffing with interest, the creature peered inside as though seeking prey.

"The freaking thing wants to eat Captain Able," James said.

"I'm just saying that thing could be a link we never knew about... between the dinosaurs and some reptilian line, or primitive bird."

"Bird?" James said, slapping his leg. The suit laughed along with him.

"There's a connection between dinosaurs and birds," said Williams, shaking her head condescendingly.

"Thought they were just big lizards." James laughed again.

"No, they are believed to be warm blooded, and sometimes hunted in packs," she replied. "Making them distinct from reptiles we have today."

Keyes shook his head. "We can study the damn thing when it's dead."

"Your current plans won't leave much left of it."

Then Keyes shrugged, indicating he didn't have a choice.

TWENTY-TWO

Kate tumbled down two levels as sections of the building cracked apart. The roof collapsed, and a hunk of concrete held together with rebar dropped through the floors below. But she slid down the detached segment unscathed.

The creature continued pounding the building, splitting the floor open. She fell through a crevice and dropped eight feet blow, landing on a desktop in a cubicle workstation. Then, the desktop gave way and she plopped onto the floor.

Now, she lay on the industrial carpet, banged up from the fall, as debris cascaded around her. Wind and rain penetrated a large hole the creature had made in the building. Kate shivered from the cold, damp air. Pain shot through her thigh after landing on craggy rubble. She feared moving to tend to the wound.

A massive yellow eye peered inside the fractured wall.

Enormous nostrils sniffed, as though sensing fare, an appetizer. Another ear-piercing roar wailed from the beast's mouth. The sound reverberated through the broken building, a shrill, driving pain into the center of Kate's head.

She desperately wanted to cover her ears but couldn't give away her position.

Then, the creature shook its head, and snot and saliva spattered throughout the demolished office space. A clump of phlegm swashed over her, matting to her flight suit. Kate hid ten meters from the beast. Foul breath wafted into the office space, and each gnarled tooth stood the size of a human.

Kate peeked through twisted office furniture, and the menacing yellow eye seemed to blink at her. The massive jaw appeared to almost smirk. A level of intelligence registered in the creature that she would never have imagined.

Ponderous steps backpedaled on the street beneath her.

Twisted metal from crushed cars echoed along the corridor of the long city street. Horns blared from the demolished automobiles below. Stepping away from the aperture, the creature's movements caused destruction around it.

Another disconcerting wink sent a chill down her spine.

The blasted thing is going to ram the building.

She sprung to her feet and ran toward the breached wall, reaching for her sidearm. Kate removed a Berretta from her shoulder holster. Standing in the opening, she planted her feet, and took steady aim.

Kate inhaled.

Squeezed the trigger.

And fired.

A bullet ripped through the air and burrowed into the menacing eye.

The creature howled in extreme pain, a deafening roar. Sound waves knocked Kate to the floor. Wailing in pain, the beast flailed. Green mucus leaked from the wound; anger and hatred registered from the provocative eye.

Furious, the creature stomped toward the building.

Kate rolled onto her stomach and sprung to her feet. Skittering through debris, she raced for an emergency staircase. She bolted down a hallway, watching for rubble on the floor while periodically scanning for exit signs.

The hallway grew darker the further she got from the broken façade. She tripped and stumbled, then regained her gait.

An exit sign hung above a metal door. Kate burst through the door and dashed down the concrete stairs. Her flight boots bustled over non-skid strips as she made the descent in haste.

A cacophony of shattered glass, followed by the building shaking, made her speed up. Legs moving rapidly, she didn't feel tired or out of breath. Dread propelled her along. The creature let out another roar and assaulted the office tower again. Everything vibrated from the tremendous blow, stairs, handrail, and walls.

Kate made a misstep and fell. Tumbling onto the next landing, her ankle flared with pain. She lifted her knee and massaged the sprain.

Emergency lighting flickered in the stairwell.

Lights went out.

A zapping sound followed; electrical wires had pulled loose. Kate stood and hobbled down the stairs. Placing weight on her right foot caused extreme pain. She'd suck it up, take the pain, but the limb kept wanting to give out. Kate held onto the handrail for balance and eased down the stairs one step at a time.

Reaching the next landing, smoke fumes wafted under the door. She flitted from stair to stair, and eventually stopped to catch a breather two floors down.

Kate felt the door. It was scorching hot.

She glanced over the railing and estimated twelve more flights of stairs to go. The building stood approximately sixteen stories tall, likely with retail space on the first floor and high ceilings, making the creature stand over sixty feet high.

Continuing down the stairs, the building shook from another blow. Steps vibrated. Kate stumbled and caught herself. Fissures ran down the concrete block and dust fluttered into the stairwell. Metal structural girders bent under the massive hits into the building.

As the steel beams deflected, eerie creaking sounds muffled through the thick walls. Concrete floors and walls supported by the beams gave way. Pieces of cement toppled onto the stairs.

She wondered if the creature might succeed in killing her.

Thoughts of the office building collapsing spurred her along. Kate grabbed hold of the handrail, and hopped down the stairs on one foot, holding the sprained ankle in the air.

Her speed increased. She reached the next landing and hobbled along.

Kate rounded the corner and returned to using the handrail; she continued hopping down the stairs. But when she got to the next landing, smoke penetrated the cracked walls and rose in thick clouds.

The fumes choked her and blurred her vision.

She wrapped a hand over her nose and opened her mouth partway, breathing through her teeth to filter the smoke, like in training for biological warfare. Kate continued down the stairs, tottering along.

Flames raged into the stairwell on the floor below, increasing the smoke and heat into the narrow space. Kate looked up. She realized the stairwell provided the perfect shaft for fire to spread upward.

Everything above her was open space, easily filled with oxygen.

She headed through the door on the second-floor landing as the conflagration erupted. *That thing starts a fucking fire wherever it goes*, Kate muttered.

A clang resounded from the door slamming shut behind her. She trotted into the second floor, limping on the bad ankle. Pain subsided into numbness, but the joint remained unstable. Everywhere she turned, Kate ran into dead ends, blocked by walls and broken floors. The space had been sub-divided into several offices for different companies.

Sprinklers finally cut on and doused everything with water.

Kate trundled into a corner and slid to the floor, hoping the creature would grow tired of battering the structure, and lose interest in pursuing a morsel of prey.

TWENTY-THREE

Hardy stood by the wooden door ready to move into position when the enemy rolled in. An ear inside the warehouse, he heard Stiles trying to finish up with the missile.

Then, the unmistakable sound of tracked vehicles clanked in the distance.

"Almost there!" Stiles called out.

But Hardy didn't respond, or head back into the building.

Stiles rushed over with a stern look in his eyes.

Hardy shook his head.

Diesel engines grumbled louder. Any moment, they would speed up the driveway and soldiers would begin another firefight.

"What is it?" Stiles said, pointing toward the road.

Hardy shook his head and held up a finger, indicating he needed a moment. Then, he pressed on his helmet listening to the communications link.

"The damn thing is ready," Stiles insisted. "We need to move out!"

Shaking his head, Hardy cackled and grinned derisively.

"What is it?" Stiles said, confused.

Hardy nodded in response to a communication, then touched the link again to speak: "We'll try to do our best."

Now, Stiles stood before him with a hand on his hip and the other tightly gripping his rifle. Hardy wasn't sure how his comrade would take the news. In fact, he was slightly daft himself after hearing what the Brass were planning next.

"You can't keep me in suspense any longer," Stiles griped.

"Well, the Brass has gone and done another *change one-thousand* on us."

Stiles looked at him, and his jaw literally dropped.

Enlisted military personnel dubbed the numerous changes back and forth from the indecisive officer corps as change one-thousands, so many revised plans, they were countless. SEALs knew the term well, and Stiles immediately registered that plans had irrevocably altered.

Hardy waited a moment, so the situation would sink in before he dropped the bomb.

Stiles stared at him impatiently. He clearly wanted to get out of there.

"A huge change in plans," Hardy said, shaking his head.

"Well... just tell me what it is," Stiles insisted.

"We've got to—"

Explosions erupted all around them.

Wooden panels splintered to bits. The SEALs ducked for cover behind the front-end of the first transport. Hardy peeked his head up. A couple of tanks creaked through the thin woods to their right.

Tank commanders popped out of both hatches, goggles strapped to their helmets. A pause in the firing, while the gunners reloaded and recalibrated.

"Let's hop into the woods behind us," Stiles said.

"We can't leave the missile here."

"Okay, we head inside." Stiles nodded. "I can make another adjustment to it, then we bust out the back of the building."

"No." Hardy shook his head. "We can't leave the missile in their hands."

"What are we supposed to do? Fight the entire North Korean Army?"

"Yeah, but only for a little while." Hardy chuckled, reaching for a concussion grenade. "I'll take the tank on the right, and you get the one on the left."

Stiles slipped along the passenger side of the truck and poked his head around the rear to break off and flank the enemy. With Stiles in position, Hardy leaned around the hood of the transport and fired a round into the neck of the tank commander on the right.

Then, he bolted toward the tank, running across the path of the approaching armored-vehicle. Stiles did the same, only he fired and ran to the left.

Machinegun fire erupted from the tanks. Bullets dug up the ground at Hardy's heels.

Hardy came up even with the tank then dashed at it from the side. Pulling the pin on his grenade, he flung his rifle around so the

MP-5 dangled from his back. Then, he jumped onto the side of the tank and tossed the MK3 inside.

He hopped off the tank and rolled away.

A blast exploded out the hatch, along with pieces of metal and limbs. The tank rolled along and bashed into the transport and came to a halt.

Immediately moving into a kneeling position, Hardy reached around for his rifle and shouldered the weapon. He readied to fire.

Nobody exited the tank.

Hardy scanned the other one.

It rolled along.

Stiles stood on top of the tank with a grenade in one hand and his SOG SEAL knife in the other. A North Korean soldier protruded halfway out of the hatch and held Stiles by the wrists. Both warriors struggled in a death dance.

Machinegun fire blasted from the tank as it circled around towards Hardy.

Hardy aimed his rifle.

And shot at the soldier fighting Stiles.

A 10mm round struck him.

He hit the North Korean behind the ear. Blood gushed out of the bullet hole. Stiles tossed the man off the tank and whipped his grenade inside. Stiles jumped from the tank, as scraps of metal and flesh rained down from the explosion.

Another diesel engine grumbled up the driveway. Hardy figured a troop transport would arrive at the scene. Blood soaked through his pant leg, and his wounded thigh burned. His chest ached from being shot repeatedly.

"Screw this!" Hardy bellowed and broke for the disabled tank.

He climbed on top and peered into the hatch, holding his sidearm ready to fire. Nothing moved within the cabin. Poking his head inside, pistol in hand, Hardy found all the occupants torn to pieces.

He slipped into the tank and shoved the driver aside.

Then, checking the engine and controls, he found the concussion grenade hadn't destroyed everything. He backed the tank up then maneuvered the turret to face the approaching driveway. Cannon loaded, he verified the trajectory, then he stepped over to the machinegun and perused the cartridge belt.

The troop transport rolled down the driveway.

Hardy fired the cannon.

A 120mm round burst through the air.

It smashed through the windshield.

The ordnance exploded and the truck burst into flames, then the transport exploded. Flames billowed into the air from the blast.

Soldiers alighted from the truck. Many held AK-47s ready to fire, while others rolled to the ground, trying to snuff out their burning uniforms.

Hardy moved to the front of the tank and opened up on them with the tank machinegun. Bullets riddled the advancing troops and dropped them in their tracks. A few soldiers darted for the woods, but Stiles took them down.

Soldiers crawled under the first transport, presenting a threat to Stiles. They fired at him from a covered, prone position.

Hardy climbed out of the tank and tossed a fragmentation grenade. It rolled under the truck.

The grenade exploded, killing soldiers, and others wailed in pain. Some lay limp, torn apart. A couple wormed out from the driver's side, and one wriggled out the passenger side. They broke around the truck. Hardy signaled to Stiles; he'd go around to the passenger side and leave one to Stiles.

Hardy cleared the hood of the large truck. He fired and a North Korean soldier dropped to the ground, a round bored into the infantryman's skull.

Hardy came around the side of the truck. The other soldier was gone.

Dropping to the ground, Hardy scanned the tree line. He'd expected the amateur to flee the scene. But the guy was smart enough to avoid getting shot running away. A bullet dinged the door of the truck above Hardy's head.

Another bullet tore up the ground in front of him.

Hardy marked the soldier's position from the second muzzle flash. He squeezed the trigger of his MP-5, and the soldier cried out in pain, toppling over. Clutching the AK-47's handgrip, the soldier compressed the trigger in the throes of death.

The Russian weapon fired rapidly, stippling the side of the truck with rounds.

Raising his rifle, Hardy plugged a hole in the man's head, putting an abrupt end to the writhing assault.

Stiles ran up beside him. "You alright?" he said to Hardy.

"Fine," Hardy replied. "How about you?"

"Doing much better than you, my friend."

They chuckled at the comment while Hardy got to his feet.

"What now?" Stiles said.

"We wait."

"You've got to be shitting me."

"Those are the orders." Hardy shook his head, wondering what other troops would emerge on the scene before they were through.

TWENTY-FOUR

Maki held Mother's hand tight. Power was out through most of the city, and the street was blanketed in darkness. They moved along slowly and she tried to glimpse the sidewalk through intermittent shadows and down-pouring rain.

Tanks rumbled by and Maki felt safe. *The military will protect us*, she thought.

Her mother pressed ahead, surefooted. But Maki tripped occasionally, unable to see the curb openings for driveways and side streets. She wondered when they could go home and hoped her father somehow found his way out of the flooded alley.

Another set of tanks rolled toward them. Then a soldier protruded from an open hatch. "Run!" he yelled to them.

Mother picked up the pace as fast as she could, impeded by the darkness.

Glancing over her shoulder, Maki noticed the soldier in the tank shaking his head. "We're going the wrong way," Maki said.

"This way leads to our apartment."

"Let's turn back," Maki insisted.

"There's nothing back there except for stagnant water."

"All those tanks…" Maki panted. "They aren't going to fight."

Her mother stopped in her tracks and looked down at Maki, baffled.

"The tanks are fleeing the monster."

Then, Mother looked all around them, and Maki did as well. Nothing but a silent roadway and empty buildings. Mother shook her head. "We'd hear commotion."

Maki stomped her rain boot, and the ground rumbled.

Her mother looked at Maki, aghast.

"It's not me," Maki said, pointing.

Mother glanced up, and her mouth dropped open.

The Kaiju slinked down the street, moving its head back and forth, sniffing, while an enormous tail whipped from side to side. Each footstep crumpled the tar beneath pointed claws, and shockwaves reverberated over the pavement.

Sidewalk and street undulated and cracked. And her mother stood motionless, paralyzed by fear, trepidation.

"We have to run!" Maki yelled, pulling her mother's arm.

"Oh, my," Mother exclaimed, trembling.

"Now!" Maki insisted.

Mother turned and dashed across the street, pulling Maki along with her. A narrow side street appeared in the shadows. "This way," Mother said.

Thunderous steps marked the creature's pursuit.

"It's after us!" Maki screamed.

Mother nodded, acknowledging their plight. She pressed onward.

The vibrations got stronger, wavering the ground beneath their feet. Maki stumbled a few times. She worried the Kaiju would close the distance before they could get to safety.

Looking back, the creature rounded the corner and stalked down the side street. Its ginormous body could barely fit between the buildings. The confined space seemed to perturb the creature.

A loud roar resounded through the tight corridor. Then, a whirlwind followed the soundwave, almost knocking Maki to the ground.

She lost pace and mother kept pulling her arm. Maki tripped and fell.

Their hands separated and her mother sped onward, unaware.

"Mother!" screamed Maki.

More thumping, and the pavement shook. The Kaiju advanced.

"Mother!" Maki called, lying on the ground.

All at once, her mother seemed to register that something wasn't right. She looked at her hand, then glanced back at Maki. Mother spun around and ran toward her, as the creature closed the distance.

The Kaiju moved near, and Maki smelled its fetid breath. She didn't have to look to know how close it had gotten. The ground shook and undulated like riding a wave.

She braced for impending doom. Maki shook her head, trying to dissuade her mother from approaching.

But her mother didn't heed Maki's warning.

She raced up and pulled Maki to her feet. "Run!" Mother blared.

Maki scrambled ahead.

She swatted for her mother's hand but snatched at air. Maki glanced back and saw her mother standing in the road, intently staring the creature down.

"Mother!" cried Maki, turning back.

"No!" Mother yelled. "Run… Maki! Run!"

Maki did as she was told. She ran ahead and sprinted until the street stopped shaking. Ran until her lungs burned and her legs wobbled.

Then, she slowed to a jog and peered over a shoulder.

The Kaiju stood in the middle of the narrow street with its head tilted back, chewing greedily. Mother was nowhere to be seen. Maki began to cry.

Blood and saliva dripped from its mouth, then a shoe spit out and floated through the stormy air, clattering on the pavement below.

The Kaiju lowered its chin then stomped forward, swallowing. A bulge wormed down its throat.

Maki took a deep breath and plugged ahead. She traversed debris in the roadway, shattered glass and chunks of concrete. Loud stamping feet trod after her. Turning a corner, she noticed a pile of rubble in the street.

A decimated building lingered before her, with the exterior torn apart. Maki ducked into the edifice, slipping out of sight.

TWENTY-FIVE

Penton sat on a canvas bench seat, leaning against the fuselage of the V-22 Osprey. The rotary engines hummed through the heavy rain, and the aircraft shifted occasionally in the heavy winds. Despite the horrendous conditions, the bird flew through the storm quite well. Droning engines allowed him to slip into a half-sleep.

A couple hours later, turbulence shook him awake. He glanced around. The crew chief sat nestled on the opposite bench. An M2 Browning .50 caliber machinegun was mounted in the rear of the aircraft. The weapon fired from the tail-end with the ramp open. Otherwise, the aircraft didn't have offensive capabilities. Penton shook his head at the design, thinking about every other Marine Corps aircraft with heavier firepower.

"We've picked up a tailwind," announced the pilot, Captain Simmons.

"How far out?" Penton replied into the communications link.

"We're descending into Tokyo, now."

"Let's drop the loading ramp."

"Sure thing."

Hydraulics hummed through the cargo space, then the ramp opened like a giant mouth, grinning at the destruction below. Wind and rain whipped inside, fluttering the sleeves and pant legs of Penton's flight suit.

"Would you like the pleasure?" This from the crew chief, Staff Sergeant Blakely.

"It's your ship," Penton said. "I'm just along for the ride."

"Had to ask... Master Gunny." Blakely tethered himself to the fuselage with a safety line. A stocky fellow, he eased up to the machinegun, while wind gusted inside the aircraft.

Blakely took a seat behind the M2, then inspected the cartridge belt and feed with the precision of a skilled professional. He turned back to Penton, grinned, and gave the thumbs up. A large ordnance emblem was plastered to the front his helmet. The omnipresent flaming bomb flanked by aviation wings was surrounded by bursting red and orange flames.

Penton wondered where he'd gotten the custom paintjob.

The Flying Tigers patch on the breast of Blakely's flight suit was standard, though. Penton's Blade Runner patch was more colorful. Marine Corps uniforms were bereft of individual unit markings, a hallmark of making Marines a cohesive fighting force, with little to distinguish various units. Only a few standouts were found on their uniforms: jump wings, aircrew wings, and the ordnance disposal badge. Unit identification was nowhere to be found, except in the airwing, where flight suits, flight jackets, and hangars adorned the patches of numerous unit command structures, a symbiotic carryover from Naval aviation.

Penton, like most Marines, collected patches from the various bases and units where he served during his time in the Marine Corps. The markings on Blakely's flight suit were a sad reminder of the comradery he'd miss upon retirement.

The Osprey dipped to the left, approaching Tokyo from the east. As the aircraft flew over the harbor and above the city, a path of massive destruction came into eyeshot. Flames blazed from burning oil and numerous structures whisked into the darkening sky.

A trail of decimated property left crushed vehicles and shattered buildings in its wake. Penton's view out the rear of the Osprey followed the monster's course. He didn't have the opportunity to observe what lay ahead.

"Christ," Captain Simmons stammered.

"This is unbelievable," the co-pilot grumbled.

Penton wondered what could be worse than what he'd seen behind them.

"I've got Admiral Keyes on the line," said Simmons.

"What are my orders?" Penton insisted.

"I'll patch him through."

Then came the admiral's voice: "Master Guns?"

"Yes, sir," Penton said.

"Glad to have you onboard," Keyes said. "We might be able to use your skills in more ways than one..."

****

The distinctive sound of rotor blades whapping through the storm woke Kate from a slumber. Clambering to her feet, she moved toward the broken wall and peered through a crevice. An Osprey circled the building, and hovered near the torn parachute caught on the corner of the roof.

Then, the aircraft flew ahead; it passed by the broken walls in the upper floors, as though inspecting the damage. Her heart raced with anxiety. She feared the rescue team would leave before she could signal her position.

Kate patted down her flight suit, not finding anything useful.

The flare gun remained attached to the ejection seat, along with a survival kit. She shook her head as the aircraft started to rise.

"Damn it!" she muttered.

She couldn't run after it. Even if her ankle hadn't been injured, the effort to descend the next couple of floors would take too much time. The Osprey flew higher into the air.

Kate reached for her sidearm, and stuck the barrel out a broken window.

She fired a 9mm round at a car on the ground, and the shot echoed down the street of broken buildings. Rain gusted inside. Kate waited a moment, then fired again, allowing the crew enough time to spot the muzzle blast.

The Osprey paused in mid-air, then quickly descended, landing in the middle of the street below. Kate's heart fluttered with elation. She holstered the pistol and made for an exit.

Descending the concrete steps, she couldn't believe how dark the stairwell had gotten. Scant light reflected through the tiny windows on the metal doors at each landing, providing just enough illumination for her to discern the steps in the shadows. Emergency lights no longer functioned in the decimated building, and the stairs were slippery from the sprinkler system.

Kate moved along carefully. She wanted to avoid slipping and injuring her ankle further. When she reached the lower landing, Kate stepped for the door leading outside. Then, she heard whimpering from a nearby hallway.

****

Penton grabbed his M-16 equipped with an M203 grenade launcher. He knew the weapon wouldn't do him any good if he ran into the creature, but having it in hand felt like the right thing to do.

He descended the ramp and stepped into a torrential downpour. Penton walked down the dark street, glancing upward at the devastated building. He stepped around rubble while scanning the broken façade for signs of Kate Able. Through the shadows and deluge, he pinpointed the location where he'd seen the muzzle flare. Then, he scouted the building in search of a likely egress point.

He headed around a corner of the tower and noticed a side street leading along the backside of the building. A metal door flung open.

Penton shouldered his rifle.

Kate hobbled outside with a young girl in tow.

He lowered the M-16 and ran to them.

Kate's face was smeared with soot and dust. She grinned from ear to ear, happy to see him. "Never expected to find you on the rescue party," Kate said, and laughed.

"It's sort of what I do," Penton said, coolly.

"Flying into decimated cities and rescuing people... that's what you do?"

Penton shrugged. "Yeah, sometimes."

"What about the rest of the time?"

"Well, I fly in and shoot the aircraft machinegun."

"Decimate the cities yourself?"

"Exactly."

Penton looked down at the girl. "Who's this?"

"This is Maki," Kate replied. "She needs our help."

"Well, you came to the right folks," Penton said to the girl. He tapped the Marine Corps logo on his name-patch.

Her sullen face lit up for a moment. Then trepidation registered in her eyes.

Penton glanced over his shoulder and felt the ground tremble, catching sight of the massive creature.

Penton couldn't reconcile the creature before him with what he'd seen on screen. The beast stood as tall as the buildings and its girth encompassed an entire side street. Scales covered the creature like plates of armor. Razor sharp talons protruded into immense claws, crimping the pavement with each thunderous step.

A knowing gleam twinkled in its yellow eyes. The beast turned its head toward the Osprey, rotors spinning in mechanical grunts.

The beast let out a roar, peeved at the grating aircraft. Spittle doused the windshield, street, and sidewalks. Observing the creature on a screen in the command center hadn't prepared Penton for the real thing. Terror shot through every fiber of his being. He shook it off and glanced at the pilot.

Simmons motioned for them to make a break toward the aircraft.

The creature took another step forward, cutting off their path. Penton calculated the distance. He knew the creature would intercept them before boarding the aircraft, or knock the Osprey from the sky upon takeoff.

Penton shook his head. It was too close for comfort.

He waved off the pilot, and shouldered his rifle.

The Osprey lifted off and hovered above the ground. Penton launched the M203 high-explosive cartridge. A whoosh hummed through the air toward the creature's neck. The round erupted on its chin, followed by a salvo of M-16 semi-automatic rifle fire.

The creature roared and stomped, confused, as flames burst in front of its eyes, obscuring its vision. With the beast distracted, Simmons got the Osprey into the sky, launching vertically until it rose above the buildings.

Then, the aircraft came around and the crew chief riddled the beast with .50 caliber rounds from the Browning.

"Let's move!" Penton said, slinging the rifle over a shoulder.

"Where to?" Kate said, stepping towards him.

"This way." Penton motioned with his chin and ran toward the building that Kate had just exited.

"Afraid you'd say that." She limped after him, holding Maki's hand tightly.

"The building's not safe," Maki muttered. "Kaiju destroyed it."

"It's all we have right now," Kate huffed for breath.

Penton shouldered the rifle and kicked the metal door open. He scanned the landing and glanced up the stairwell as far as he could see, searching for looters. "Clear!" he yelled.

Kate hobbled past him and ascended the stairs, while Penton held the rifle steady with the barrel pointed over her shoulder. Maki padded up the stairs behind her.

Reaching the next level, Kate instinctively stepped to the side and allowed Penton to swing the door open. He performed another hasty scan, then waved for them to enter the hallway.

"Which way from here?" Kate said.

Penton had already hustled down the corridor, instinctively tracing his way to the back of the building and away from the creature out front. He moved swiftly, not expecting to encounter hostiles, but proceeded cautiously enough to engage if necessary.

At the end of the hall, he found the corridor turned to the right. An exit sign was located partway down. Penton made for the stairwell with Kate and Maki trailing behind. Maki's rain boots slogged on the carpet and her knapsack slapped against her back, a thwacking sound emanated from her slicker.

He pushed the door open and checked the landing, then glanced up and down the staircase. "All clear!"

Kate entered the doorway and traipsed past him.

Just as Maki's boots squeaked on the concrete landing, Penton noticed movement out of the corner of his eye. Down the hallway, two men stepped from an office carrying computers. They must not have heard the new arrivals because both men looked up in shock at Penton, holding the M-16 pointed at them.

They stopped in their tracks, gripping the computers tightly.

Square-jawed and young, the men wore designer jeans and leather motorcycle jackets. They didn't look Japanese, and were clearly looting the building. Penton did not have the time or inclination to intervene and police the situation. He shook his head, as if indicating they could go on their way.

Both men looked relieved.

Penton nodded a good-bye, then started for the stairwell.

Another man stepped from the room down the hall. He didn't carry computers, but held an Uzi 9mm machine-pistol in his hand. Registering the situation, a sardonic grin crossed his face.

Then, he raised the machine-pistol and opened fire.

Bullets ripped down the hallway, digging into drywall and ricocheting off metal and concrete block. Penton stepped through the threshold just in time to avoid getting hit from the staccato of automatic weapon fire.

"Go!" Penton yelled down the stairs to Kate.

She'd already made it to the first landing and busted out a door.

The blasting Uzi let up. Penton heard plastic clatter on the floor then footsteps hurried down the hallway after him. He pulled out his sidearm and reached around the doorjamb, firing three shots in the direction of the pursuers.

A man cried out in agony and dropped to the floor hard.

The Uzi ripped a few more wild shots, followed by the sound of a door slamming shut. Penton poked his head out and glanced down the hall. A man lay on the floor clutching his leg. His confederates were nowhere to be seen.

Lights flickered in the building, followed by a shockwave rippling through the floor, and the distinctive sound of concrete fracturing. Chunks of the building broke loose and dropped to the street below. Then, a menacing roar echoed throughout the shattered building. The structure wouldn't hold together much longer.

Penton holstered the pistol and descended the stairs, two at a time. He pushed through a door at the bottom and found himself in a narrow alley. The area was illuminated by an emergency spotlight.

A motorcycle and a sports car were parked in the alleyway. He checked the ignitions of each vehicle. Both were empty. No keys.

He reached for his fighting knife, strapped upside-down over the left side of his chest. Penton punctured the rear tire on the motorcycle and the front tires of the car. Then, he started down the alley after Kate.

Penton made it past the hood of the car when a blow knocked him to the ground.

His communication link broke on the pavement. He scrambled to get to his feet, and a designer boot struck him in the ribs.

A shot whizzed by his head. He rolled to the right and reached for the K-bar.

Penton jumped up and swung the fighting knife around, clutching the leather handle in a fist, with the sharp edge pointed away from him.

The attacker stumbled forward, and the knife cut into the man's neck, cleaving it open. Blood gurgled from his throat and the man collapsed to his knees, reaching for the wound in vain.

A pistol clattered onto the pavement.

Penton reached for the weapon lying on the deck. He identified the QSZ-92 immediately as a Chinese military issue semi-automatic weapon.

Kate sauntered up the alley, shaking her head. The dead man hadn't come out the back hatch. "Must have been a lookout," Penton said. He wiped his blade on the man's silk shirt, then sheathed the K-bar. Penton studied the man's face. He clearly wasn't one of the thugs Penton had encountered in the hallway.

"I'd say more like a wheelman." Kate pointed at the car.

"What?" Penton stammered.

The far door was flung wide-open.

"He was inside the car?"

"Yup. And he got the drop on you."

Penton shook his head. "Can't believe I missed that."

"Nice work, Rambo," Kate said, laughing.

"Rambo was Army." Penton smiled. "Don't confuse me with him."

Another roar let loose and the foundation shook.

"We've got to move," Kate said. "Not sure this area is safe."

"No kidding." Penton hustled down the alley.

****

Penton turned down a side street and jogged away from the decimated building. Kate and Maki plodded after him. He held the M-16 by the pistol grip, with the barrel pointed upward.

Looking back to check on the others, Kate limped along, and Maki churned her stout legs, pitter-pattering to keep up.

"You need any help?" Penton called to Kate.

"Faster if I limp along," she replied, panting for breath.

"What about her?" Penton said.

"She's going as fast as I can go... so we're all set."

They turned another corner and Penton slowed to a brisk walk. Kate and Maki ambled up beside him.

"My communications link is busted," Penton said.

Kate shook her head. "So, we can't get in touch with the flight crew on the Osprey. What are we going to do?"

"Your generation of warriors are always stuck on being in contact with command." Penton laughed. "When I was a lance corporal, they'd send out an ad hoc patrol without any radios, no helmets or body armor. Just a war-belt and a rifle. And the leader of the patrol was usually a twenty year old... lance corporal or corporal."

"You're hard Corps," Kate laughed.

"We'll figure this out."

"I know... 'Improvise, adapt, and overcome.'"

"Exactly," Penton said, pressing ahead.

Just as his boot smacked the ground, the pavement rumbled, and a fierce explosion erupted behind them. Only the blast wasn't from ordnance but rather the building behind them giving way.

Penton looked over his shoulder. The top of the building dropped and clouds of dust billowed up.

The ground vibrated.

Pavement surged in a wave.

Knocking them down.

Strewn on the crumbled street, dust rolled away from the building. Thunderous steps plodded toward them, shaking the ground.

"Run!" Penton screamed.

A puzzled look crossed Kate's face, but she scrambled to her feet, pulling Maki from the asphalt.

"What's going on?" Maki said, trotting after her.

"The building is falling," Kate replied.

"That's not all—" Penton halted.

Chunks of debris tumbled to the ground from the falling structure, and concrete broke loose on a nearby building.

"Keep going!" Penton yelled, turning around.

A colossal head snaked out of the smoky side street, wavering above the ground on a long neck. The falling building got hung up on an adjacent tower. Massive jaws snatched open and lunged at him. Saliva whipped through the air.

Penton tumbled backward and landed on his rear.

Gigantic teeth snapped shut, a near miss. The beast snarled and then jerked its head back, sniffed the air, and eyeballed him for a moment.

Another deafening stomp moved the beast closer. The Kaiju lashed out again.

The beast moved in for the kill, sinister yellow eyes, with its teeth bared, ravenous for the taste of blood and flesh.

Penton shouldered his rifle.

Giant muzzle and sharp teeth advanced.

He fired the M203 grenade canister.

The cartridge launched toward the predator, striking a heaving nostril, and exploded into flames. Shaking its head and exhaling, the creature snuffed out the blaze. A menacing roar followed, hitting Penton like a gale wind.

Then it took another step forward, moving its haunches through the side street. A haunch rubbed the tottering building and a high-pitched grind resounded from the towers. This time, it really began to collapse. Like watching contractors demolish an office building, except charges are set to implode the structure. An eerie creak emanated through the city streets, then the damn thing toppled toward them.

An office building stood alongside the structure the creature had assaulted. It was twelve stories tall, shorter than the falling building. The larger edifice collapsed and crumbled onto the smaller one, breaking through the roof, and dislodging chunks of concrete and shattering glass.

Debris rained on the street below, crushing down on the creature's back, knocking the beast to the ground. Penton clambered to his feet and bolted after Kate and the girl. He caught up to them and paused long enough to scoop Maki into a fireman's carry, then he raced away from the fallout.

****

Later, Penton slowed his gait and put Maki down. Kate gimped along, but kept pace with the ordnance chief and young girl. Rounding a corner, they put another building between them and the destruction.

"What now?" Kate asked.

Penton liked her spunk. "Give me a moment."

"The creature won't stay occupied in the rubble for very long."

He nodded in agreement, then glanced around, thinking.

The area had been evacuated at the start of the crisis. Penton took in the surroundings through the overcast conditions and emergency lighting emanating from some of the surrounding buildings. Parked cars lined both sides of the street.

He checked the vehicles. Some were owned by office workers, and others appeared to be people visiting downtown with shopping bags in their cars.

"I bet when the shit hit the fan," Penton said, "the streets were jam-packed."

Kate shrugged. "Probably… but why does that matter?"

"They took off in a hurry, unable to drive out of here."

"So?" Kate said, shrugging.

"You need to get some urban warfare training."

They both laughed.

Penton peeked into a few cars then broke a window. He reached inside and grabbed a cellphone. "See," he said, showing her the phone.

"How did you know?" said Kate.

"Easy, people get in a hurry, and forget things in the car," Penton said. "They rush off and forget their phone, or they misplace it. When things got dicey, this person didn't have time to gather everything."

"So, what are you going to do?"

"I'm going to call the main number at the airbase and have them put me in touch with the colonel."

"Good luck with that," Kate said.

Penton tried getting through to the command center, but the various safety protocols that duty Marines follow didn't allow him to reach anyone right away. Finally, he hung up the phone in frustration.

"Told you so," Kate said, smirking.

"Let's see if this works," Penton said, trying to recall Top Anderson's phone number. He shook his head.

"What is it?" Kate asked.

"A problem with all of this technology and speed dial," Penton replied. "You can't even remember your buddy's phone number."

"Yeah, I know… you used to have twenty phone numbers memorized."

"Pretty much," Penton said, trying a number he hoped worked.

The phone rang for a bit. "He's probably dozed off."

"I'd be in bed by now if I weren't on duty."

The call went to voicemail, but it was Anderson's voice on the other end. At least Penton remembered the correct number. He left a message, then hung up.

"Well, you got the right number at least," Kate said.

"I was thinking the same thing. Hope he checks messages before morning."

"So, we're going to have to come up with something else."

Penton nodded. He took a moment to reload his grenade launcher. Then, he scanned the street looking for the best place to go. Dust had filtered past the demolished buildings and floated over a few city blocks to where they stood. It covered his boots and clung to his flight suit.

A roar emanated from around the corner, and the ground shook. The beast was afoot.

"This way," Penton said, pointing to a narrow alley across the street.

TWENTY-SIX

Hardy checked his watch. The extraction team would be there shortly. He tapped Stiles on the shoulder. "Come on," Hardy said. "I've got an idea."

They went back into the warehouse, and Hardy opened the big doors at the far end of the building. Then, he walked over to the trailer holding the Tochka missile and motioned for Stiles to join him.

"We're going to push this thing outside." Hardy pointed toward the back doors.

"What the hell for?" Stiles griped, shaking his head.

"My guess..." Hardy adjusted the sling to his MP-5. "From what I've been told, which is very little, the Brass want to take this thing. An acquisition of sorts."

"You mean steal it?" Stiles shook his head again.

Hardy shrugged. "Sure, I mean *steal* it."

Stiles sneered. "We had orders to dismantle this thing from any potential use, and now they want to abscond with the damn thing. The entire proposition is dangerous."

Hardy looked at the younger sailor. "We're hired guns... that's it."

"They could be violating a treaty." Stiles took a deep breath. "We're not supposed to follow unlawful orders."

"I know," Hardy agreed. "And it's our asses if something goes wrong." He looked Stiles over sternly.

"So... what then?" Stiles demanded an honest answer.

"Dismantling the missile," Hardy explained, "or turning it over to our own government... it's the same thing to us. We're not putting it to use, so we wouldn't be involved in violating a nuclear treaty. This is for the Brass to figure out. For all we know, they just want to make sure no one can ever use it."

"That's bullshit and you know it."

"But a treaty isn't violated just because we take it."

"Agreed," Stiles barked.

"Okay, then help me move the damn thing outside."

Stiles finally nodded in agreement.

They got behind the trailer, leaning into it with their shoulders and pushing hard from their legs. After the inertia of getting it moving, they peddled their feet and kept the momentum up. They rolled the trailer outside and swung it across the gravel parking area.

Hardy felt it picking up speed and thought it might get away from them, but the tires snagged in a depression of loose gravel. They brought the trailer to a halt, jerking the rig back with a clang. It stopped twenty feet from the building. "Perfect," Hardy said.

He looked toward the sky and wondered how long before the Marines would arrive. A reliable lot, he could always count on them taking the fight to the lion's door.

Stiles countenance reflected his misgivings. Hardy wasn't sure if it was the nonsense about the treaty or the questionable judgment involved in changing up the objective in the middle of a mission. But the younger SEAL had reason to be miffed.

Keeping one ear to the sky, listening for a chopper, and the other focused on the road, Hardy wasn't surprised at what he heard first.

TWENTY-SEVEN

Penton hustled down an alley then stepped onto a main street, a good distance from the monster. He scanned each direction and plotted a course toward several abandoned cars.

The vehicles weren't parked on the street, but rather deserted in a jumble in the middle of the roadway. Gridlock had caused the drivers to flee their automobiles and take to the street by foot. Penton wanted to commandeer a vehicle and get some distance from the creature rampaging the desolate city.

The cellphone in his pocket rang. Penton reached for it and recognized the number. Top Anderson was calling him back.

"Penton, here," he said, answering.

"Why are you calling me after hours?"

"I'm on the ground with that thing chasing us."

"Told you to leave the rescue mission to younger folks."

"I need to get patched through to the command center," Penton griped. "The duty Marines wouldn't break protocols."

"Whatever happened to improvise, adapt, and overcome?"

"Free thinking isn't part of today's fighting forces."

"You said it, not me."

"Can you help me out?"

There was a slight pause, then a laugh. "Already headed down the stairwell, now," Top Anderson said with a chuckle.

"Put me on speaker when you get there."

Penton stretched it out, walking among the forsaken vehicles. He glanced into cars for keys in the ignition, while waiting for the Brass to get on the horn. About fifteen minutes later, the phone rang and Penton answered: "Hello."

"Colonel Tomkins, here."

"We're on the ground in Tokyo, looking for extraction."

"We've got you on speaker phone, Master Gunnery Sergeant Penton."

"That's perfectly fine with me," said Penton.

"I've already patched Admiral Keyes into the call."

Penton listened intently.

"This is Admiral Keyes. How are you holding up out there, Master Gunnery Sergeant?"

"We're doing just fine. The monster is trying to sniff us out, though."

"The joint-task force has devised a plan," Keyes said. "We want to take the creature out but need to draw it away from the heavily populated area."

They're going to use nukes, Penton thought.

"We need your assistance..."

"How so?"

Penton kept checking the vehicles for keys. He was surprised at how many people fled their vehicles but thought to take the keys with them. Static buzzed their connection, taking it in and out. "How so?" he repeated.

"Need someone... to draw the thing away from the city."

"Not sure how exactly we could do it."

"The thing hates noise," Keyes said. "Find a way to attract its attention by making noise. Then, the damn thing will chase you."

"Like bait..."

"Afraid so."

"What's the plan?"

"We've been in touch with the captain of the Seawolf, a submarine located in the Sea of Japan." Keyes breathed heavily. "Can't say anymore right now."

"Guess we have our orders," Penton said, ready to hang up.

"Master Gunnery Sergeant..." Keyes continued.

"Yes, sir," said Penton.

"Keep the phone handy. You might be our only hope."

"Understood, sir."

Penton ended the call and peered into a work van. Keys dangled from the ignition. He considered the find then figured people in company vehicles would be more likely to abandon property than owners.

He glanced up the road and spotted a bigger van. Logos were plastered all over the side. A local radio station's mobile broadcasting studio. Penton ran up the street and looked inside. He spotted a key-fob in the dash. Stepping back, he checked the tires and noted announcement speakers near the roofline.

Penton waved to Kate. She trotted over to the van with a puzzled look on her face. But Maki seemed interested.

"Got orders to lure the thing out of the city," Penton said.

"Acting like *bait*?" Kate snapped.

Penton laughed. "Precisely what I told them, but someone's got to do the job."

"Why us?" Kate griped. "The Defense Forces can handle this."

"There isn't an *us*," Penton replied, shaking his head.

"What do you mean?" Kate said.

"This is a dangerous job. I've got to do it alone."

"You think dive-bombing that thing wasn't a dangerous job."

"Not saying that you can't handle a tough assignment—"

"What then?" Kate cut in.

Penton shrugged and gestured toward the girl. Kate looked down at Maki and the girl stared up at them, expectantly. "Can't leave her here, alone."

"We can both go," Maki said, stepping toward the van.

"Afraid it's not necessary to put you both at risk." Penton shook his head. "You've got enough ammunition for your sidearm?"

Kate nodded. Penton climbed into the driver's seat and waved good-bye. She looked askance at him as he closed the door.

He started the engine then backed into the car behind him. Crunching metal clamored as a row of vehicles jumbled into one another. He pulled to the right and drove up onto the sidewalk, trying to clear the cars stopped in the traffic jam.

Then, the steering wheel and seat vibrated. Penton worried the van had mechanical problems. Another tremor and he understood the problem wasn't with the vehicle. He braked and flung open the door. "Get in!" he yelled.

Kate scooped the girl into her arms and dashed toward the van. She ran with an awkward gait, limping. Like her ankle might give way, but she didn't chance a slow getaway. The beast was upon them.

She opened the passenger door and slid Maki onto the seat. The girl had enough sense to climb in back then Kate hopped inside. Before she closed the door, Penton hit the gas, rocking her backward into the seat. Maki staggered and fell hard.

"You all right back there?" Penton said.

"My leg hurts," Maki replied. "But I'll be fine."

"Just stay put on the floorboards for now."

Penton took a right and worked his way toward the coastline on the far side of the harbor. He cut down dark city streets as rain cascaded on the windshield, then he made abrupt turns, attempting to lose the creature.

A roar emanated from behind them, as the creature marked its pursuit.

"The Kaiju is after us," Maki said.

"We'll lose the damn thing when we get to an open road."

"Thought our goal was to have it chase us," said Kate.

Penton shrugged. "We will put some distance between it and us, but let the thing keep coming."

He made another turn and the beast closed in. Its stomping shook the van. Pavement cracked in the road in front of them.

Penton worried the creature might derail their escape.

Rounding turns slowed the van down, but the creature didn't seem to lose a beat. Penton accelerated hard on the straightaways to keep the thing at bay. He made another turn, intending to take them out of the city. The street was gridlocked with abandoned cars.

"What now?" Kate said, exasperated.

"Not like we own this damn van," Penton said, pulling over the curb and onto a grassy strip.

"Where are we going?" Kate demanded.

"We're headed out to the Chiba Prefecture."

"And we're going to drive off-road?"

"For *now*... at least."

The van jostled over the uneven ground, but pressed ahead at 30 mph alongside National Route 14, moving away from Tokyo. Maki peered out the back window and reported on the creature's progress. "It's still back there," she said. "But it's not getting any closer."

Kate breathed a sigh of relief, and Penton longed to do the same. But his gut told him they had more to contend with before the day was through. He made it around the slog of stopped cars and eased over the curb and back onto the roadway. The van bounced as the rear tires found the road.

He accelerated and put more distance between them and the creature. Rain bounced off the macadam.

Penton finally inhaled deeply. He heard snickering and looked over at Kate. "What?" he said, trying to find the humor.

"You… that's what."

"Not sure what you meant."

"We've been fairly safe for about twenty minutes."

"And?" Penton said, confused.

"And… you're just letting loose now."

He shook his head. "Doesn't behoove a warrior to relax, ever."

Kate laughed. Maki giggled in the back, showing the first sign of shock subsiding.

The road stretched out in front of them, leaving the metropolis of tall buildings behind and a landscape of undulating hills ahead. Large houses with layered levels and sweeping Japanese roof lines peppered the hillsides, barely discernible in the darkness and rain.

A vibration shook Penton's leg. He checked the mirrors for the creature, thinking it had gained on them, but the beast ambled safely in the distance. Then, he remembered the phone and reached into his pocket.

"Master Gunnery Sergeant Penton, here."

"This is Admiral Keyes. How are you holding up?"

"We've got the thing behind us, but the van's been pulling away."

"We had sight of you through Defense Forces cameras, but now that you've left the city, all we've got are satellite shots." Keyes exhaled into the phone, frustration from a long day with little progress registered in his tone.

"Not much to report," Penton said after a moment.

"We'll, I'm sure you know satellite images aren't the best."

"The few that I've seen," Penton said, "look like old movies left in someone's attic for decades."

Keyes chuckled at the comment.

"So, what now?"

"We really need you to keep that thing after you."

"Afraid it might lose interest," Penton said, glancing in the rearview mirror.

"You've got to do something to get the thing headed over toward the coast," Keyes pled. "Get on Route 296 and take it from Funabashi out toward Sosa. You know the way?"

"Been out there… while on leave before," Penton replied.

"Okay, so you know what to do?" said Keyes.

"Sure, draw the thing out towards the coast."

"You've got it. Check in with you soon."

"Sure thing," Penton said. He ended the call and wondered how to keep the creature chasing them.

"The Kaiju doesn't like noise," Maki said, as though reading his mind.

"What?" Penton replied, dumbfounded.

"You're wondering how to get the Kaiju to chase us," Maki said, leaning forward between the seats. "It doesn't like noise."

"Apparently not," Kate cut in.

"So, what are you saying?" Penton pressed.

"Kaiju doesn't like loud sounds." Maki grinned. "All sounds are noise."

"We just need to broadcast loud sounds?"

"Exactly right," Maki said.

Penton grinned. Kate turned on the sound system and broadcasted the Rolling Stones from the loudspeakers attached to the roof. A roar followed immediately after the music blared, and the road trembled as they turned onto National Route 296.

The sound annoyed the creature. It broke into a run, marking its prey in hot pursuit.

TWENTY-EIGHT

Hardy heard the whop-whop of helicopter rotors, then spotted a Sikorsky Super Stallion hovering toward them just above the tree tops.

The missile rest on a trailer in the middle of a parking area behind the warehouse. He figured the operation would be over in less than fifteen minutes. Then the SEALs could hightail it out of there.

A moment later, the faint sound of a truck engine rumbled under the buzz of the approaching helicopter.

"We've got company," Hardy said.

Stiles shook his head and checked over his M-16.

"I'll contact the Marines and let them know."

The younger SEAL nodded in agreement.

"This is the team leader on the ground," Hardy spoke into his comm-link.

"Roger, we're approaching fast," the pilot replied.

Hardy grinned at the successful connection. The barrel of a .50 caliber GAU-15/A machinegun poked from the port side of the aircraft. Converging on the scene, the chopper's nose dipped toward the ground; it headed toward the other side of the warehouse.

"We've got a troop transport closing in on our position."

"Affirmative, we can see them from here."

"How far away?" said Hardy.

"Moving in too close for us to extract without incident."

Hardy looked at Stiles and shrugged. He flipped off the safety to his MP-5 and shouldered the weapon.

Stiles shook his head again. "We could've just disarmed that thing and been long gone by now."

"We're in this now!" Hardy stepped away from the missile.

The helicopter flew past their position and hovered above the trees. Rotors blasted gusts, kicking up sand and dirt from the far side of the warehouse. Bursts of machinegun fire ignited from the aerial gunner's window.

Hardy trotted around the side of the building. And Stiles broke oblique to the right.

Brakes locked and the transport halted in the driveway. Squad leaders barked orders as boots hit the ground. The GAU-15/A strafed the truck and tore through the canvas top. Rounds riddled through fabric and flesh. Wounded soldiers spilled over the sides while infantryman on the ground erupted a volley of AK-47 fire at the Super Stallion.

Hardy advanced, then dropped to the ground in a prone position. He aimed carefully and squeezed the trigger, hitting a senior non-commissioned officer in the head. Then, he fired at soldiers engaging the helicopter.

Bullets tore up the ground around the North Koreans and plugged holes in the stalled transport. Hardy shot the infantryman closest to him then worked his way down to the line.

The aerial gunner sent many of the infantrymen flailing into death dances. As .50 caliber bullets ripped the enemy to pieces, Hardy fired away and Stiles maneuvered around the first disabled truck and took position to the right, flanking the newcomers.

Stiles' rifle fire took down troops on the right side of the truck, who were protected from the Super Stallion's gunner and the senior SEAL on the ground.

Bodies dropped on the right side of the truck, legs kicking in the throes of death. A few .50 caliber rounds ripped through the canvas top of the transport, hitting soldiers on the other side of the vehicle. Stiles took care of the rest with deadly aim.

A few minutes after the firefight had begun, return fire from the North Koreans ceased altogether.

Hardy and Stiles double-timed back to the missile, while the Super Stallion circled around and hovered above them. Cargo straps dropped from the aircraft and unfolded, tumbling to the ground. A line remained tethered to the helicopter.

The SEALs attached the straps to the trailer and secured the missile for delivery. Hardy stepped back and waved to the crew chief. Then, the helicopter lifted upward, pulling the straps taut. Flying higher in the air, it strained the lines. Rotors blew gusts toward the SEALs on the ground. They stepped back as the trailer jockeyed off the gravel parking lot. Once the cargo rose a few feet above the ground, and the load hung secured, the Super Stallion whisked into the sky then cruised off toward the coastline and the ocean beyond.

Noise from the helicopter blocked out everything else.

A moment later, the familiar creaking of a tracked vehicle came from behind them. Metal scraping echoed through the rural location, followed by a crash and wood splintering.

The tank broke through the warehouse wall behind them, bits of wood flew everywhere. Hardy and Stiles bolted across the parking lot. They reached the tree line just as the machine gunner opened fire.

Rounds tore up the gravel driveway and nipped at their heels.

Stiles and Hardy ducked into the woods. The terrain dropped off considerably. Both SEALs dashed downhill through scrub, quickly descending below the trajectory of the deadly machinegun.

Still, rounds ripped through the tree branches above them. Hardy glanced back and breathed a sigh of relief. The tank came to rest at the edge of the woods, while the gunner tried to angle the machinegun down the embankment. Hardy tapped Stiles on the shoulder and ducked behind a large rock.

The turret lit up with more machinegun fire. Bullets dug into the ground and ricocheted off rocks. Stiles bellowed in pain. He went down hard. Another burst cut down the trees and shrubs behind him. Hardy reached for his comrade's war-belt and yanked the fallen SEAL behind the rock.

More machinegun fire stippled the foliage all around them, cutting holes in the dense leaves and ripping into trees and earth.

Stiles shook his head, a defeated look in his eyes.

A pause in the attack gave Hardy some hope. He looked over Stiles' injuries. Blood gushed from a large bullet hole in the leg. Hardy rolled him over and saw an exit wound. He unzipped his jumpsuit and pulled the web-belt from his trousers and used it as a tourniquet. Then, he quickly applied a field dressing to the lacerated flesh.

Other wounds leaked blood from the chest area, but his body armor and trajectory angles had prevented the large caliber rounds from penetrating all the way through the vest.

All commotion from the assault went quiet. Hardy figured the enemy had given up. Then, the unmistakable sound of the cannon turret moving into position sent a chill down his spine.

"Move!" Hardy commanded. Rising to his feet, he slung Stiles over his shoulders in a fireman's carry.

He thundered downhill, pain from his own wounds spiking through his chest and leg. A blast erupted from behind, and Hardy braced for impact. A shell that could immediately launch them both into the darkness of death.

An explosion from behind sent fragments of rock cascading down on them. The tank's cannon blew up the boulder they'd used for cover. Hardy hustled further into the woods, seeking cover from foliage and tree trunks. The machine gunner started up again, riddling the forest with large caliber rounds.

Terrain dropped off a steep cliff to the left. Hardy put his comrade down and eased over the ridge, placing his boots on a ledge. Then, he grabbed Stiles by the war-belt and slid him toward the edge. He scooped him up like a new bride and lowered him onto the ledge. Glancing down, Hardy noted more ledges that he could use for makeshift steps, and continued the process, relieved the stray bullets would only whiz overhead.

When he reached the bottom, a few soldiers shuffled to the ridge. They stood at the edge, yelling and pointing down, appearing as silhouettes in the dark evening. The infantrymen fired at the SEALs. Hardy grabbed Stiles and pressed them both against the base of the cliff. Bullets dug into the dirt nearby.

The soldiers understood their futility and started down the craggy slope.

Hardy locked and loaded his MP-5, then stepped away from the protective cover and trained a beam on the top of the ledge. As he suspected, a soldier remained above ready to shoot if the SEALs fled into the open.

Taking advantage of surprise, Hardy squeezed off a shot and bore a hole into the man's skull. Soldiers climbing down the cliff stopped on ledges to take up the fight, while others scurried down the rock-face, trying to get to a solid position.

Hardy focused on the soldiers shooting at him. As he shot two of them, bullets kicked up dust all around his boots.

He ran hard at the base of the cliff, ducking out of view, then he jogged along the rock-face and popped out at another location. Hardy got off two quick shots before they could return fire. A couple more soldiers dropped, but three remained, dug into fortified positions on ledges in prone positions. He couldn't get a good bead on them.

Running back to cover, he caught up with Stiles and slipped his rifle over a shoulder. He heaved Stiles into a fireman's carry and worked his way along the base of the cliff, keeping out of sight, but putting distance between them and the infantry soldiers on the side of the hill above. Then Hardy bolted toward a grove of trees. A few desperate shots rang out behind them as the SEALs slipped out of eyeshot.

Once back in the woods, he carried Stiles to the SEAL Delivery Vehicle. They found the apparatus intact and eased it into the water. Both SEALs donned their scuba gear and dove into the safety of the ocean depths.

TWENTY-NINE

A while later, Penton eased off the gas and lured the creature closer, then he sped up to keep a safe distance between them. The beast roared in anger at the sound of the music blaring from speakers on the roof. Dawn began to break on the horizon and the weather reflected signs of the storm breaking off soon.

"What's the plan?" Kate asked, leaning over to look at the dash.

"Lead the damn thing further out to the coast so they can take it out."

"Well, you should know… we are running low on gas," Kate said, pointing at the fuel gauge.

Penton glanced down and shook his head. "Always has to be a wrinkle."

"Do you have enough gas to get out there?" Kate said.

"Probably," Penton replied, "but it's hard to tell."

"We need to keep far enough ahead of it to give us time."

He sped up to put more distance between them and the creature. Pavement vibrated from the beast's pursuit and shook the van toward the edge of the road. Fighting to keep the vehicle on the road, Penton jerked the wheel.

The van went off the road and slid on the soft shoulder. He slowed down and straightened out the vehicle.

Penton looked in the mirror. The creature closed the distance fast, as though it realized they were vulnerable. "The thing's smart," Penton said.

"Yeah, and it never seems to get tired or worn out."

He pulled back onto the highway and hit the gas. The road still rumbled and he had to fight to keep the vehicle straight. Penton sped up even more to get ahead of the tremors.

They cruised along with the creature stalking after them. It showed no signs of letting up. All its wounds were superficial. Penton couldn't believe the amount of ordnance it had withstood. The creature's head bobbed back and forth as it trod behind them, resembling the gait of an enormous bird.

A short time later, the magnificent coast came into view. Rugged mountains covered the coastline, dropping off steep cliffs to the ocean below. The rural highway cut along the edge, and the van undulated over the roadway.

Spectacular panoramas caught their attention. Everyone sat quiet inside the vehicle, glancing at the scenery below. For a moment, Penton forgot about the creature keeping pace behind them. The twisty road caused him to slow down. He glanced at the fuel gauge and noticed the needle getting closer to the empty mark.

He wondered if there was any place in the vicinity to fuel up.

Another vibration ran up his leg. Penton instinctively looked in the mirror to chart the pace of the creature. It continued plodding at a safe distance. Then, he reached into a pocket and pulled out the cellphone. "Penton here."

"Master Guns," Keyes said. "How are you holding up?"

"We're doing just fine. Except we are running low on gas."

"Got enough to keep you going for another ten minutes?"

"Think so..." said Penton. "Why?"

"We're ready to make our move. You just pull ahead and get to a safe distance."

"What's the plan?" Penton said. "If you don't mind me asking."

There was a pause on the other end of the line.

"Admiral Keyes... are you still there?"

Another pause.

"Admiral Keyes?"

"Just high-tail it out of there," Keyes finally said.

"Roger." Penton ended the call and shoved the phone into his pocket. He looked over at Kate. A dire concern registered on her face. She shook her head, obviously understanding that Penton figured they planned to use a nuclear weapon.

He nodded to confirm the assumption.

"This can't really be happening," Kate muttered.

"No time for us to ponder misgivings. We need to put some real distance between us and the target."

He stepped on the gas. The van raced along the coastal highway, swerving around curves, and skittering off the side of the road. Yet the creature kept up its pursuit as giant feet pounded the asphalt behind them.

****

Keyes shifted in his command seat while staring at the video screen. He chewed the nub of an unlit cigar and habitually swirled coffee into his mouth. Dark stains ran down the side of the mug and smeared a picture of the Gipper on the front.

He scanned the room to make sure the suit was still in the head. "What's the status of the Seawolf?" Keyes asked his Executive Officer James.

"She's ready to fire on your order, sir."

"What's the distance from the beast to the decoy?"

"They've pulled about two hundred yards in front of the creature," Commander James replied. "Somehow that thing is keeping pace."

Keyes studied the screen. The van and coastal highway appeared in black and white from the satellite video. Behind them, the monster stomped upon the roadway, cracking pavement and thundering along.

"What's the perimeter of the fallout?" Keyes asked, knowing the answer.

"Well beyond two hundred yards." This from Williams the intelligence officer.

"There's no aircraft in position to extract them," Commander James chimed in. "What are your orders, sir?"

James grasped a phone in his hand, tied into the ship's communication network. Keyes knew his executive officer already had the captain of the Seawolf on the line. He looked at the monitor again. The beast had moved into the most viable strike zone, where civilian population was the least dense.

"Sir?" Commander James repeated.

Keyes thought about making another call to the master gunnery sergeant. He thought about providing a warning.

"Sir, there's no time…"

Keyes ground his teeth into the cigar.

"Sir?"

Everything seemed to stand down for a moment. Keyes watched the van and the creature chasing after it. Finally, he nodded to the executive officer. "Give the order," Keyes said flatly.

"Fire away," Commander James said into the phone.

Another window appeared in the corner of the screen. Choppy waves bashed into the hull of a submarine, and a grey sky lingered overhead. The images on the screen changed up. And the submarine exchanged places with the road scene on the bigger monitor.

A hatch in the back of the submarine opened. Then, a Tomahawk missile shot from the opening. Exhaust burned through the air as the missile raced skyward. The trajectory of the Tomahawk traced east.

The intelligence officer abruptly stood up. "I cannot watch this," Williams said, heading for the door.

Keyes pounded a fist on the table. "You think this is easy for me!"

She halted by the door and looked at him.

He pointed at the small window on the screen. "Those Marines are heroes… and we've got to watch them die."

****

Glancing in the rearview mirror, Penton noticed the creature getting smaller and smaller. At last, the beast finally let up its pace. Penton breathed a sigh of relief.

"What's next?" Kate demanded.

"We've got to get some distance from the creature."

"An atomic blast… even from a small missile… will engulf us."

Penton nodded. He glanced out the window at the rocky coastline. "Maybe we can find some cover. Wait for the fallout to clear."

"That could work if we get far enough away. And if we find protection."

The van crested a hill and a small cinderblock building caught his attention. Some sort of power control station, the building lay far down a hillside. A driveway led to the building, secured from the road by metal gates.

"Probably our best bet," Penton said.

"How much time do we have? Maybe we've got a better option."

"Something tells me… we're about out of time."

Penton steered toward the driveway and stepped on the gas. The van broke through the gate and the chain snapped apart. Pieces of metal links danced off the windshield, and the steel arms swung open.

He drove toward the building at speed. The walls looked solid and the roof was flat, so he suspected poured concrete covered the rooftop. Electrical wires ran into a conduit on the façade and likely worked through a control panel and exited through the opposite side, then snaked through an underground pipeline.

They closed in on the building fast. Kate grabbed the door handle, as though bracing for an impact. Penton braked hard and the van decelerated, halting with the nose plunging down, then the vehicle surged backward. He shoved the shifter into park and alighted from the van.

Penton bolted for the door, while Kate helped Maki out of the vehicle.

He grabbed the knob and found the door locked.

Penton stepped back and scanned it over. A heavy steel door with the hinges on the inside. He noted a lock in the doorknob and a keyhole for a deadbolt right above it. The place was shut up tighter than Fort Knox.

Kate ran up beside him, with Maki's little feet scampering a few steps behind. "Not a window in the frigging place?" Kate said, huffing.

"Makes it the perfect place to hide. Just difficult to get in."

Kate looked at Penton. He nodded, and then she grabbed Maki's hand and headed around the side of the building. Penton took a few steps back, pulled out his sidearm, and aimed at the deadbolt.

A whoosh resonated through the sky.

Penton's heart raced. A nuclear missile was closing in. He blasted away at the lock, squeezing off four .45 caliber rounds. Then, he fired two more at the doorknob.

"Run!" he screamed to Kate.

Penton stepped forward and kicked the knob with the heel of his boot. The door shifted inward, but held together. Kate and Maki rounded the corner, as the sound of an intense explosion ripped through the air.

They fell to the ground, and Penton staggered, losing his step.

The door held steady.

Penton stepped back, reloading.

He fired madly at the knob and lock mechanism, drilling holes into the steel.

Then, he took a step and leapt toward the door. His heel struck the knob and snapped it off, but the force broke the door open. It swung wide and smashed into the cinderblock wall inside, clanging metal reverberated through the empty building.

He flew through the doorway and landed on a musty, concrete floor.

Penton rolled onto his chest and shot upright. By the time he wheeled around, Kate was inside with Maki in tow.

Penton slammed the door shut and braced it closed with a coil of cable he'd found on the floor.

The room fell into darkness, and he wondered if the distance, mountainside, and concrete building would protect them from the blast. Kate hit the deck and told Maki to lie down next to her. Penton followed suit and dropped beside them.

Kate reached for his hand. Comforted by her touch in their plight, Penton couldn't help but think about his daughter back in North Carolina.

THIRTY

The Tomahawk missile cruised through the early morning sky as the sun poked out from behind the clouds. Keyes couldn't help but appreciate the marvel of the sight, even though it meant certain death for anyone located near the blast.

A white tail of exhaust fumes spat from the missile. The nose dipped and the Tomahawk's trajectory angled toward the target. Below, the creature stopped in its tracks and canted its head, listening. Then, the beast tilted its snout toward the sky, as though sniffing the air.

"The damn thing knows it's coming," Keyes blurted.

"Ten seconds to impact," Executive Officer James said calmly.

Keyes shook his head, worried about the execution of their plan. He glanced around the room. All eyes were glued to the screen.

"We've got him," said Executive Officer James, reassuringly.

The nose dropped considerably as the missile raced toward the creature. Now, the Tomahawk sped almost vertically downward, rapidly closing the distance. Both the beast and missile appeared on the same screen. The missile driving downward, and the creature looking upward into the sky, made the serene coastal landscape appear out of place.

Everything stood frozen in time, as the nuclear weapon homed in on its target. Keyes clenched his fists, waiting.

"Five seconds to impact," Executive Officer James counted.

The creature stood motionless, continuing to glance skyward, with its head slightly tilted to one side. *Maybe the thing's confused*, Keyes hoped.

"Three seconds."

Or thinking.

Two.

Calculating.

One.

And the beast leapt toward the cliffs, bounding over the precipice.

The missile impacted the ground where the creature had been standing. It exploded, sending rock and debris hurling in every direction. Then, a small mushroom cloud billowed and spread gently over the countryside.

When the dust cleared, there wasn't any sign of the creature or its remains.

THIRTY-ONE

Penton heard the blast and placed the explosion a half-mile away. A reverberation shook the building, but the sensation passed in a moment. He waited for the nuclear wave to follow, expecting it to shake or topple the building. But nothing happened more than a tremor.

He groped in his pocket for the cellphone and found purchase. Penton pulled it out and flipped on the light.

Kate looked at him desperately.

She was probably thinking the same, frightened of the radioactivity. He shrugged, trying to suggest maybe they had a chance. Her eyes lit up. "We're in a valley," Kate said, hopefully. "The nuclear blast might not reach us through the dense, rocky terrain."

"We'll have to wait it out," Penton replied. "This building might serve us well as a fallout bunker."

"The sort that people built during the cold war were in basements."

"Tell me about it," said Penton, rolling his eyes.

She smiled. "Hard to believe you look that good and go back so long... I meant that you're in great shape for your age."

"Couldn't have been that I look good?" Penton said, laughing.

Kate didn't respond, and the discussion fell into an awkward silence. He stood up and stretched out his back. The room was ten by twelve feet and it connected to another room that was closed off and padlocked shut. He figured an electrical control panel laid beyond the next door, maybe even a radio.

The tight quarters wouldn't allow him too many opportunities to shoot at the padlock. A missed shot could send a bullet ricocheting off the cinderblock walls. Someone might get injured, and he didn't trust the conditions in the environment to send them outside, even for a few seconds.

Penton checked the phone and noticed that he had juice for about twenty minutes. Then, he looked at the signal strength and saw the bars were at minimal. He hit recent calls and tried to reach Admiral Keyes.

The phone rang for a moment then cut off without going to voicemail. Penton tried it again with the same result.

"Looks like we're going to be here for a while."

"Do you think they were successful?"

"If not, that thing might come this way. And we'd be sitting ducks."

"That's what I'm afraid might happen."

"Right now, the nuclear blast is more of a concern than the giant creature."

"A nuclear bomb won't kill a Kaiju," Maki broke in.

"What makes you say that?" said Kate.

"My grandfather told us stories about when the Kaiju attacked long ago. The military tried to use a nuclear bomb. Some thought the creature was destroyed, and others felt that it went back to sleep somewhere deep in the ocean."

"Maybe the Kaiju from your grandfather's time was killed by the nuclear weapon," Kate offered, touching Maki's shoulder.

Maki shook her head. "My grandfather didn't think so."

Penton looked at the girl, so sure of herself.

"I'd bet this is the same one," Maki continued. "And it has come back from the ocean depths. Maybe it wants revenge."

"Well, either way, it seems like we'll be stuck here for a while," said Penton. He cut off the light and slipped the phone into his pocket.

He sat on the floor with Maki's dire look burned into his mind.

THIRTY-TWO

Keyes reported the result of the strike to General Yoshi. The commanders decided to take precautionary measures. They dispatched a squadron of F-2 fighters from the closest Japan Air-Self-Defense Force base.

The planes took off during a lull in the storm in early morning hours. Silver fuselages were embossed with the distinctive JASDF insignia. Each plane was loaded with missiles, bombs, and machineguns. Although conventional weapons hadn't worked, Keyes hoped if the creature lived through the Tomahawk strike, it would be wounded and vulnerable to attack.

At day break, a naval ship from the Japan Maritime Self-Defense Force moved into action. The *Izumo* plotted a course toward coastal waters off Sosa. The ship served as a destroyer and helicopter carrier, loaded with seven anti-submarine helicopters, and two search-and-rescue helicopters.

Keyes figured bringing the ship into play served as a safety measure rather than a tactical strike option. Treaties signed after World War II had stripped Japan's military down to a protective force. All offensive capabilities were strictly prohibited. Japan was not permitted to own nuclear missiles, aircraft carriers, or amphibious assault ships. The *Izumo* pushed the envelope on such requirements and only passed muster by loading the vessel with defensive-type helicopters.

The screen in the command room was tied into communications with the Japanese Defense Forces. General Yoshi issued orders, while Keyes monitored events and gave tactical feedback. With the storm dying down, a United States Air Force surveillance plane flew out of Yokota Air Base. The pilot patched through to the command center.

"This is Major Charles Weber," a voice crackled over the speakers.

"Major… Rear Admiral Keyes, here."

"Roger, Admiral."

"We don't have visual from your plane."

"All systems are go," said Major Weber.

"Maybe it's on our end."

"We're nearing the coast and everything looks clear."

Keyes studied the satellite vision on his monitor. "Any sign of the creature?"

"Negative," Major Weber replied. "The target area appears below… and it's just a crater with debris in the usual blast pattern. Earth and rocks scattered in every direction. Must have blown the thing to bits."

Keyes shook his head in disbelief. "Afraid I'm not satisfied. Have your crew check the visual systems, and circle around to get a good look at the coastline."

"Understood," Weber said. Then the buzz of straining propellers muffled in the communications systems.

The corner of Keyes' screen wavered. A picture of General Yoshi was replaced by a visual of the coast from the observation plane. Everything appeared serene and peaceful with no sign of the nuclear destruction nearby.

Then the camera view abruptly shot upward, as though the pilot had jerked back on the controls. Only the overcast sky appeared on the screen.

"What the hell is that thing?" Weber mumbled.

"I've got no idea." This from the co-pilot.

"Let's circle back around to get a better look."

"What do you have in sight?" Keyes demanded.

There was a long pause. "Perhaps the creature that you're looking for," Weber finally replied.

Keyes pictured the beast strewn on the sand, injured or dead from the blast and its fall off the cliff. He couldn't see how the thing could have survived intact. "What condition is the creature in?"

"Looks like some sort of prehistoric dinosaur… gigantic."

"Yeah, but what shape is it in?" Keyes snapped.

"The thing appears to be perfectly fine."

"Get me a damn visual!"

The nose of the plane evened out. An image came back on the screen. The creature walked along the coastline, partly on the sand,

and a massive leg sloshed through the surf. It stood three-quarters of the height of the cliffs.

Keyes shook his head. "The damn thing avoided the missile."

"Do you want to try another launch from the Seawolf?" Executive Officer James encouraged.

Keyes waved him off. "A Tomahawk won't do the trick."

Everyone sat mute for a moment, waiting for Keyes to give the next order.

He stuck the cigar back in his mouth and chomped on the end, about ready to light the damn thing. Then, he leaned back and glanced at the screen. "What does the terrain look like around the creature?"

"Appears to have steep cliffs along the coast for quite a way," said Weber.

"We've got the beast pinned down... for a while, anyway."

"What are your orders?" James pressed.

"Have we been able to reach those folks on the ground?"

"No, sir," Intelligence Officer Williams replied.

"Why the hell not?"

"Cellphone reception isn't working." She shrugged. "They're probably holed up in a bunker or coastal cave."

"Well, let's hope that's the case for their sake... in terms of protection from radiation." Keyes tossed the chewed-up cigar on the table. "But it certainly doesn't bode well for communicating with them."

"No, sir," Williams said, anxiously.

Keyes pulled a face and snapped her a look. *A bunch of damn fools*, he thought. *Navy officers can't think for themselves anymore.*

"So, what do you propose we do?" James repeated.

"Like I don't know that time is of the essence," Keyes berated him.

"Sorry, sir," James said, meekly.

"You've got to think these things through."

"Understood."

"Not sure that you do."

The visual of the creature on the screen got bigger as the search plane moved closer. And then the beast turned and looked towards the aircraft.

A beam of blue light shot from its mouth. Then an explosion echoed through the communications link. The video cut out, and General Yoshi appeared on the screen.

"What the hell was that?" Williams muttered.

"The Kaiju took out your plane," General Yoshi said.

Keyes pounded the table with his fist.

"Our fighters are loaded with ordnance and en route as we speak," Yoshi advised. "And the *Izumo* is moving into position."

"The ship is defensive oriented," Keyes said. "We need to *attack* that thing."

"We have some offensive capabilities through the defensive weapons systems," General Yoshi explained. "The RIM-116 Rolling Airframe Missile can be used to attack the Kaiju."

"Let's see what you can do," Keyes replied. "But we need to move forward with our backup plan."

General Yoshi shrugged. "Let's wait and see."

The suit walked back into the room. Keyes eye-balled his officers, as though indicating to keep their mouths shut about the Tomahawk missile.

*****

A moment later, the screen turned into a blurred satellite visual of the coast. Keyes noted the creature made progress up the coastline. He figured the Japanese Defense Forces could at least slow the beast down while he tried to get his backup plan in play.

A squadron of F-2 fighters buzzed across the screen and released rockets as they swooped past the creature.

Keyes shook his head in dismay. Even as the missiles exploded into the thick hide, he knew they wouldn't be effective. They'd already been through this with Captain Able and figured out that the attack had to be close to the creature to inflict any damage.

Another sortie flew through the air. It repeated the rocket launch with similar results. The creature canted its head and roared at the planes as they raced away. It stamped a massive foot in the surf and water shot twenty feet into the air.

The third and final wave of planes cut across the sky.

Long before the jets reached the target, a blue beam of light shot from the creature's mouth. The laser hit the nose of a fighter and smacked the fuselage of another. Instantly, the planes exploded in mid-air. Scraps of wings and a tail spiraled through the sky, as three fighters maneuvered to avoid the falling debris.

Two jets pulled up and the other broke left. A moment after the fighters careened upward, they collided with each other and exploded into flames. The remaining jet rushed toward the craggy coast, and the pilot yanked on the thrust levers.

The nose shot upward and the plane rose rapidly along the rock-face. As the jet cleared the escarpment, a beam of blue light shot through the air and blasted the fighter to pieces. The jet burst into tiny pieces, leaving mere fragments of debris floating through the sky and trickling into the ocean below.

Keyes glanced at the small window in the corner of his screen. Devastation registered on General Yoshi's face. The creature appeared unstoppable. Keyes hit the mute button and turned to his staff officers.

"What do you make of this laser beam?" Keyes said.

"The creature did not have that capability before," Williams replied.

"Do you think our *attack* had an impact on it?"

"Anything is possible… but we really don't know much about the creature."

"Maybe we helped arm the damn thing…"

Then the large screen lit up with blasts from explosions as the remaining fighters dropped bombs on the creature. Earth and dust billowed up and obscured the beast. A volley of missiles launched from the *Izumo*. Ordnance whipped across the screen and sailed into the wavering haze.

Several missiles exploded in the center of the smoky clouds. Direct hits caused the creature to writhe and stumble.

Other missiles cruised into the cliff-side, erupting in the rock. Debris hurled down the slope and cascaded upon the monster. The creature shook its head and stammered toward the surf. Then, a squadron of fighters zipped across the screen.

The jets swooped in closer this time, releasing a barrage of missiles and letting rip their aircraft machineguns.

Missiles pounded into the creature and burst into its hide. Bullets dug into the thick scales. Keyes watched the creature stumbled. *We just might have a chance*, he thought.

And then the beast lost his footing and tripped. It stumbled and fell into the water.

Cheers erupted from around the command table. A wave of bombs dropped from the sky. Explosions sent sand and water bursting into the air. The creature tossed in the shallow water, trying to right itself.

More bombs descended on the beachhead from another wave of jets.

Explosions broke up the coastline and clouds of smoke and debris shrouded the creature from view. Keyes moved to the edge of his seat in anticipation. He wondered if attempts at taking the beast down could really turn so favorably.

"We've got the Kaiju, now!" General Yoshi blurted from the corner of the screen.

"Let's hold off on the celebration until the dust clears," Keyes said.

"He's down in the water, probably drowning to death."

Keyes shook his head, guarded about the outcome. He recalled one of the stories he'd heard in the last twenty-four hours, about how the Kaiju had attacked in the 1960s. After an atomic blast, it was presumed dead, but old-timers told tales of the beast creeping to the bottom of the ocean, stealing away in a crevice or deep-sea canyon. Now, the creature had come back and stalked through Tokyo, decimating buildings.

General Yoshi continued smiling at the coastal destruction. Slapping a thigh, the general smiled again. Keyes couldn't bring himself to celebrate. He wondered how Penton and Able had fared after the nuclear blast.

Then, a blue beam shot from the billowing smoke, an explosion ignited the sky, and debris from a plane drifted across the screen. Another zap from the blue beam and the fuselage of a jet dropped from the sky.

Keyes shook his head, disappointed.

The creature rose from the dust of the battle zone. It shook its head and let out a menacing roar, revealing rows of sharp teeth and a long, forked tongue. Another roar, then it glanced toward the open water.

Laser beams whisked out of its mouth and shot across the water. The beams traced for the Japanese warship. A laser struck the ship in the hull, blasting open a large hole, then an explosion blew flames through the open cavity. Another explosion burst from the command bridge. Then, the ship keeled to the starboard side and rolled over, sinking bow first below the waterline. Within a few minutes, two more fighters dropped from the sky and the ship had disappeared beneath choppy waves.

The creature stepped deeper into the surf then its head dipped beneath the water. Waves splashed the plates running along its back. And then the Kaiju plummeted toward the ocean depths. A flick of its tail revealed the creature was headed north.

A couple of pilots ejected in time. Parachutes gently floated toward the sea, dotted with castaways, adrift in the undulating water. The assault on the creature had concluded in utter failure.

General Yoshi stared at Keyes and nodded. "You should go forward with the plan."

THIRTY-THREE

The squat industrial building shook with each blast from bombs dropping on the beachhead. Scant light reflected through the bullet holes in the door.

Penton discerned the sounds of bombs exploding and rockets bursting. But the faint humming noise, followed by explosions emanating high in the sky, and a massive eruption far out to sea, made him wonder if a new weapon had been called into use or whether the creature had more offensive capabilities than he'd imagined.

He reached into his pocket for the cellphone and tried again with little luck. Reception was unavailable through the cinderblock walls. Their fortuitous hold up in the small building had gone from a stroke of luck to an excruciating wait.

"What do you think is going on out there?" Kate said in the darkness.

"Another attack on the creature. Planes and a warship."

"They won't be able to kill the Kaiju," Maki muttered, assuredly.

"We'll have to wait here until the attack blows over," Penton said. "And it will help us to have some time for the winds to carry the fallout away."

The discussion fell into an awkward pause.

Kate rolled over. Her flight boots kicked the floor as though she were sitting up. "Don't you think we should get out of here soon?" Kate finally asked him.

"Makes sense to button down... and ride this out, here."

"But—"

"But... what?"

She panted, trying to get the words out.

"Are you all right?"

"No."

Kate scrambled toward a corner, hands slapping the concrete floor and boots scraping along behind her.

"What is it?" Penton demanded.

She didn't respond.

Then, she vomited into a nook near the outside door. Puke splashed against the wall, and the stench wafted around the room. Penton could barely hold down his urge to throw up.

"Gross," Maki mumbled, tucking her face under his arm.

Penton shuffled over to help. Kate rocked back on her butt and desperately wiped at her face. Smacking cheeks echoed through the dark room.

He wondered if she was ill, or pregnant.

"We've got to get out of here," Kate insisted.

"What's wrong?"

Another long pause. "The radiation has leaked into the building," she eventually said. "Just a matter of time and Maki will feel it, and you'll get radiation sickness, too."

Penton shook his head, discouraged.

He rubbed her back gently to comfort her. Kate latched onto his hand, grasping it tightly. She squeezed his fist then massaged it, comforting him when she was the person in need.

"The dose cannot be that high," he offered.

"Well, I am feeling it."

"We're a good half mile or more from the blast. And the building is located beneath a rock-face."

She leaned over and threw up again.

He reached for his first-aid kit and fumbled in the darkness. Almost every six months for thirty years, he'd either been given NBC training, or taught the courses. Penton never figured he'd put Nuclear, Biological, and Chemical warfare training to use. But now he was searching for the syringes in his kit.

Kate sat back and wiped her mouth again.

"I'm going to administer a dose to all of us," Penton said. "But it's too dark in here to see what I'm doing."

"What do you want to do?"

"We can either open the door, or take our chances blasting through the inside door."

"Where will that get us?" Kate said, groggily.

"Might be a window on the front of the building… It would help us to see—"

"And?"

"Maybe there's a phone or computer we could use."

"Sounds like a plan."

Penton paused before getting up. "Look, firing at the lock might be dangerous. A bullet could ricochet around the cinderblock walls."

"I'm not inclined to open that *fucking* door."

"Okay," he said.

"Rather take my chances with a bullet, than a higher dose of radiation."

He stood up and walked toward the inside door. Penton held his hands out in front of him, feeling for the wall or door. His boots shuffled across the cement floor, and then finally, his hands banged into the cinderblock wall.

The wall felt cool and rough on his hands. He slapped at it, moving to the left, trying to feel the steel hatch.

His left hand smacked the cold, metal door.

Penton shuffled further until both hands were pressed against the door. Then, he slid his left hand down, groping in the dark for the knob. He found purchase on the doorknob, and then traced his right hand up and felt the padlock.

"This is going to be tricky…" he said, "shooting in the dark."

"Go ahead," Kate said, squirming toward the center of the room.

"Roger," he replied, reaching for his sidearm.

Kate hunkered down and murmured something to Maki. The young girl's rain boots kicked on the floor, and he pictured Kate covering her. "Okay," Kate said after a moment.

He reached for the phone and shined a dim light on the lock.

Then Penton stepped back and fired several rounds at the door.

The shots blasted away, ringing his ears as the clamor echoed around the small room. A bullet struck the lock and a metal fragment dug into his thigh. Two of the rounds penetrated the door and pounded into equipment on the other side. Cracked plastic and a metallic ding echoed through the steel hatch.

Another bullet rebounded off the door and ricocheted around the room.

Kate yelled from the noise. He figured she'd been hit, but the sound continued as the bullet slammed around the tight space. A silence immediately followed and pain burned in his upper leg.

Penton's ears rung from the blasts. He felt disoriented.

Shaking it off, he reached for the door and it held secure. Penton holstered his pistol and kicked at the knob with the heel of his boot. The metal doorframe reverberated, but held strong.

He kicked it again. Daylight crept through a fissure.

Penton's heart raced with anticipation. He gave it another try. Stepping back and rushing at the door, he threw his weight into the blow.

Still, the door held firm. Momentum was lost when he leapt into the air.

The first two attempts delivered solid blows to the door. Penton backed up and charged the door, hurling his body into it. His shoulder struck the door.

Something cracked. He prayed he wasn't injured.

The door flung open. Penton hurled into the room and fell on the floor. His eyes went blind from bright light. A moment later, Kate pulled him to his feet, and then she took a deep breath to gather herself. He glanced around and noticed a large window overlooking the ragged coastline. The room resembled a small office, with a desk, computer, phone, and electrical equipment.

He reached for the phone. Pain shot through his shoulder, and a sensation tingled down his forearm into his pinky. He shook out his arm and cracked his neck. Then, Penton squeezed his hand open and closed. Feeling slowly came back into his fingers.

He reached for the phone. Penton held it to his ear. Dead.

"No connection," he said, dispassionately.

"You don't sound surprised."

"All that bombing along the beachhead..." Penton said, shrugging. "Figured the chance of an underground cable making it through was less than fifty percent."

Kate nodded, understanding.

He tried the computer, but it didn't come on. "Power line is out."

"Doesn't the thing have a battery?"

Penton looked around the dusty room. "Likely died months ago." He shook his head. "Doesn't seem like anyone gets out here very often."

"Mine has a battery." A faint voice muttered from behind them.

They both turned to find Maki standing in the doorway. She smiled widely. "I've got a computer in my backpack and the battery works." Maki grinned proudly.

"Sweetheart, why didn't you say something sooner?" said Kate.

"Nobody asked." Maki shrugged her little shoulders.

Penton stepped over to the girl. Maki removed her backpack and handed it to him. He opened it and found the laptop inside, and then he placed her computer on the desk.

"That thing might be able to put a call through," Kate said, gasping for air.

"How so?" Penton inquired.

"Skype."

"Here, you get it running," he said, stepping back.

Kate took a seat at the desk and began booting up the computer. Her skin looked pale, but she seemed to gather herself, as though trying to steady a dizzy head. She fiddled with wires and linked the computer to the phone line. Surprisingly, the laptop kicked on and buzzed with the outdated connection through the phone system.

Penton sat down in a nearby chair and pulled out his first-aid kit. He set it on the desk and then reached for the zipper on his flight suit. "Might want to look away."

Kate grinned. "I've seen it all before."

"Not like this, you haven't." Penton grinned, then slid down his utilities and scoped out the damage. A metal fragment protruded from his quadricep, and the bullet grazed through flesh at mid-thigh.

He clamped his teeth, then ripped the metal fragment loose. Blood percolated from the open cut. Penton applied pressure with his thumb to help clot the wound. He glanced up. Kate clacked away at the keyboard, while sweat dripped from her brow. Then, he felt his stomach turn queasy.

"Guess you're right about the radiation," Penton said.

"How so?" Kate responded without looking up.

"Think I feel the sickness setting in."

She turned to him with a doleful countenance. "We've got to get moving along," she said, nodding at her own comment.

"Not sure it will be better for us out there."

"What are we supposed to do?" Kate snapped. "Are we just going to sit here and slowly die?"

The last bit came out as a rhetorical statement and not a question. Penton didn't respond. He busied himself by treating his injuries. After applying an antibiotic cream, he dressed the wounds, then reorganized the medical supplies.

He reached into the first-aid kit and grabbed a few syringes.

Kate glanced up from the computer screen. "Let me finish this up... I'm almost logged in."

Penton shook his head. "No time."

He broke open the packaging and tugged a syringe loose. Kate slid over and unzipped her flight suit. She wiggled it down, revealing her athletic body and black panties and bra. She looked an entire 115 pounds of lean muscle. Kate caught him peeking and smiled.

Then, she flashed him a mock disapproving frown. Mischievous. She poked him in the nose. "Keep your mind focused on the task at hand," Kate admonished him.

He laughed and then pressed the needle into her thigh. Penton pulled back the plunger and injected the serum. Kate winced but didn't cry out. He removed the needle and wiped the pin-hole with antibiotic gauze.

She pulled up her flight suit then he reached toward her with the needle in hand.

"What are you doing?" she said.

"Got to tie this off on your uniform."

"What?"

He slid the end of the needle around the hole in her zipper, then bent the needle back so the syringe hung from it. "This shows how many injections you've been administered," he explained. "You can't have more than two, or you'll die of an overdose."

"So, when the reinforcements finally arrive, I can only have two of these hanging on my uniform."

"Something like that," Penton replied.

He administered a dose on himself, then pulled up his flight suit, and tied his syringe off on the zipper. There were only two doses left. He figured Maki could only handle one, and the other would go to Kate.

"Why hasn't she been affected yet?" Kate said, indicating to Maki.

"Probably has a higher tolerance than us," Penton offered. "Maybe from past family exposure. Her ancestors likely survived an atrocity."

Kate nodded. The prospect of an atavism that might help the girl was obvious. "Still, we should keep an eye on her."

"I've got a needle for her and another for you," Penton said, tapping the first-aid kit. Then, he shook his head in disappointment.

"What?" Kate insisted.

"Really burns my ass that young officers don't recall the basics of NBC training." He shook his head again.

Kate seemed chagrinned.

Penton grabbed the first-aid kit and stowed it away in his flight suit. Kate didn't respond, though. A confused look glazed over her face.

"They rush us through that training," she finally said.

"Sure," Penton replied. "And it's the kind of mistake that can get someone killed. Enlisted Marines are taught NBC in boot camp, and they get refreshers at least twice a year. Meritorious promotions and Marine of the Month awards often have NBC questioning as part of the process. You can't get either without knowing your stuff."

Kate turned back to the computer. "Sorry, I didn't measure up…"

She clacked away at the keyboard, ignoring him. Penton wanted to caress her shoulder, let her know that he didn't mean to be so harsh. But she was a Marine and needed to take good criticism along with the bad. Instead, he stepped over to Maki and checked her vital signs.

A moment later, Kate was talking to someone on the computer screen.

Penton glanced at the screen and saw a lieutenant commander staring back at them. The naval officer appeared to be in a communications room, likely Pearl Harbor. Kate explained the situation and the lieutenant commander nodded gravely. He didn't seem to doubt her story for a moment.

"We'll see what we can do," he said, then the screen went blank.

Kate looked up at Penton hopefully. She smiled. "Maybe they can get through and send us a rescue team. Airlift us out of here."

Penton looked out the window at the grey morning sky. The wind and rain had let up, but he wasn't sure the storm had ended. On the other hand, they'd definitely heard a major air strike, and so aircraft were able to take flight more readily than during the main thrust of the storm.

Maybe there was still hope for a rescue, but he wondered about the creature.

THIRTY-FOUR

Keyes looked at the screen and shook his head. The entire beachhead depicted mass destruction. Fuselages of broken planes washed up on shore and smoke wisped in the overcast sky. Sailors clung to life vests, bobbing in the water, futilely kicking toward shore. Others floated on the surface, motionless, a tableau of death.

A crack of morning sunlight appeared on the horizon, breaking through the grey haze. Weapons were silent, and the creature had slithered away. Somehow, the tragic spectacle grew serene. The images were ghastly, but the calm after a major storm, and the pause in battle, ratcheted down adrenaline, causing a numbness to creep into the soul where fear, anxiety, and rage had seized dominion.

Everyone in the command room knew to keep quiet. They sat still, waiting for the cue from the admiral.

Keyes glanced around and felt the air squeeze out of the room.

He knew that General Yoshi would come on-line and press for next steps. The Joint Task Force would have to move into further action. But he wasn't sure about the wisest approach in tackling the creature, a relatively unknown enemy.

He stood up and grabbed his cigar, then nodded at the executive officer, indicating for Commander James to follow him from the room. Keyes stepped past the suit and exited through a hatch into a narrow hallway then he strode toward the head.

He relieved himself quickly while James stood outside.

Then, the two senior sailors headed up several sets of steep, metal stairwells, and turned down a tight passageway. Keyes spun the handle to a thick, steel hatch and stepped onto the upper deck. Brisk wind battered the ship and whipped at his uniform.

Keyes grabbed the handrail and took a deep breath. He looked across the choppy salt water at the endless sea.

Commander James stood alongside him. They'd been together long enough the executive officer understood it wasn't the time to begin a discussion. Keyes needed a moment to contemplate the situation, process options, and then he'd seek input from the younger officer.

Keyes stuffed the cigar in his mouth and reached into a pocket for his zippo. A chrome lighter with the Navy logo on the side, he'd bought it at a base exchange during his first tour as an enlisted sailor.

He flipped the top back and struck the flint wheel with his thumb. A flame shot from the lighter, wavered in the wind, but didn't go out. He grinned. "These things are perfect for an old-salt officer," Keyes said. "Never lose their flame... no matter what the conditions."

Commander James smiled and nodded in agreement.

Then, Keyes leaned over and cupped a hand to block the wind, lit the end of the cigar, and puffed to get the tobacco ignited. He flipped the lighter closed and shoved it into his pocket.

Admiral Keyes calmly smoked the stogy and stared out at the sea. When the post-battle jitters subsided, he turned toward James. "What do you think?" Keyes said.

His executive officer nodded, understanding the drill. Keyes would seek his input then blow holes in the advice, trying to work through the best options. Commander James grabbed hold of the railing and shook his head. He inhaled, leaden with the pressure of taking part in command. "Conventional weapons are of no use," James finally said. "We've got to hit it with something harder."

Keyes nodded, acknowledging the point. "I just don't know," he replied.

"We don't have many options," James pressed.

"You're talking about using a bigger nuke," said Keyes. "The Tomahawk didn't work... in fact, it seemed to make the thing stronger. That damn ray-beam wasn't coming out of its mouth... until after we used the nuke."

"We didn't use a big enough nuclear weapon."

"You think a bigger nuclear weapon will destroy the thing?"

"Damn straight," James replied.

"You can't possibly know that..." Keyes snapped.

"The first strike wasn't a direct hit. And something from the fallout made it stronger. A Tomahawk just isn't all that powerful a weapon. It is a surgical strike missile that missed the target. We need something bigger, stronger, with more blast range… Blow the thing to bits."

"Releasing more radiation into the environment is a huge issue."

"We'd only do it because the Japanese Defense Force agrees."

"The responsibility for the use of such a weapon remains entirely with us." Keyes shook his head. "We've got a treaty in place right now, which restricts the use of nuclear weapons. Even if we are successful and kill the beast, we'll likely face criticisms from foreign countries."

"We are the ones dealing with the situation in the moment. You always told me that the critic isn't the one that counts, the person in the arena, marred in blood and sweat, that's the one who makes all the difference."

Keyes grinned. "Didn't think you were listening."

Commander James laughed. "I've always listened to you."

"Well, it's *my* ass on the line," Keyes said. "This isn't the situation where you're deciding whether or not to respond to hostiles. We're talking about potential treaty violations… getting called before Congress."

"This is a big decision," James said. "And I don't envy your position in the least."

"Maybe we should wait it out," Keyes postulated. "The storm has died down. We could get a boatload of more conventional weapons into the mix. Hell, this ship will be within striking distance in a matter of hours."

"The creature is halfway to Iwaki by now. It decimated Tokyo and will ravage another city, killing thousands. We simply don't have time."

Keyes took a puff from the cigar and stared out at the water. He knew that his comrade was right. But he could picture himself seated at a table in front of a Congressional Committee. "Nobody could blame us for taking the conservative approach."

"So, now it's *us*," the younger officer jibed him.

"You know what I mean," Keyes said. "Just a hard call to make."

"Understood." James crossed his arms. "Potentially a career-ending decision."

"Potentially a career-ending decision," Keyes repeated.

"Unless—"

"Unless... what?"

"We handle it as a covert operation. Like the old days."

Keyes thought about the Soviet nuclear missile. "We could put that Tochka to good use. It has the payload to create a large blast area. And the swath would hit the beast hard, as long as it strikes close by."

He glanced out at the immense ocean, thinking.

At last, he nodded; Keyes ripped the cigar from his mouth and tossed it overboard. "Let's get going," he said, heading for the command room.

****

A moment later, Keyes hustled down the steep stairwells and walked through the narrow passageways. He moved like a seasoned veteran aboard ship. And he didn't pay the cables and pipes running along the bare metal walls any mind.

Commander James fell a few paces behind. By the time Keyes reentered the command room, his executive officer was trailing down the hallway.

The officers sat up straight when Keyes entered the room. The suit sat slumped in a chair. As he expected, General Yoshi appeared in the corner of the viewing screen. General Yoshi had a dire concern on his face. Keyes glanced around the room, taking in the audience, and considered what he was getting ready to do.

"Everyone out, except the XO and Intelligence Officer," Keyes barked.

The officers sitting around the command room didn't seem to register his order right away. Many of them appeared baffled, perhaps not believing or uncertain of what they'd heard. When the chief of the boat stood up, a few of the officers settled back down, likely thinking Keyes meant for enlisted personnel to leave.

"Out!" Keyes screamed. He kicked a chair with the heel of his shoe for effect.

Suddenly, the officers sprung from their chairs and bolted out of the room as though they were back in basic training. Officers hustled out of the hatch in single file. The suit stood up with his palms held out, questioning. Keyes grunted at him. A moment later, only Admiral Keyes and the intelligence officer remained in the room.

"Where the hell is James?" Keyes snapped.

"Right here," Commander James said before the intelligence officer could respond. He'd evidently gotten tied up in the hall, waiting for the parade of officers to clear the room. Keyes shook his head at the situation.

"Both of you take a seat," Keyes said, motioning toward the plush sofa.

They sat down as directed, but he remained standing with command of the room. Keyes looked up to the screen and addressed General Yoshi, bowing slightly as a salutation.

"Admiral, please explain the meaning of this," General Yoshi said.

"Sir, please advise if you are in a secure location."

Yoshi glanced around then nodded in affirmative.

"Anyone able to listen in on my conversation with you?"

The general smiled and shook his head. "I've been having my discussions with you from my briefing room, alone."

Keyes smiled at the response.

"Then, I fill in my staff officers after we talk. At least this is our approach since we first discussed the use of the missile."

"Yes, the use of the missile is very sensitive information."

General Yoshi smiled kindly then nodded.

"We feel the recent attack on the monster," Keyes continued, "did not fare well."

"No, it certainly did not."

"We were thinking…" Keyes motioned toward his officers, "that conventional weapons of any sort may not work on this creature."

Yoshi nodded. "Even if we overwhelm the creature with a stronger wave of attacks, you think that we will fail."

"The storm has settled down. We could try it, but I do not expect it will work."

"A heavy attack would cause the creature to seek safety out at sea," said General Yoshi. "The Kaiju would resurface and ravage the mainland again."

"I'm afraid so." Keyes shrugged. "You know more about the creature's capabilities than us. But the initial assault came because of the beast surfacing in Tokyo Harbor. This creature is amphibious and can live on land and under the water. Your theory is sound."

"Japan is doomed, then." Yoshi shook his head, dismayed.

"Perhaps not," Admiral Keyes postulated.

"Go on, then." General Yoshi stared back at him with interest.

"We might have an alternative," Keyes explained. "Another nuclear missile that might blow the creature apart."

Yoshi nodded, and said, "Continue…"

"Our special operators have commandeered a cold war missile." Keyes paced about the command room. "An old Soviet Tochka OTR-21."

"We are familiar with this missile," Yoshi said, grinning.

"The Tochka has a wider blast radius than the Tomahawk. We are thinking that if it strikes near the creature, the missile will blow it to pieces. Our concern is with the much higher level of radiation."

"My concern is with the stability of such an antiquated weapon."

"We admit there is some risk involved."

"How do you plan to get the missile into place and fire it?"

"These are all good questions," Keyes replied. "We've got a cold war veteran on the ground, highly experienced with ordnance."

"Sounds like a makeshift launch." Yoshi shook his head.

Keyes glanced over at his executive officer. The reaction wasn't promising, and Keyes wondered if General Yoshi might decide to try another volley of conventional weapons, drive the creature back into the sea, and live to regroup and fight another day. Ultimately, it was Yoshi's call and his country would suffer the consequences. Keyes didn't want to press the use of the missile but merely provide it as an option.

"The decision is entirely yours," Keyes finally said.

"My concern is not with the fallout after a successful blast," General Yoshi said after a moment. "But rather taking the chance of putting it to use and having to deal with the nuclear effects without even getting it off the ground."

"A valid point," Keyes admitted. "We have confidence in our technician, though."

General Yoshi seemed to contemplate the situation. "Time is of the essence," he finally said. "The Kaiju is likely headed north and will reach Mito soon. Waiting will mean the end of that city. And we will lose the opportunity to take the Kaiju down in the countryside."

Keyes felt adrenaline pump through him. He anticipated permission for attack.

"Let's move forward with the missile launch," Yoshi said. "Ready your forces for a wave of joint conventional attack should the effort fail."

"Yes, sir!" Keyes replied, already in motion. He turned to address the two officers in the room.

"Admiral?" Yoshi murmured.

Keyes looked back toward the screen.

"Let's hope your ordnance technician is up to the task."

The screen faded and Keyes felt a sinking feeling in his gut. Such a plan had never been attempted before. He wondered if they could really pull it off.

A vision crossed his mind of the missile exploding a few feet above the ground.

THIRTY-FIVE

Penton administered another dose of medicine to Kate and gave Maki her injection. Everyone seemed to be holding together, and he wasn't feeling very sick himself. Sunlight broke through the dissipating storm clouds. He gazed out the window at the waves plying toward shore at a northern angle.

Then, he looked at the crabgrass, fluttering in the same direction, away from the small industrial building. "The wind is blowing the fallout north," Penton said.

"Well, that's certainly helpful…" Kate sounded despondent.

"Maybe we'll get out of this—"

"Yeah, so long as that beast doesn't head this way."

He listened intently but couldn't hear a sound from outside. The creature habitually thumped the ground and caused vibrations when chasing after them. "Something tells me that it's headed away from us."

"What makes you say that?" Kate asked.

"Too damn quiet. The creature made a lot of noise chasing us."

"We were on city streets and a highway. Now, the thing could be walking on soft earth. I'm not convinced that it headed in the other direction."

"The creature would have been upon us by now."

Kate shrugged, conceding to his point. Then, she reached for the computer screen and pressed the Skype icon. A frustrated face appeared on the screen. The admiral's nostrils flared with heavy breathing, and his brow tightened into wrinkles.

Stepping toward the computer, Penton noticed the mouth moving, but he couldn't hear any words. "We've got a technical problem with the audio," Penton said to Kate.

Then she fumbled with the computer and the sound of Keyes' voice boomed through the small industrial office. "About time!" Keyes shook his head. "We've got a major crisis and the two of you are standing there playing guessing games about things we already know."

They both glanced at the screen, dumbfounded.

"Just because you couldn't hear me… doesn't mean I couldn't hear you."

"We were just trying to prepare—"

"Enough!" Keyes paused and adjusted the collar of his shirt. He looked back up at them with an earnest twinkle in his eyes. "The creature was headed north the last time he appeared on our satellite video."

"What happened to the satellite feed?" Kate asked.

"Nothing," Keyes said, shaking his head. "The damn thing slipped back into the water. Our last view of it… indicated that the creature tracked to the north."

"So, we might not be in the clear," Kate concluded.

"Most likely… it's headed north."

"Are we being extracted?"

"Sort of…"

Penton moved closer to the computer, leaning over Kate's shoulder with his hands on his hips. He perused Admiral Keyes' demeanor, trying to discern the politician that lurks beneath high-ranking officers.

Keyes took a deep breath and stared at them for a moment. "We've got a Super Stallion headed your way."

"So, we *are* being extracted," Kate said.

"The helo is carrying some delicate cargo," Keyes replied.

"What do you mean?" Penton interjected.

Keyes forced a smile and then divulged the plan.

Penton shook his head. A vision of the missile launching ten feet into the air and exploding with him nearby came to mind. And the vaccinations on hand were used up.

Looks like this is it, he thought shaking his head. *My final stand… and it will be in a covert op handling unauthorized nukes.*

****

A while later, the *whop-whop* of massive rotors brought Penton out of deep thought. He sat up in the metal folding chair, trying to pinpoint the distance of the approaching helicopter.

"They're here," Kate said, pointing toward the sky.

"Not quite," Penton corrected. "About half a click out."

"But it sounds so close…"

"They are coming in right over the water, fast. The sound carries to low points like where we are situated."

Kate smiled, admiring his experience.

"We should get a move on it now, anyway."

Penton stood and adrenaline rushed up his spine. Marines learn how to wait for dire situations in laid-back ways. They curl up in helicopters, transport trucks, and assault vehicles, often sleeping until the moment to disembark. Then, they rush ahead, fueled by adrenaline, senses honed and acute.

He'd noticed a steel ladder bolted to the concrete block wall in a corner of the office. It led to the rooftop where he planned to meet the arriving helicopter. Penton mounted the metal rails and climbed the ladder. Maki followed after him, assisted by Kate.

Penton worked a bolt loose and flipped the steel hatch open. It clanged on the deck as he scrambled onto the roof. He looked over the conditions: a flat rooftop with gravel covering a thick membrane; a wall rose above the roofline with a radio tower from bygone days bolted to the brick.

Making his way to the edge of the roof, Penton scanned the horizon and saw the Super Stallion moving swiftly across the water. The helicopter was painted olive drab. He hadn't known whether it would be a Navy chopper or the Marines. Silver would have signified a Navy aircraft. Soon, he observed the word Marines written in block letters on the tail.

Penton smiled at the sight of his comrades flying in to the rescue. A moment later, Maki shuffled up beside him and grabbed his fingers. He gently tightened his fist around her little hand. "You'll be in safe hands soon," he said, smiling.

Kate stepped beside him and the three of them watched the helicopter buzz over the choppy ocean waters.

While waiting for the chopper, Penton had wondered if he could even pull off the assignment. He also thought about how to say good-bye to his daughter, concerned about the prospect of never seeing her again.

Now, his mind laid out the tasks at hand; he contemplated what had to be accomplished, step-by-step. Every fiber of his being channeled energy at the colossal undertaking, and failure no longer became a consideration.

He turned toward Kate and put his hands on his hips. "That chopper is coming in fast," he said. "And we don't have time to argue. I want you to extract with the girl pronto. I'll stay behind and get the missile ready."

Kate shook her head. "The mission is more important than either of us. I'll stay behind and lend you a hand."

Penton admired her spunk. He looked into her eyes and felt a tinge of regret.

"Don't try and stop me," Kate said. "I out-rank you."

"Someone has to look after the girl," he reasoned.

"There's an entire aircraft full of capable Marines that can watch out for her." Kate pointed toward the incoming Super Stallion.

"What about your ankle? How's it doing?"

"A lot better, now that I've given it some rest."

"Maybe you should tighten up your boot, just to make sure."

"Good idea," Kate said, bending down and reworking her laces.

Wind gusts whipped at Penton's flight suit as the helicopter closed in. Rotor blades squealed and blasted air-current down at them. She kept talking, but he didn't hear a word from a few feet away.

The Super Stallion hovered overhead with the Tochka missile slung under its belly. Moving into position, the pilot steadied the aircraft. Then the ramp at the rear of the helicopter slowly began to open. Hydraulics eased the ramp down, and a thick rope dropped toward the deck, with one end fastened to the rear fuselage and the other cascading down to the rooftop.

A Marine in a flight suit stepped across the open ramp, wind gusting into the aircraft. He gingerly walked over the metal decking, a few stories above the ground. The job wasn't for someone with a fear of heights.

He wrapped his leg around the rope and dropped from the bird. Flight boots pinched off the rope, slowing his descent.

Nobody followed after him. Penton realized it was a skeleton crew aboard the Super Stallion.

The crew chief hit the deck and ambled over toward them. His aviator's helmet had an ordnance symbol painted above the visor:

an antiquated bomb with a flame, flanked by large aviation wings. A grim reaper sticker was plastered behind the ear-piece. He was short with a West Coast smile.

"Master Gunnery Sergeant..." the crew chief said to Penton, offering his hand.

Penton shook his hand quickly. "Thanks for dropping by."

"I'm Staff Sergeant Bishop. Here to help you unload that bastard."

Bishop pointed toward the missile. Penton looked up. It hung in a harness, lying horizontal to the deck. Shaking his head, Penton looked at the lad doubtfully. The kid cracked another California grin. His sandy blonde hair crept out from under the flight helmet, grown to the maximum regulation length.

"Guess we should get started," Penton said, moving into position.

"Just hope we can do it... without the darn thing dropping on our heads."

Penton registered a twang in his voice, a mountain state. The kid had joined the Marines from some rural town and took a liking to the West Coast lifestyle. A Hollywood Marine, probably went to boot camp in San Diego, and spent most of his career at Marine Corps Air Station – Pendleton.

"Let's improvise, adapt, and overcome," Penton said, but his words carried away with gusts of wind from the rotor blast. Bishop had already moved into position.

The remaining flight crew on the aircraft lowered the tail of the missile, dipping it toward the roof. A moment later, they slowly released the main line, tethering the missile to the helicopter. The large ordnance eased closer and closer to the deck as the pilot worked to steady the chopper in position above the rooftop.

Lower tailfins touched the roof deck, then Penton and Bishop grabbed hold of the top fins and yanked the missile off the gavel. They made for the radio tower, pulling on the missile, while the pilot slowly veered to the left.

Penton felt the helicopter bob right, and the missile lunged back, causing him to stumble. He caught his balance just as Bishop tripped. The younger Marine fell, landing splayed across the rear of the missile. Tailfins clanged into the gravel, and the missile slid in the harness, dropping down, fins reverberated another clunk onto the roof deck.

Staring up at the straps holding the missile, Penton realized they could not allow it to lift off the deck again. The darn thing would drop from the harness and go straight through the roof, then fall into the basement below.

He stepped away and signaled to a crew member. Freeze!

A young Marine peered from the open hatch at the rear of the aircraft and nodded. Harnessed to the fuselage, he leaned out and observed the situation below. The Marine nodded again. He seemed to be talking into the communications link.

The helicopter remained hovering in place.

Moments later, the young Marine leaned down and gave a thumbs-up to Penton. They would hold the position until Penton told them to move.

Penton pictured the pilot desperately working the foot pedals. He knew they didn't have much time. He stepped over to Bishop.

"We're going to have to drop her... right here!" Penton yelled.

Bishop looked confused and glanced over toward the radio tower, as though trying to measure the distance.

Penton pointed to the unraveled rigging. "No way!"

He'd punch the kid before letting him foul up the situation worse.

"Get the tail down," Penton said, "and I'll work them through righting it up."

Bishop nodded and grabbed hold of the tail.

Penton admired the kid's courage. The missile could easily slip loose and crush him to death.

Stepping back, Penton made visual contact with the pilot.

Penton rose his arms into the air like a referee showing a completed field goal. And then he slowly moved them to the left, like a tree bending in a storm. The pilot nodded and the helicopter shifted left.

The missile straightened up. But it happened too fast.

Penton held up the sign to freeze.

The chopper whined in a steady hover. Penton grinned at the pilot's control of the aircraft. He looked at the tail. Bishop had two fins securely planted on the deck. Just a little further and it would be standing tall. Netting had come further unraveled, though.

If the pilot pushed it too far left, the missile would topple over.

The fall could cause a spark of static electricity. And the age of the missile could allow a current to set it off. Maybe it would rocket out to sea or merely explode on the rooftop.

Penton didn't like the idea of Kate and the girl standing nearby. He wished they'd been loaded into the chopper before attempting to deliver the missile.

The missile continued tipping left. And the other fins contacted the roof with a *thunk*.

Then the nose moved and the missile titled to the left, with the fins on the right side coming off the deck.

Penton waved Bishop away and instinctively stepped toward the missile.

He pushed on it in futility. The missile refused to budge, but then it ceased moving. It teetered on two fins and the pilot steadied the helicopter. Penton glanced up and noticed the harness almost completely unraveled. A piece of rope barely ensnared the nose. Even a slight jar and the missile might come loose.

The helicopter shuddered in a pocket of turbulence.

And the missile shifted to the right. It didn't break loose of the harness, but the fins were now a couple inches from the deck.

Penton looked at Bishop and the young Marine seemed to read his mind. Bishop shook his head.

"We have to take the chance!" Penton said.

"It might fall over!" Bishop yelled in the rotor blast.

"Nose is going to come loose." Penton pointed. "Any movement from the helo and the missile will tip over for sure."

Then Bishop shrugged, acquiescing.

Penton stepped back and signaled the crew member looking down. He made a swipe motion, indicating to cut the line.

The crew member talked into the communications link. A moment later, the line dropped from the belly of the Super Stallion.

The missile tipped right.

Fins pulled away from the roof.

It wavered then tipped left.

Penton rushed toward the missile and gave it a shove. His effort was like pushing against a dump truck.

But the missile teetered on two fins and didn't topple over. Instead, the dense ordnance just hung in the air for a moment. Then, it titled back to the right and landed with a heavy thud. A reverberation ran across the deck.

Penton let out a sigh. He looked over and Bishop breathed easier.

Then he spun around and Kate smiled at him.

She stepped toward him with Maki in tow as the helicopter pulled away.

"That was close," Penton said.

"I didn't doubt you for a second." Kate sounded sincere.

"I doubted me the whole time." Penton laughed.

"Where's the helicopter going?"

"Just circling around," Penton replied. "Holding it steady that long is a drain on the pilot. Something you fixed-wing jockeys don't to have to worry about."

"I'm a Harrier pilot. Totally get it." She laughed and Bishop snickered.

Penton nodded. "He'll be back in a moment."

"Figured as much," Kate said.

"They can't leave this guy behind," said Penton, thumbing toward Bishop.

The younger Marine grinned, a flawless West Coast smile. "Much obliged to work for you... Master Guns. But I'll appreciate taking to the air again."

Penton shrugged, thinking the creature could be anywhere.

Kate looked down at Maki. "We're going to have to leave you with this kind gentleman." She indicated toward Bishop.

Maki frowned. "Aren't you coming with me?"

"We have some important work to do."

"I want to stay," Maki pouted.

"We'd like you to stay, too."

"Really?"

"Yes, but it's too dangerous," Kate insisted. "We're going to join up with you soon, though."

Penton shook his head.

"What?" Kate said.

"You need to get going with her."

"I'll stay and help you."

"You're not an ordnance technician."

"Yeah, but you can use the help. And someone needs to team up to extract you later. Besides… I out-rank you."

Her words were spoken with finality.

Bishop stepped over as the helicopter circled around. The rotors blew hard and a line lowered with a large basket. A yellow inflatable lifeboat was folded up inside. "I'll take her up with me. And you two use the boat to get out of here."

Penton looked out at the breaking waves, doubtfully.

"We've got paddles, too." Kate pulled the gear out of the basket.

The prospect of getting the missile launched and clearing the potential blast area was daunting. Penton didn't like relying upon the antiquated weapon. He was old-school and missed some of the ways from the past.

And the prospect of using such antiquated ordnance was unprecedented.

****

Penton watched the basket rise into the air with Bishop and Maki inside. She waved down to them, sadly. Maki had lost her parents and stoically plodded ahead. Now, she might wonder about ever seeing the two of them again. He shook his head, disheartened.

The lifeboat lay on the deck. Maki's computer sat on top of it, and a toolbox was set on the gravel nearby.

He grabbed a handful of tools and headed over to the missile. Kate followed him and offered to help. "Like a nurse aiding a surgeon," she said.

"Yeah, but when surgery goes wrong… only the patient dies."

Penton unscrewed a control panel and looked inside. Surprisingly, the wiring and control systems had been updated. He shook his head and laughed.

"What is it?" said Kate.

"This might be easier than I thought."

"Really?"

"Sure, at least getting the launch started." Penton considered her eyes in earnest. "Doesn't mean the bloody thing won't explode three feet off the deck, though."

"We'll do the best we can." Kate slapped his shoulder.

He admired her gusto. Kate was a true Marine, focused on the task at hand, trying her best to achieve a great result, pushing aside fear and doubt.

Penton walked over and retrieved the laptop. He handed it to Kate and hardwired the computer to the missile's electrical system. Then, he clacked away at the keyboard while she held the computer.

The launch sequencing was just as he'd anticipated. But someone had attempted to disarm the damn thing. Penton reworked the codes. Then, he programmed the control panel to release an electrical current that would ignite the missile motor and send it flying into the air. "This is almost too easy," he repeated.

"Let's not count our blessings too soon."

"Agreed." He smirked, then set the warhead to detonate on impact. Penton would rather have it explode in the air at a strategic point, but his approach was more conventional. It had a better chance of success, or at least a lower chance of failure.

He reached into his flight suit and pulled out the cellphone.

Penton punched in the number for Admiral Keyes. A moment later, Keyes was on the horn.

"How are we doing?" Keyes said, calm and collected.

"Got her ready to roll," Penton replied. "Now, we just need to program the detonation point. Do you guys have the coordinates for that thing?"

No response. An awkward silence.

"Well?" Penton insisted.

"There's a bit of a snag," Keyes finally said.

"We can't wait for you to find that thing." Penton felt nauseous again. He knew they had to clear the area soon before radiation sickness took its toll.

"That's not the problem…"

Penton gulped.

Silence.

"It's headed back this way, right?"

"Exactly."

"Do you know the coordinates?"

"Yeah, we can give them to you," Keyes replied. "The trouble is that the thing took to the water and we expect it's going to surface right near you… You're on top of the damn thing."

"Just give me the coordinates," Penton snapped. "*We'll* worry about extraction."

"The missile is basically going to go straight up and down."

"That close…"

"Yup."

Penton reached into his flight suit. He pulled out a crumpled notepad and stubby pencil with a worn tip. He got the coordinates for the monster from the admiral. The creature swam through the ocean half a click away, tracking right toward his location. Then, he got the previous four points of its location from Keyes and charted the creature's course.

He scribbled on the notepad. The beast would likely surface on the beach about three hundred yards from his current location. Extraction would be dangerously close.

"Got it," Penton finally said.

"Just try to do your best… and get the hell out of there."

"Will do."

"Take care, Master Guns."

"You too, Admiral."

Penton ended the call and shoved the phone into a pocket in his flight suit. He turned toward Kate. "Made a huge mistake letting you stay behind."

"Letting me…"

"You know what I mean." He shook his head.

"No time to discuss this *now*."

"You should take the lifeboat and get out of here."

"How would you extract, then?"

Penton stared into her eyes. "Don't worry about me," he said. "I can hightail it out of this place on foot."

"Are you crazy?" Kate snapped. "You'll never clear the blast zone."

"Well, I can try…"

"At least with the lifeboat, we have a chance."

"You'd have an even *better* chance if you left right now."

Penton felt queasy and reached for his stomach. The radiation from the blast was taking a toll on him. He bent over and breathed deeply, getting some relief. The moment passed and he stood up straight.

"I'm not leaving you alone," Kate insisted. "Besides, the mission is too important."

Penton nodded, conceding to her point.

If he keeled over and didn't get the missile armed and ready to launch, an opportunity would be lost. Kate had taken two injections; she was much smaller and younger, and so their chances were better with her in the mix.

"Let's get going," Penton said.

"Roger that."

"Hand me the computer," he said, reaching out with the notepad. Kate gave him the computer and took the notes. "Read me the coordinates when I say go."

"Got it," Kate said, perusing the notepad.

Penton dropped a knee and placed the computer on the other. He tapped away at the keyboard, setting the launch code, and configuring the time sequence. "Go!"

Kate rattled off the coordinates, pausing every so often to allow his unorthodox typing to catch up.

He clacked at the keyboard. The missile's control panel registered on his screen. Responding like a new weapon, the Tochka confirmed each instruction path he programmed into its control system.

A moment later, the screen read: ARMED.

Then a digital clock began ticking a countdown from five minutes.

Seconds began clicking at a breakneck pace.

"We've got to move!" Penton hollered.

Kate grabbed the lifeboat and bolted for the stairwell while he unhooked the computer from the missile.

She quickly disappeared down the hatch.

Penton checked over the Tochka. It appeared solid and ready to fly.

He shut the control panel cover. And then he snatched up loose tools and shoved them into the toolbox. He grabbed it and the computer and stepped to the side of the building and then dropped them over the edge. Any fodder on the takeoff deck could easily turn into a projectile hurled at them during extraction.

Penton glanced out toward the water at the choppy surf. He doubted they could traverse the turbulent current in time to clear the blast area.

Then, he hustled toward the stairwell and felt his head swirl. He stumbled and teetered toward the opening in the rooftop. Penton dropped to the deck and his knees dug into the coarse gravel.

He inched over to the ladder and gingerly slid a leg over the edge. Reaching out with a flight boot, he found purchase on a rung, then latched onto the ladder with both hands and heaved himself through the open hatch.

Everything blurred and he felt as though he might fall.

His grip seemed rubbery and weak.

Penton stepped down the ladder, one rung at a time.

He made it halfway down when the toe of his boot slipped off the metal. Penton dropped like an anchor, chin striking a rung as he fell. Hitting the concrete deck, he toppled onto the floor.

Pain shot through his stomach. He curled into a ball and clenched his gut.

This is it, he thought. Penton trembled and threw up.

An image of his daughter in North Carolina came to mind, just the two of them walking on a vast beach. So many regrets. Much to make up for in a chaotic military life, ruled by his demanding career.

Fever burned throughout his head, obscuring his vision, and turning his thoughts dull, incomprehensible. Everything was blurry.

He lay on the floor, immobilized by his condition.

And then he considered Kate out there alone, struggling with the rough surf. He wanted to help her escape the fallout.

Penton gritted his teeth and squeezed his fists. He took a deep breath and tried to level the delirious feeling, like shaking off a bad drunkenness. Moving into a seated position took all the mental strength he could muster.

His stomach turned again. Penton wretched and felt a little better.

Eyes blurry, the room eventually came into focus.

Penton took three deep breaths, then crawled toward the ladder. He used it to hoist himself onto his feet. The dizziness waned. He started for the door, leaning forward and throwing one foot out in front of the other.

As his body veered from side to side, he used forward momentum to remain upright. Penton stumbled through the backroom of the industrial building then cleared the open door.

Outside, he staggered downhill headed for the beachhead. Penton zigzagged toward Kate and the lifeboat, fighting to remain on his feet.

He reached the sand and got within ten feet of her when his head whirled again.

Penton wobbled on shaky footing, and then stumbled toward the lifeboat. He caught a hazy image of a massive head, rising from the surf, water cascading off a spiked hide and enormous hide.

And then Penton toppled head-first into the sea foam.

THIRTY-SIX

Kate managed to prepare the lifeboat with an automatic inflation device. Then, she worked at assembling the paddles. Each one had come in three sections. They felt flimsy, and she wondered how the makeshift boat would fair in the harsh waves under extreme conditions.

A thud at her feet caused her to raise a paddle in defense. Just as she recognized Penton strewn on the sand, head in the surf, another movement caught her attention. The creature rose from the water less than fifty yards away. Its attention was drawn to the industrial building. Kate figured the beast had acute hearing and expected the missile heating up had it preoccupied.

She tossed the paddles into the lifeboat and then reached for Penton.

The Marine was large and nothing but dead weight. He'd fallen completely unconscious, without any ability to assist her. *Improvise, adapt, and overcome*, she thought.

Kate grabbed Penton under the arms and dragged him to the dingy. She backpedaled and kicked up sand and water but managed to get him alongside the lifeboat, post-haste. Then, she heaved him headfirst into the boat.

His legs and flight boots dangled over the edge.

Wrapping her arms around his boots, she shoved them upward, and then pivoted his hips and released him. Penton's lower torso dropped into the boat with a thud. Kate glanced at the creature. The Kaiju meandered onto shore and started up the beach toward higher ground.

A moment later, huge legs and feet plodded uphill, claws crimping the ground.

She grabbed onto a rope, slung around the lifeboat, and shoved the boat from the rear. The lifeboat didn't budge. "Shit!" she yelled.

Kate dug into the sand with her powerful legs and calves. Then, she pushed forward, while lifting the rear of the boat, and shoving it toward the open water. The boat inched ahead but didn't make much progress.

Shaking her head, she decided to try another approach.

This time, she circled the boat and grabbed the rope at the bow. Backpedaling and yanking the boat hard, Kate got it moving ahead. Soon, the lifeboat tossed against the rolling surf.

She worked her way around to the stern and pushed the boat against the pounding waves. Kate maneuvered the lifeboat until she waded through water chest high. Then, she climbed in and shoved each paddle through a plastic oarlock.

Kate rowed like mad. The little dingy shot over waves, moving further out to sea. The beachhead got smaller and smaller, but she doubted they'd clear the blast zone. She wanted desperately to wake Penton and share their last moment together.

But giving in wasn't an option for a Marine, so Kate kept rowing.

THIRTY-SEVEN

An hour beforehand, Rear Admiral Keyes stood on the bridge of the Gipper and watched a squadron of F/A-18 Super Hornets take flight. The fighters were loaded for bear with an assortment of weapons.

Ordnance technicians, wearing the distinguished red shirts, had prepared the planes, while Keyes instructed the flight crews in a briefing room below deck. He'd explained the combat zone would be hot with radiation, and that the attack had to be swift, with only a couple passes at the target.

Now, he sat in the command room with the theater of operations on the large screen and had General Yoshi in a smaller screen to the upper left. They fed a visual of the satellite to Yoshi's command room. Both leaders impatiently awaited the result of the Joint Task Force plan. Whether success or failure, they'd disclaim any involvement with the nuclear weapon, blaming its use on unknown militants who'd absconded with a relic of the cold war.

Keyes shifted in the command seat. Then, he sat up straight with his back locked, as though an arrow ran along his spine. An image of the creature rising from the ocean-depths appeared. Water cascaded over its scaly hide in torrents. The beast rose high into the air and bounded toward shore.

The industrial building, with the missile on its roof, appeared miniscule as the creature stomped onto land.

"The Kaiju will destroy the rocket!" Yoshi exclaimed.

"Let's give it a moment," Keyes said, trying to placate the general.

"Somehow, it knows of our plans to destroy it…"

"This could just be a coincidence—"

"Look!" said Yoshi. "The Kaiju is headed directly toward the building."

Keyes couldn't debate the comment. He watched as the creature stomped toward the industrial building. The squat building stood on a knoll overlooking the ocean. A rocky hillside and a stretch of beach divided it from the creature. The sandy path cutting through a gap in the craggy hillside was too small for the beast to pass through. Keyes hoped the slight hillside would slow the creature down, at least long enough to allow the missile time for launch.

"We're not going to have enough time," Yoshi postulated.

Everyone in both command rooms gasped at the comment. Keyes shook his head and longed for a cigar. "Just give it a moment," Keyes said, confidently.

The comment appeased them, and then they sat quiet, watching.

But he had serious doubts, and his pulse raced with anxiety.

Keyes mused over the prospect of where Penton might have set the coordinates. Surely, he wouldn't have armed the missile and set it to shoot straight up and down. The information that Keyes had provided the Master Gunnery Sargent would have set the target about a half mile up the beach. Now, Keyes wondered if he'd made a crucial mistake. *Maybe the missile would miss the target and serve to make the creature stronger.*

The Kaiju reached the rocky hillside and stopped. It canted its head and peered up at the industrial building.

"The missile is heating up!" Keyes bellowed with excitement.

"He hears the rocket," Yoshi confirmed.

"We'll have launch in a moment."

Then the creature scaled the knoll, teetering from side to side as it advanced, an immense tail dragging along behind it.

Ascending the hill, the creature crested the top in no time.

Keyes watched for exhaust emitting from under the missile, but nothing happened.

The beast stomped directly toward the building. Brick shook and the missile vibrated. It continued to approach the building, turning its massive head every so often.

"The Kaiju is drawn by the noise!" Yoshi said.

Reaching the building, the creature looked down at the rooftop and let out a resounding roar. It turned its head and wrinkled its snout in anger.

Next, the creature wound up its massive tail.

The Kaiju whipped the tail with all its might, and the dense appendage hurled toward the tiny brick building.

Just as the tail hit the building, shattering brick, and crumpling concrete behind it, the missile ignited and blasted from the deck. The Tochka shot into the air, and the Kaiju swatted at exhaust fumes.

The missile soared into the sky and disappeared from view.

Everyone in the command room erupted with cheers. Yoshi grinned in the corner screen.

Keyes wondered where the damn thing was headed. Even if Penton had done a great job programming the missile, the blasted thing was almost as old as Keyes. It could navigate off course and detonate anywhere.

He began to doubt the wisdom of utilizing such an untrustworthy weapon.

THIRTY-EIGHT

Kate rowed furiously over steep waves, while Penton lay on the bottom of the dingy unconscious. The effort pushed them forward only to be driven back. And then another stoic effort would cause them to crest a wave beating toward shore.

Once over the top of a wave, the lifeboat surged ahead. Through her struggle, they slowly crept further and further out to sea. Kate's efforts were almost done in futility, without making much progress. But when she finally took a breath and looked toward shore, the infinitesimal advances added up.

They made it a quarter mile from the beachhead and even further from the industrial building. Having cleared the huge breaking waves, they now undulated over choppy ocean waters.

Kate shoved the paddles deep into the water and pulled back hard, propelling them in longer distances between each stroke. Fear of the missile exploding on takeoff had fueled her rowing labor. Now, the Tochka soared high into the air and flew out of sight. The creature stood at the base of the squat building, battering the structure with its massive tail.

Although the lifeboat moved into calmer waters, she'd grown tired and drained from clearing the breakwaters. Regardless, Kate stepped up her efforts, anxiety fed the exertion.

Marine training always tested endurance beyond reasonable conditioning. And now she had a clearer understanding of the method to the madness. The Marine Corps had a proud tradition of winning against great odds and overcoming dire circumstances. Kate understood a large factor, spanning generations of victories, drew from a single trait: perseverance.

She didn't plan to become radioactive fodder. Her arms tensed, firm, like ropes, and her back and shoulders contracted, tightening sharply with each stroke. Abdominal muscles flexed tirelessly from her physical fitness training. Gritting her teeth, she rowed even harder. *There will be time to rest when you're dead*, she thought.

The lifeboat moved further from the shoreline, but she worried they wouldn't make it far enough to avoid the fireball blast.

THIRTY-NINE

Keyes watched the missile reappear on the screen. Everyone sat in the room with their mouths agape. He grinned at the image.

"What is it?" said Williams.

"The Master Guns really knows his stuff…"

"Why do you say that?"

Stepping toward the large screen, Keyes traced his finger from the missile trajectory toward the creature. A straight angle, the missile would likely detonate on the target. "He adjusted the Dead Reckoning coordinates based upon the creature's prior travel path," Keyes explained. "The Jarhead got it just about perfect."

Keyes stepped back and stood by the edge of the table. He noticed Yoshi in the top corner window smiling widely. "We're not out of this yet," Keyes cautioned.

"True, very, very true," Yoshi replied. "But this is looking good."

"Don't count your chickens before they've hatched."

Yoshi smiled, nodding. "We'll see soon enough."

The missile cut through the sky, rocketing downward at a tremendous velocity. Keyes expected it would impact the earth at the creature's feet. Then, he heard General Yoshi mutter something incoherent.

Searching the screen, Keyes quickly found the source of the alarm. The creature had decimated the little industrial building, battering the brick and concrete blocks. Cement dust billowed around the Kaiju, creating a smoke screen that concealed the beast.

"No way to determine the success of the attack," Yoshi stammered.

"Get me the sortie leader on the comm-link," Keyes demanded.

"Yes, sir!" Williams worked the keyboard swiftly.

A headshot of a pilot flying through cloudy skies appeared in the right-hand corner, across from Yoshi. "What's the word?" Lieutenant Commander Donovan said.

"We've lost visual of the creature," Keyes replied.

"Understood," said Donovan.

"Your squadron is going to follow up the missile with a strike on the target," Keyes explained. "You'll only be able to make a single pass."

"Roger," Donovan said.

"Let everything loose," Keyes said. "And get out of there, pronto."

"Understood." Donovan cleared his throat. "Any word on the missile's success?"

"On time and on target," Keyes responded.

"So, we're batting cleanup…"

Keyes looked at the screen. Dust billowed in the air and continued to obscure the scene. A silhouette of the creature appeared to be stomping on the ruined building, crumpling it to bits. But Keyes just couldn't be certain.

"With loss of visual, we can't be entirely sure," Keyes admitted.

"We'll do our best," Donovan said.

"I know that you will."

"Over," said Donovan.

"Godspeed."

The window in the right corner of the screen fuzzed out, and the image of Lieutenant Commander Donovan flicked off. Keyes returned his attention to the descending missile. Shooting downward, the Tochka picked up speed.

Then, the missile rocketed into the earth, smashing into the center of the billowing sediment. An explosion erupted, blasting a mushroom cloud into the air.

Building fragments, mixed with shrapnel, soil, and rock erupted across the terrain. The mushroom cloud wavered, then spread horizontally over the landscape and radiated across the sea. Keyes held his breath watching the fire blast, trying to ascertain its course and breadth.

"Will the Marines make it?" This from James his executive officer.

"A Tochka is supposed to have 100 kilotons of nuclear warhead," explained Williams the intelligence officer. "The cloud should reach about 40 thousand feet high and extend a blast radius half as wide. Anyone clearing the target zone by half a mile will escape immediate burns, and the further they get away, the more likely to survive the radiation."

"So, how far away is considered safe?" James said.

"Depending on winds... they'd need to clear at least a mile to be safe." She crossed her arms, thinking. "Three miles would be about a sure thing."

"Not sure if they even got much past the half-mile point," Keyes muttered, trying to make sense of the speck on the screen representing the lifeboat.

Williams sighed. "They need to keep that boat moving away from the blast."

"This is all conjecture," Keyes said, shaking his head. "We don't know for certain how much they packed into the warhead. The thing could be loaded with more nukes... for all we know the blast will engulf them no matter how hard they try to get away."

****

Kate rowed at a breakneck pace. The lifeboat rose and fell over choppy waves, moving further out to sea. She dug her flight boots into Penton's side, using his body for leverage as she torqued on the aluminum oars.

Having a clear view of their path, she'd watched the monster demolish the industrial building, whacking it repeatedly with its tail, then it stomped the concrete block and bricks into rubble.

A cloud of dust had wafted up and surrounded the creature, obscuring it.

Then, the missile whizzed out of the sky with flames projecting from its tail. She pulled the oars into the boat and covered both ears. And a moment later, the missile impacted into the middle of debris from the obliterated building.

An explosion erupted from the site, sending debris flying in every direction. The ground shook and coastal waters undulated.

A bright cloud shot into the air, mushrooming at its apex.

Kate tried closing her eyes but couldn't help peeking at the destruction. The fire blast didn't even reach the shoreline. A small nuclear warhead, the radius of damage appeared fairly contained. She breathed a sigh of relief. Further devastation ensued.

Rings of glowing light shot from the center of the cloud formation, like branches emanating off a tree trunk. The shockwave whisked across the water.

She grabbed the oars and desperately began rowing again.

The lifeboat whipped across the water in futility. Outpacing them, the shockwaves moved rapidly, closing the distance.

Still, her instinct to fight for survival held strong. *Endurance for one moment more*, she thought. Kate rowed and rowed, vigorously battling fatigue and ocean currents. Every ounce of her being infused into the rowing. Panting and heaving the oars with all her might, she pushed to her physical limits and beyond, arms and lungs burning.

The glowing rings extended a quarter mile out to sea, wavered and then dissipated from sight altogether.

Kate rowed the lifeboat a good three-quarters of a mile from the blast site. They were far from safety. Radioactive fallout would catch on the wind and travel in sundry directions. She caught her breath and then kept rowing.

****

Keyes stared at the screen in disbelief. Movement stirred from ground zero as smoke and dust from the blast dissipated.

"The Kaiju lives!" Yoshi declared.

Sure enough, rubble shifted and the creature rolled onto its side. The beast tried to raise its head and appeared disoriented; the large snout dipped and turned from side to side, as though the creature had lost its senses.

Another cloud of dust wafted into the air, as the beast's massive tail whapped the detritus strewn on the blast site.

"Yeah, but it got knocked down pretty good," Keyes said, pointing.

Yoshi nodded, acknowledging the blow.

"Donovan... what's your ETA?" Keyes demanded.

"Two minutes from the target zone," Donovan replied.

"Our missile launch was a success, but the creature remains alive."

"We're prepared to strike," Donovan confirmed.

"Move in fast and hit the damn thing hard," Keyes instructed. "Then get the hell out of there."

"Roger," Donovan responded.

A moment later, the squadron of F-18s whizzed across the screen. The jets approached the fallen beast, rapidly closing the distance. Donovan flew in the lead, with the other four planes set in a standard "V" formation, wingtip to wingtip.

The fighters surged downward, racing toward the target zone.

Squirming on the ground, the creature kicked and whipped its tail, trying to right itself without success. More dust whisked into the air, but visibility remained clear. The lead jet pulled away from the others and dove toward the monster.

Donovan swooped within fifty yards of the creature and let his missiles loose in two bursts. Motors ignited as the ordnance released from the undercarriage. The AGM-65 Maverick air-to-surface missiles ripped through the air toward the target.

The Kaiju found his footing and started to rise, wavering on weak legs.

Donovan's jet pulled up as the missiles impacted the creature. Explosions burst flames and smoke into the sky.

He veered right then another two jets dove towards the creature. More missiles ripped through the air, detonating on the monster's hide. The fighters broke in separate directions, leaving a clear path for the next two planes.

Emboldened by the success of the first two sorties, the last two planes buzzed in close to the creature. AGM-65 Mavericks were released from the fighters. Missile motors burned through the hazy, smoke-filled scene. The volley of ordnance pounded into the creature, erupting with multiple blasts.

The Kaiju stumbled as the fighters tore away from the target.

As the creature fell, it tilted its head and shot a ray of blue light at the trailing plane. The jet exploded on contact with the laser beam. No sign of the pilot ejecting, as plane fragments hurled through the sky.

The squadron reassembled and buzzed over the flailing creature.

Keyes leaned over and whispered to his intelligence officer: "Cut the video feed to Yoshi, now," he said.

Williams nodded, understanding.

A moment later, the small window in the corner of the screen wavered. General Yoshi disappeared from the screen, replaced by fuzzy static.

The fighters made another pass, riddling the monster with machinegun fire from Vulcan six-barrel rotary canons mounted to the nose of each plane. Bullets dug into the dense hide, causing it to roar in anger.

A buffeting so intense, the Kaiju wailed in fury and began to rise from the ashes.

Donovan led a squadron of jets high into the sky while the fourth broke across the ocean. The undercarriage of the solo fighter appeared to be empty. Keyes figured it had been loaded entirely with Mavericks.

Circling around after reaching altitude, the small sortie buzzed toward the target zone.

The creature staggered to its feet and canted its head from side to side as though listening for the jets. Glancing into the sky, the Kaiju shot a blue beam into the clouds. The beam shot past the nose of Donovan's fighter, barely missing him.

Reaching the target zone, the F-18 Hornets released the remaining ordnance. A payload of B61 – Nuclear Bombs whisked toward the lumbering creature. The bombs were 340 kilotons and over three times the yield of the Tochka missile.

The cluster of nukes hit the target simultaneously. Bombs exploded into a mushroom cloud almost three times the size of the previous one, erupting skyward and shooting a fire blast over the tranquil landscape and ocean waters.

Donovan's sortie throttled away from the combat zone toward safety.

When the smoke cleared, the Kaiju was nowhere to be found. A moment later, the screen wavered, then General Yoshi reappeared with a bewildered expression on his face. He wasted no time. "What is the meaning of this?" Yoshi demanded.

"We had a brief technical difficulty," Keyes replied.

"What sort of difficulty?" Yoshi snapped, incredulously.

"Not to worry, my friend," Keyes reassured him. "Everything is under control. Systems are back on-line. And look… the Kaiju has been defeated."

Yoshi skeptically glanced at the satellite feed. A smile crept across his face, and he nodded with satisfaction. "Very good work, Admiral."

"Thank you, my good friend," Keyes responded. "But this was a joint operation, and the credit belongs to everyone."

"Indeed," said Yoshi. "We've all endured much sacrifice, here."

"We'll follow up with full reporting soon."

"Agreed."

Keyes smiled kindly at his peer and hoped the Japanese government would brush the situation under the rug. Yoshi had a doubtful countenance, but retained the gleam in his eye, as though he suspected there was more to the situation but didn't care to learn the details. The end justified the means.

Yoshi nodded again then the small window clicked off and he was gone.

Williams leaned toward Keyes. "Admiral, if we had nuclear capability… three times as strong as the Tochka, why did we jeopardize the lives of those Marines?"

"Cover," Keyes replied coolly.

"That's it?" Her eyebrows raised.

"Look, we live in difficult times," Keyes explained. "The world stage would not stand for release of nuclear weapons… reportedly against some monster that many people would never admit even existed. We needed cover and blaming the blast on a stolen cold war missile, launched by unknown zealots was our best option."

"Those Marines could die from a mission undertaken solely for political reasons."

"Many people died fighting that creature, and even more perished while it ravaged Tokyo." Keyes shook his head, dismissively.

"It doesn't seem right," she said.

"None of it is *right*," Keyes replied. "You've got a lot to learn. Most of the time that we send our people on covert missions, we spin the story for political reasons. We do what we must do. Everyone has their role to play."

Keyes glanced back at the screen. A Sikorsky Super Stallion buzzed across the water toward a lifeboat bobbing in the water. Nobody moved inside the boat.

FORTY

By the time the volley of bombs exploded, Kate had rowed over a mile and a half from the blast zone. Winded and struggling against strained muscles, arms and shoulders aching, she paddled at a slow pace.

The mushroom clouds dissipated, and the fire blasts didn't reach them, fading out as the flames shot across the ocean. Radioactive particles would drift along with the sea breeze. Kate couldn't outrun the fallout drifting with the wind. A stoic effort, their fate was sealed from the moment she'd launched the lifeboat.

She wished they'd set more time on the launch code then thought about the monster pounding the building. Any more time and the operation would have been a failure. Nearing the brink of a painful death, she still considered the importance of the mission.

Penton finally stirred in the bottom of the boat.

"Wake up, Marine!" she barked.

The harsh tone caught his attention. Penton raised his head off the rubber decking. He instinctively responded to her command, ready to move into action. "What?" he replied, trying to get up.

"Relax," she said. "We're past the worst of it."

Penton stared back at her, befuddled.

"You've got a bit of radiation sickness," Kate explained.

Recollection of the situation crossed his face.

"Not sure if we're going to make it, though."

A grin crossed Penton's face.

Kate couldn't understand the expression.

Rain drops landed on his cheek, and the unmistakable *whop-whop* of a helicopter resounded in the distance.

EPILOGUE

Penton woke to the sound of pitter-pattering by his bedside. Multiple footsteps trod on the steel deck. He tried sitting up, but medical equipment restrained him. First-aid tape and intravenous tubing impeded his movement.

He found himself in the sickbay of a large vessel. Penton had been aboard ship many times in his career, mostly LHPs and the like; amphibious assault ships that house a contingency of Marines and close-combat support aircraft. This space appeared vast, so he figured it was a naval aircraft carrier.

Kate leaned over the bunk and smiled. "How you holding up, Master Guns?"

He forced a grin and pain radiated through his chest and stomach.

"That good," Kate said, grinning.

"Feel like shit."

"Quiet, we have mixed company."

She leaned over and hoisted Maki onto the edge of the bed. The young girl looked at him with a twinkle in her eye. "You promised that we'd see each other again." Maki shrugged innocently. "But I didn't believe it."

"Sorry about that, kid," said Penton.

"No need to be... *sorry*." Maki canted her head. "You were right."

Kate looked at Penton and beamed with excitement.

"What's next?" Penton said after a moment.

"The docs have checked you over and expect you'll pull through just fine."

"And what about you two?"

"We've checked out even better," Kate said. "The wind blew most of the particles toward shore. And remnants from the storm brought a heavy rain that saturated the rest of radioactive particles."

"So, you're not sick, too?"

"Minor, very minor," Kate said. "I'll be returned to full-time active duty in a few weeks. And Maki is doing quite well, too."

"You gave me your vaccination," Maki said kindly.

Penton nodded, feeling touched by the child's understanding and appreciation.

A groan emanated from a bed nearby.

Turning his head, Penton scanned the sickbay. He looked at the next rack over, empty. Someone moved a few beds away. A stout sailor lay on the rack and threw back his covers. His leg and abdomen were dressed in bandages.

He stared at Penton for a moment then grinned.

"Do we know each other?" Penton said.

"No, but we've all heard about you," he replied. "Chief Petty Officer Hardy…"

"Well, it's nice to meet you, Chief," said Penton.

"Pleasure is all mine," Hardy said.

Penton looked at him, confused.

"You're quite the hero," Hardy explained.

"Not me," Penton responded, shaking his head.

"A select number of us have heard the story. You've pulled off the mission."

"She's the hero," Penton said, pointing at Kate.

Hardy cracked a smile and shook his head knowingly. "The two of you have plenty of time to figure it out."

Penton looked to Kate for answers.

"I'm not sure—"

"She's been by your side," Hardy explained, "the entire time you've been out. And the grief was more than a comrade in arms… if you catch my drift."

Another sailor laughed at the comment from a few beds away.

Penton shook his head. Sometimes another person needs to state the obvious before feelings can be professed. He thought about his daughter in North Carolina and figured the crystal coast was a good a place as any to retire.

"Ever thought about being stationed at Cherry Point?" Penton finally said.

Kate grinned and nodded. "Sure, but only recently."

"North Carolina is a great place to live."

She laughed. "I'm sure."

A pile of personal items sat on a supply bin next to the rack. Penton stretched out his arm and grabbed the cellphone. He punched in the number for his daughter then paused and considered how to explain the news.

THE END

John W. Dennehy is a writer of Horror & Suspense. His first book Clockwork Universe is out now from Severed Press. He has two more books expected from Severed Press in 2017, including Pacific Rising and Deepwater Drift. His stories have appeared in SQ Mag, Disturbed Digest, Typehouse Literary Magazine, Beyond Science Fiction, and in anthologies such as Winter Shivers, Bones III, and SNAFU: Wolves at the Door, and many others. Currently, he is working on a Supernatural Horror novel.

After graduating from Pinkerton Academy, he enlisted in the U.S. Marines, serving with MALS-26 Patriots. Then John earned a degree in English/Creative Writing at UNC Wilmington. John is a member of HWA, MWA, and NEHW. He lives in New England and can be found at http://johnwdennehy.com/.

CHECK OUT OTHER GREAT KAIJU NOVELS

ATOMIC REX
by Matthew Dennion

The war is over, humanity has lost, and the Kaiju rule the earth.

Three years have passed since the US government attempted to use giant mechs to fight off an incursion of kaiju. The eight most powerful kaiju have carved up North America into their respective territories and their mutant offspring also roam the continent. The remnants of humanity are gathered in a remote settlement with Steel Samurai, the last of the remaining mechs, as their only protection. The mech is piloted by Captain Chris Myers who realizes that humanity will not survive if they stay at the settlement. In order to preserve the human race, he leaves the settlement unprotected as he engages on a desperate plan to draw the eight kaiju into each other's territories. His hope is that the kaiju will destroy each other. Chris will encounter horrors including the amorphous Amebos, Tortiraus the Giant turtle , and the nuclear powered mutant dinosaur Atomic Rex!

KAIJU DEADFALL
by JE Gurley

Death from space. The first meteor landed in the Pacific Ocean near San Francisco, causing an earthquake and a tsunami. The second wiped out a small Indiana city. The third struck the deserts of Nevada. When gigantic monsters- Ishom, Girra, and Nusku- emerge from the impact craters, the world faces a threat unlike any it had ever known - Kaiju . NASA catastrophist Gate Rutherford and Special Ops Captain Aiden Walker must find a way to stop the creatures before they destroy every major city in America..

CHECK OUT OTHER GREAT
KAIJU NOVELS

KAIJU SPAWN
by David Robbins
& Eric S Brown

Wally didn't believe it was really the end of the world until he saw the Kaiju with his own eyes. The great beasts rose from the Earth's oceans, laying waste to civilization. Now Wally must fight his way across the Kaiju ravaged wasteland of modern day America in search of his daughter. He is the only hope she has left . . . and the clock is ticking.

From authors David Robbins (Endworld) and Eric S Brown (Kaiju Apocalypse), Kaiju Spawn is an action packed, horror tale of desperate determination and the battle to overcome impossible odds.

KUA MAU
by Mark Onspaugh

The Spider Islands. A mysterious ship has completed a treacherous journey to this hidden island chain. Their mission: to capture the legendary monster, Kua'Mau. Thinking they are successful, they sail back to the United States, where the terrifying creature will be displayed at a new luxury casino in Las Vegas. But the crew has made a horrible mistake - they did not trap Kua'Mau, they took her offspring. Now hot on their heels comes a living nightmare, a two hundred foot, one hundred ton tentacled horror, Kua'Mau, Kaiju Mother of Wrath, who will stop at nothing to safeguard her young. As she tears across California heading towards Vegas, she leaves a monumental body-count in her wake, and not even the U. S. military or private black ops can stop this city-crushing, havoc-wreaking monstrous mother of all Kaiju as she seeks her revenge.

CHECK OUT OTHER GREAT KAIJU NOVELS

ATOMIC REX: WRATH OF THE POLAR YETI
by Matthew Dennion

It has been fifteen years since Captain Chris Myers used his giant mech to draw the kaiju of North America into each other's territory to have them destroy each other. Once all of the kaiju had battled to the death only Atomic Rex was left standing. In Antarctica, the kaiju known as Armorsaur has entered the frozen valley of the yetis and attacked them. Devouring all but one alpha male yeti who was exposed to the kaiju's blood and left dying in the snow. The yeti awoke to find himself transformed into a kaiju with an obsession to destroy Armorsaur. Chris and Kate are forced to protect the people of their settlement by drawing Atomic Rex into South America where he will battle the kaiju there to usurp their territory and claim their hunting grounds as his own. As Atomic Rex enters South America from the north the enraged Polar Yeti enters the continent from the south. The two most powerful kaiju in the world will battle their way through a multitude of giant monsters as they are set on a collision course with each other!

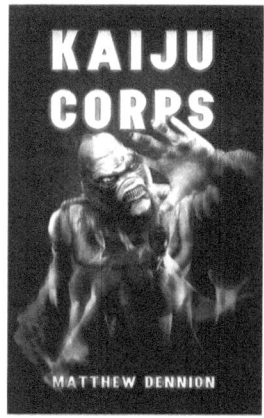

KAIJU CORPS
by Matthew Dennion

They are four soldiers who were genetically created to be mankind's last line of defense against potential world ending threats. They are soldiers who can transform themselves into gigantic monsters. They are the Kaiju Corps and they are facing a threat that is beyond the scope of even their fantastic abilities.

CHECK OUT OTHER GREAT KAIJU NOVELS

POLAR YETI AND THE BEASTS OF PREHISTORY
by Matthew Dennion

A team from Princeton University searching for a lost tribe in Antartica discover a hidden valley filled with wooly mammoths, saber toothed tigers and other Ice Age beasts. Seizing the opportunity of a lifetime, the team set up camp to study the amazing creatures. But there is something else that lives in the Valley. Something terrifying. Something beyond imagination. POLAR YETI!

TITAN WARS
by M.C. Norris

Millions of microscopic alien life forms escape a sample canister of water from the frigid depths of outer space. Invisible to the naked eye, a menacing menagerie of more than seventy deadly species react to Earth's warm and fertile seas by launching into metabolic overdrive. Waves of gargantuan abominations begin to rise from the sea, transforming our world into a zoo without cages, where humans plunge to the bottom of the food chain.

In dire need of a zookeeper, the Allied Navy turns to "Psyjack," a bickering geek squad with an outrageous plan to hack into the minds of the megafauna with some reengineered neurosurgical technology. The young gamers hope to level the uneven playing field by fighting monsters with monsters, but they couldn't have anticipated how deadly their technology could be, if it ever fell into the wrong hands ...

www.ingramcontent.com/pod-product-compliance
Lightning Source LLC
Chambersburg PA
CBHW030157200626
46812CB00017B/2441